TESS

TESS

EMMA TENNANT

230131

HarperCollins*Publishers*

HarperCollins*Publishers*
77–85 Fulham Palace Road,
Hammersmith, London W6 8JB

Published by HarperCollins*Publishers* 1993
1 3 5 7 9 8 6 4 2

A catalogue record for this book is
available from the British Library

ISBN 0 246 13664 2

Set in Linotron Janson by
Rowland Phototypesetting Ltd
Bury St Edmunds, Suffolk

Printed in Great Britain by
HarperCollinsManufacturing Glasgow

For Renée Wayne Golden
with affection

'Everything has already been lived and relived a thousand times by those who have disappeared but whom we carry in the very fibres of our being, just as we also carry in us the thousands of beings who will one day live after us. The only question which incessantly poses itself is why, of all these innumerable particles floating in each of us, certain ones come to the surface rather than others'

and

'. . . how strange each existence is, where everything floats past like an ever-flowing stream and only those things which matter, instead of sinking to the depths, rise to the surface and finally reach, together with us, the sea'.

MARGUERITE YOURCENAR, *Two Lives and a Dream*

Part One

Where You Are

My mother used to say she could always tell a first-timer from a soul that had been around before. Even with the youngest babies it was there: a fierce, incredulous look – no one had prepared you for *this*! – while the revenants, if you could so call them, had an air of acceptance, of resignation, even if their destiny was likely to be as violent or unpredictable as you could get.

The minute I saw you I knew you belonged to the first lot.

And let's hope, if you've really broken the chain, that we can all start anew. Kill the deadening sense of repetition, where every single thing you do has the taste of being done by a woman standing just ahead of you: your mother and then her mother and all the mothers together, as they go back into the fog of their unchronicled days. Go into a new world.

– But soon there won't be any world, says Ella, the eleven-year-old who no longer goes to school. And I can't tell her any different – unless making sense of all our past will give her a sense of how the world could have been different all along, if life's tape had been played another way. So there could be time still to change it.

You came as I always knew you would. On an afternoon in September when the seas are beginning to build up – and smash their way through to the very edge of the cliffs, sucking the brown clayey base and further weakening the defences against the rising tide. We don't have long – neither you, nor I, nor Nature – so listen carefully and there's just one chance in a million that we'll turn back the waves and put the earth back in kilter again. Queen Canute, you might say.

*

3

I shall call you Baby Tess. I don't know what your mother called you and she didn't have the grace to tell me, after she'd rung the bell of the Mill and shoved you in at me with a dummy stuck in your mouth that looked as if it had been there so long it was growing out of your poor face. I don't know your age either – but I'd say there hadn't been a Full Moon shining down on you at midsummer: the world didn't know you were coming, then.

No, you're here in time for the harvest. The last in two thousand years since the birth of that other child – whose advent brought grief and conflict and joy. You have come to change the pattern, to reverse the code and give a new message of hope.

If it's not too late. Tomorrow they'll come and find her. Either here – or in a little market town where Thomas Hardy loved to go wooing his latest incarnation of Tess.

They'll find the woman, last in a long line, who loved – and was abandoned – and took her revenge in the end in the only way she knew how.

My sister. Your grandmother. Tess.

And Ella – who squats on the stones of Chesil Beach and peels an apple with the penknife she stole in a fight the last time she went on a school outing (she was a rough girl, Ella, until Mr Pagden slapped her down in front of all the others and she went quiet and decided to stop going to Weymouth High altogether) – Ella grins up at me as I begin to tell the story of where we are and what we are to the baby I have named Tess after all the luckless Tesses before her.

– Tell her about the ghost at the Mill, Ella says. Please, Liza-Lu!

But it's my turn to feel impatient with this child – this truant who lives in our little village near Abbotsbury by the sea and attaches herself to me, wherever I go.

I tell her she should learn history properly, and not just listen to ghost stories. (And I'm hurt, too, of course: the ghost the villagers say they see is Mary Hewitt, my mother; and even dead they can't leave her alone. She's mad, they say, as if the spirit, that fierce independence that my mother had, that I see already in the eyes of Baby Tess, must always be spoken of in the present tense. Mad Mary Hewitt: she's come back to haunt us. Little wonder the rich folk who come down from London, and from Los Angeles and all over the joined-up world, don't like a mill with the ghost of a madwoman roaming about in it.)

– But I don't like history, Ella says, and pouts. She wants another kind of history lesson – different from the potted, dead scraps of information her mother sells in the tourist brochures from the kiosk by the gate of the tropical gardens and the swannery. Utterly unlike the succession of lifeless kings and stale-smelling politicians Mr Pagden beats into his pupils at Weymouth High.
    – You can stay and listen if you're good, I say.

So here goes. The baby – whose mother I knew once when she was a little girl –
    How can I say to Baby Tess: of course I knew your mother. She's the daughter of my sister, Tess. Tess the murderess, you know –
    How can I explain to you, Ella, that little girls can never be too careful? That there is danger everywhere, and no man can be trusted?
    How could anyone with a heart say that to a young member of the human race – and then tell that person to go and listen to Mr Pagden's history lessons at Weymouth High?

So, while there's time, I'll try to tell you both the history – of the Then, the Here and the Now.

And I'll show you how the story Thomas Hardy wrote – the story of Tess, 'A Pure Woman, Faithfully Presented', who was seduced by Alec D'Urberville and murdered him for the love of a man who betrayed her a million times worse – how this story comes up again and again and now is the time it must end.
    We'll leave the story of the Old Mill, where my father and my mother lived and were in love once – and where Tess, the beautiful one, grew up more worshipped by her father than the swans he tended down there in the saltwater lagoon.

We'll walk back, when the sun goes down across the sea, and Lyme Bay with its wooded hills looks as if it's swimming out to join the fingers of the setting sun on the water.

Then you'll know how Tess loved. And why my mother went mad. And whose ghost it is that really walks all this area – this ancient place neither of my parents would ever have dreamt of leaving.

Ella frowns at me. The tide is going out and she has gone down crab-like on her bottom to shining, coarse sand that has half-mussel shells and cuttlefish thrown casually over it as if by a decorator's hand.

A couple walk by; they're each holding a brochure from Ella's mum's kiosk. They stop, as if to ask me a question – but for some reason when they see Baby Tess they change their minds and walk on.

The man of the couple – he has a tense face, you can see he's not enjoying himself and the woman isn't either – tosses his shiny paper down on the beach and it flutters towards us on the breeze. The woman remonstrates with him for making litter – but he shrugs, and they walk on, ill at ease with each other.

Ella retrieves the brochure and twists it into a cone to place on the battlements of the damp, grainy castle she has scooped up from the newly naked beach.

– Wessex! she says, as she pulls at the cone, reading the words on the bright cover of sea and greensward, with the sharp, pointed and white-moustached face of Thomas Hardy inset against a touched-up photograph of the birthplace of the famous man at Bockhampton.

– Wessex! I think that's a silly word, Liza-Lu, Ella says. Why is it called that?

But I'm too busy changing little Baby Tess and giving her the Ribena bottle her mother at least had the sense to tuck into the carry-cot under the stained little blankets, to answer Ella.

*

6

– Later, I say. And I tell Ella if she wants to hear some of the story she'll have to learn to look after the baby and give her a bottle when she starts to cry.

And when we've settled Baby Tess and made her comfortable, I begin.

A Summer Game

It's the end of summer, 1954.

We're lying on a bank of pebbles – my elder sister and Retty from down the road, and Alec and a boy called Victor who seems to have escaped from the caravan site on a permanent basis and roams the beach with one of those stubby fishing-rods everyone except townies knows never catch anything at all.

All the same, Victor is holding up a fish – it's a mullet and he says he caught it in the Fleet, a few miles down – and we wonder why he bothers when it's so obviously three days dead.

Anyway, there are other things on our minds. For the first time since they closed Abbotsbury Swannery a week ago we have the place to ourselves: no sightseers, no hikers over the narrow bridle paths that wind between the reed beds and the sharp green hill where the chapel of St Catherine stands in ruins, looking out over the sea. No trudging, dragging steps of walkers on the shingle bank as they go two steps forward, one step back, and slide down, when they lose their balance, to the water's edge.

We're on our own, half in the long eelgrass and half on rough sand, under a tamarisk hedge and facing a wall of white stones that is as brightly lit by the late September sun as the walls of an operating theatre.

I am five years old, my sister Tess is seven – and so is Retty – and the boys are a bit older, which seems a lot at that time.

7

All summer we knew we were going to play this game. The 'scientists' (Alec and Victor, of course) and the Nurse – poor Retty – are slowly covering Tess's body with stones.

Then it will be my turn. But while I wait – nervous, both wanting the game and wanting to run away from it – I stare at Tess's face and wonder if they'll even remember to get round to me once they've finished with her.

For Tess is the pretty one. (The word 'pretty' – how I came to hate it in the long evenings in the Mill when neighbours called in: How pretty she is, how pretty, they said of Tess, and looked away from me as though I were a household pet, ugly but for some reason kept there, for what use was I if I couldn't be pretty, at least?) Pretty Tess.

And, just like everything else, the looks passed down from grand-mother to granddaughter as if the original beauty, minted God knows how long ago, must stand as currency until the exploitation of the beauty of women is finally stamped out.

It doesn't let you down, Tess's beauty. From whichever angle you look at it, there is perfection. The mouth – some grandmothers ago – was called Eve's mouth: lips just slightly open, full and Cupid-bowed, as if the apple of the tree in Eden is just about to get its first, gleaming bite.

That dark hair. Not black, dark. Some said those dark looks, with eyes so brown-black too, came from the Spanish invaders when they plundered Cornwall and spread their blood into the rest of the Southwest.

And the nose. Tess's nose is delightful, so small and delicate that it suggests she's never far from making a witty or teasing remark and throwing her head back in the air, so you can see the fine arch of her nose. And it's true. Tess is known for her spirit and wit. (Although it's hard to remember just what it was she said, afterwards.) Now, however, she looks very solemn indeed as the 'scientists' come up with their handfuls of stones. She slips off her dress as if she did it every day in front of other people.

I pray it will never be my turn, when I see Tess's small breasts, nipples like starfish on the pebble-white of her skin, move tenta-tively upwards as Alec and Victor come near.

8

– So where were we? as my mother used to say.

She'd put aside her spectacles, and lay the book on the wide lip of the windowsill and say: I must have been dreaming.

But we all knew she wasn't dreaming at all. Nor did she read from the book that was always pulled out of the bookcase after tea, and had bright pictures by Walter Crane of tangled tree trunks and frogs sitting right in the gold platter of the fairy princess.

What my mother told us wasn't a fairy tale at all.

And as it's the truth – and as you've come here as they always said you would: just like that – mysteriously – I'll tell you where here is. Where you are now, in the last season of the last year of the millennium – and where we were then, on that hot September day in 1954. And long before that and ever since, too,

on

Chesil Bank

Chesil Bank is one of the geological wonders of the world. It is twenty-one miles in length and runs along the southern coast of Dorset, which is in turn in the very south of England before it slopes down to the far west; and it is formed entirely of shingle. It is a natural barrier made by the sea against itself; and the strangest thing, as you will learn when you are older, is that the stones of the shingle are small at the western end (West Bay) and are known as pea-gravel; whereas at the eastern end (Portland) they're so large you could take them for the eggs the swans in the old swannery are encouraged to lay.

This giant bank of sea-shaped pebbles has only been overcome by the sea once – in the great gale of 1824. Then, the church in the village of East Fleet – along with the rest of the village – was destroyed, and the smugglers' passageway through the vault was inundated. You can see the brasses of the Mohune family; and under them is the vault where they stored their contraband.

If things weren't being smuggled in, along this stretch of flat, wild beach (and there was a brisk smugglers' trade, over waters with so strong an undertow that poor Retty Priddle didn't last five minutes when she threw herself in: but that's another story), then they were literally tossed in, all the way from Spanish America, people said. Gold coins, pieces of eight, have been washed up on Chesil Beach. Flotsam so unexpected no one stopped to think what wreck it might have come from, before helping themselves: porcelain cups, wafer-thin, encrusted with barnacles; mother-of-pearl-handled knives and forks fit for a king on board his schooner, singing and dancing on the night the ship went down. There was a merman once – long ago, mind you. A merman thirteen feet in length, they say. And if he comes again, there'll be a storm far worse than the one before and we'll all be swept out of our beds, to a watery grave somewhere miles inland from that natural sea wall.

Of course there's a lot of superstition in a place where the sea has acted so unusually, has created, in fact, an oddly tropical landscape by its formation of a lagoon that lies landlocked on its nearside and could be mistaken, with its brackish waters and warm temperatures, for a lake in Africa. There's a feeling that anything might fly out from the gardens – tropical, too – which the Fox-Strangways family planted in the late eighteenth century, and where palms and creepers and great bushes of early flowering camellias reinforce the impression of an England gone literally barmy. People walk quickly by the stone wall, that should enclose a park with chestnuts and oaks and is instead as wild with lush vegetation as the first Pacific isle Captain Cook laid his eyes on. Because that flapping in the trees, while obviously only a pigeon or a crow, seems to summon up something foreign and intensely familiar at the same time. A *sou-criant*, maybe, or a great bright bird that just doesn't belong in this part of the world at all.

Any more than you do, my dear.

When Did it Begin?

I have to choose another name for our village – more a hamlet, really – where I grew up and have come back to today, to find you waiting. As was foretold.

I shall call it Nasebury. The secrecy comes not from a desire to be coy but from the need to protect the place from prying eyes, from further curiosity about the unsolved crime of thirty years ago.

Was it here, people would ask, that the bloodstained sheet that had been used to wrap the body of a man was found lying so carelessly by the reed beds? Was it on this stretch of Chesil Bank that poor Retty Priddle, so in love with the angel from Beaminster that she took to drink and lost her senses, plunged over stones to the treacherous undertow of the sea? Isn't there a small pile of stones to mark the spot?

All the other names of the places are real. Abbotsbury . . . West Bexington . . . Rodden with the beautiful house set down cheek by jowl with humble cottages . . . Langton Herring; and, of course, that royal resort of a mad monarch, George III – Weymouth.

Just as the people I shall tell you about are real: Thomas Hardy, who so dominates this whole landscape; his wives and his loves.

Some of the people I shall tell you about seem more real by now than their progenitor and his long-ago loves, the mad wife and the scheming secretary who succeeded Emma and inherited her unhappiness. These people have a life-blood which nothing can staunch: the flippant seductions of Alec D'Urberville linger still in all this part of Dorset; and Tess's heart-rending voice, whether uttering the low diapason of the baptism of her dying child, or singing songs with the other dairymaids at Talbothays, still echoes when the winter wind whistles, when the larks sing on the high ground at Evershot.

And this is because the story is true, true as an old ballad. And long after Hardy was laid to rest at Stinsford between his wives – his ashes, significantly, in the burial place of famous men, Westminster Abbey – his heart with the women he caused such suffering – the ballad is played and played again.

I will explain.

But first, the facts of our life at Nasebury.

It was here – a stone's throw from Abbotsbury, literally, that Alec and Victor, to attract our attention, would take one of those medium-sized stones from Chesil Bank (here, we're at the halfway mark between the pea-gravel of West Bay, near Bridport at the western end, and the giant egg stones in the eastern tip) and throw it plop! into our garden at the side of the Mill as an invitation – a warning? – they were coming to 'play'. And it was there that my mother lived when she married my father, and then stayed on as caretaker when London folk bought the Mill in 1968.

The Mill wasn't working as such when my father lived there. It had fallen into disrepair. My mother heard ghostly feet on their first night there, in the black-out in 1942. But it was a family of white owls that was walking about in the loft over the old beams.

No ghosts here, my mother used to say when we asked about all the tales of Dorset hauntings. My sister Tess said she'd seen the stone eagles from the gateposts at Mapperton fly down the beach on their way to the sea – as they were supposed to do, each midsummer.

– Swans flying in, my mother said, without so much as look-ing up.

But, I shouldn't be so sure, my father teased her; and Tess always believed him, you could see that: as if the beauty she had from her grandmother, her Tess beauty, made her all the more susceptible to old stories. It was as if she'd lived through it all before – and alas!, as we know now, was due to live through it all over again in her own lifetime.

Not I. The plain younger sister. The goose, half-formed. Yet, as in a fairy story where the ending has gone horribly wrong and the goose fails to turn into a swan, fated to live out her life with the prince. The snag being that the prince doesn't love her.

That I will explain to you, too. Just remember, for now, that I am Liza-Lu; Lizzie; Liz – whatever they choose to call me when my turn comes to play my part. And surely, by now, I have played it long enough.

My father was a romantic. After he was demobbed at the end of the war, he decided to buy the Mill (it had only been rented up till then); but his family, the Hewitts, did come from Dorset, from the wide streets of Bridport where they'd had a chandler's business. (Bridport is the main centre in Britain for rope-making and hemp. To be 'stabbed by a Bridport dagger' is to hang on a rope by the neck until you are dead. As Tess did. But that's to tell you later.)

My father had no desire to go into the business. He'd come into a small sum of money from his family, and, as I say, he bought this mill with its long garden on the side of the hill, a garden invisible from the road and bordered by a brown stream that chuckles and clatters over pale stones to the millpond under the house. Above the Mill, at the top of the steep green slopes, stands St Catherine's Chapel.

St Catherine, patron saint of spinsters.

My mother used to say it was odd that she ended up here, when we were nothing to do with spinsters at all, but descendants of a long line of unmarried mothers – as our species was then known.

St Catherine would have laughed, my mother said. But don't deride spinsters, Liza-Lu. Spinsters belonged to the first guilds, in medieval times, that women could join and have control over their own wealth. People came here to buy their lace and linen handkerchiefs.

My father – I keep starting again with those words, and perhaps it's because we none of us had any real sense of having a father that the words stick in my throat and I go careening off to the genetic structures of our ancient ballad, most lately taken up by Thomas Hardy and certain to remain here until the structure of society and life are utterly changed.

It wasn't that our father was distant, just that he seemed totally irrelevant to us and to the future we saw so clearly marked out for us as girls. The romantic streak in him seemed to obfuscate the facts of the difference between his and our outlook and expectations of life.

My father helped tend the swans at the old swannery at Abbotsbury between February and September. By the side of the brackish water of the lagoon he built artificial nests, to encourage laying. These are mute swans and they aren't fierce; so he encouraged people to walk among them, on the shingle shore of their colony, and by the side of the river (the same as flows through our garden at the Mill) where hydrangeas and bamboo grow to a gigantic height in the subtropical climate.

It was as if the swans were all my father needed in the world.

But you will ask, one day, about my father's family, and the best way I can answer you, I believe, is to say that that is the wrong direction to look altogether.

You must look at your mother, and her mother before her, and all the long line of women born without names of their own, given or sold to names that would never be truly theirs: as nameless, as interchangeable as the eyeless fertility statues found in the old settlements all over Europe and Britain, with mammae and thighs and vulvas as marked and carved as the old worship sites cut in the clay. The history of these women is the history of you and your mother. And, because, for all these women, the suffering and the song was the same: toil, childbirth, death; and for those who fell outside, another song repeated itself: rape, childbirth, desertion or betrayal, let me tell you your history as I must tell it to Ella, who no longer goes to school.

Think of me in 1958, as I daydreamed my way through the lessons Mrs Moores gave in our little school, where she tried so hard to expel us from our narrow shelf of land behind Chesil Beach and into the world – the 'real' world, of politics and money and men.

But we were already conditioned to be girls.

– Which twin has the Toni?

– Did you hear that Retty Priddle ran away to the caravan site last night and her mum found her and Victor on the beach at Charmouth?

– Did you see that jumper in Mullens in Bridport?

– No, it's not my shade. Might suit Retty, that lilac.

– You're *green* with envy, Liza-Lu. That's your trouble –

Poor Mrs Moores. She had to bring out the strap. A strap of leather about an inch thick – and down it came on the palms of our hands, for chattering and giggling right through the Stuart kings.

But what can you expect? Those kings seem distant to a bunch of girls. And the boys at Nasebury school: they don't pay much attention either, as they doodle in their books and score initials and rude words in the still-left-over-from-wartime desks.

But the boys will inherit the sceptre of the kings.

The girls will knit. We will work as shop-girls at Mullens or waitress in a tea-shop in Weymouth or serve in the Marks and Spencer when it comes.

Behind our eyes, as we lead the teenager to those shelves so finely packed with whaleboned bras in layers of crinkly tissue, or Granny to the outsize rail, where tweed skirts like the flanks of battleships hang fiercely together – behind our eyes, as I say, there is only the dream that is always the same: the house, two bedrooms, the playroom that's built on later in an extension at the back. Roses over the door – that goes without saying.

And it makes no difference how many times the old song is sung: 'betrayal, heartache, loneliness, death' – it'll always be a song that's sung for others and not for us.

The husband's step on the path.

The kiss goodbye in the morning.

And for us, Ella and Baby Tess (for, Ella, I am exploiting you shamelessly already, using you as childminder when you should be at school), there was all the excitement of a new world, built from machines.

For the first time in history, all the chores were done for us. Our dishes were washed and rinsed and came out piping hot and gleaming. On the first TV sets we saw ourselves in the act of choosing soap powders, like a sultan's wives tasting delicacies in the harem while his eunuch stands over the proceedings and smiles at us, before leading us back to the seraglio.

A house!

Think, children, of the miracle of a house! And a car! For many, a 'two-car family', as if people had been subsumed altogether by the machines.

The tumble dryer. The Tupperware party.

Little wonder our eyes dreamed, in those jobs that were just a prelude to the important part of life.

Just as much as all the nameless women and eyeless, vastly burgeoning fuck-goddesses of extreme antiquity, we were, despite all the machines, sacrifices on the altar of fertility.

And what we couldn't know, in this Brave New World, was that the song was just the same as it always had been. That if you don't take responsibility for your own life, the song will always be sung through you.

So it's best to return to Chesil Beach, on that late September day in 1954, and ask ourselves two questions:

What happened, since the beginning of Life on Earth, to knock women from their first, all-embracing position of power? What happened to reduce them to the status of the female sea-urchin (you can tell the female by the white pebble placed, as a claim of proprietorship, on her spiky back by the male); and what causes them to be, tens of thousands of years after the perfecting of brain and intellect, still preponderantly waiting for the placing of that fatal stone – and if bravely struggling away from it, toiling as mother alone, struggling, struggling?

And what happened, when the body of a man was taken in a boat up the coast and hidden, on that day thirty years ago (and that a full fifteen years since the day Tess and Liza-Lu and Retty Priddle and Alec and Victor played 'scientists' on Chesil Beach), on September 22nd, 1969, to be precise?

How can a body disappear, just like that?

We'll have to go back – several millennia at first – before we can
begin to find the answers.

But for the moment we have Tess – yes, up to her neck in stones
on the beach.

Everyone knows the next stage of the game but no one wants to
be caught doing it.

Tess doesn't care. She wants more than anything in the world
for Alec Field to lie down beside her on the beach and pull off the
stones one by one – except for one, which he will push, slowly and
then more and more insistently, right up her vagina, so that as she
gasps with pain and pleasure she sees a white plateau of rock inside
her – a platform, hung with mosses and submerged by secret canals
and waterways, where Alec's finger will at last walk away from the
obstacle of the stone and begin to tickle her proper.

Victor and Retty Priddle will have to stand around, to provide a
sort of human windbreak.

And when the stone is pulled out it's a different colour from the
other stones that form the great barrier of Chesil Beach.

It's not white but grey and blue, veined, soaked by Tess's just-
discovered inner sea.

To return to the stones.

The problem – in the first place – lay in explaining just how
these stone fish and shells could possibly be found on dry land.
Ammonites whose secret is in a spiral like a stowed ladder of evolution; burrows and trails of worms preserved in sandstone; the
droppings of reptiles (which are called coprolites) had no right to
be above the water-mark like this. The land had been formed by
God on the third day of Creation; and that day itself was no more
than six thousand years ago, at the time of the expulsion of Adam
and Eve from a garden assuredly not littered with these relics of a
marine past.

The Flood must explain it all.

And so the diluvialists, as they called themselves, kept right up to the seventeenth century their theory of Noah floating above the mountaintops and the fish swimming below him, waiting to be petrified in the receding flood.

Only with Lamarck – whose life spanned the greatest change to date in the living organism of society – the French Revolution – a life which ended five years after the flood of 1824 that rose above Chesil Beach and obliterated the village of East Fleet – came new ideas of evolution and geological durations of time.

The cliffs behind us – as we sit on the beach enjoying the late summer sun – are Jurassic, known as Fuller's earth. Far down there, beyond the last of the shingle beach, are the cliffs of Kimmeridge clay. Fossils from these cliffs can be extracted easily. Or you can find them lying among the stones: chipped, coiled mementoes of the Palaeozoic era.

It's with one of these fossils – actually it seems to be a prehistoric flint-head (there are plenty of them here, too) – that Alec, in the summer of 1954, is stroking the white stomach of Tess.

While I have been explaining to you, the game has gone on.

But before we go back to that September day in 1954 – and its consequences, reaching as they do as far into the future as your presence here (your presence in the world, one might say); and stretching as far back as the waves of the sea, each responsible for its successor and pushed by its predecessor into an eternal present – let me explain just one more thing.

It may help explain our story; and its eternal recurrence.

Lamarck's theory of the inheritance of acquired characteristics has been long discredited. We are all Darwinians, like our grandparents before us.

Yet for us, Baby Tess, there is a truth in Lamarck's wild scientific poetry. He says:

> It is not the orphans, that is, the nature and form of parts of an animal, which gave rise to its habits and specific faculties; on the contrary, its habits, its way of life and the circumstances in which the individuals from which it

has descended, found themselves, have, with time, constituted the form of its body and the number and state of its organs, and ultimately its faculties.

Then,

> Fluids moving in the soft parts of organisms which contain them, characteristically clear for themselves passages, settling places and outlets; they create canals and hence various organs; they vary the canals and organs either by different movements or by different fluids ... they enlarge, lengthen, divide and build up these canals and organs by the materials which form and which are constantly separated out from the moving fluids.

Lamarck believed in the unity of Nature. He put forward the claim that minerals were produced by decaying living matter, making a cyclical relationship between living and inert nature. 'Without exception, the raw compounds which form most of the earth's external crust and continuously modify it by their changes all result from the remains and residues of living organisms.' When an organism died there was nothing to hold the complex substances together any more and they gradually disintegrated, only to be recombined by new living beings, in a perpetual cycle.

And minerals could be understood in terms of the historical sequences they passed through.

On the day we return to believing this – when we are as fully aware of ourselves and the landscape irrevocably interrelated and producing of each other in as unending a chain of happening as the waves of the sea, we will be able to save the planet.

And our own bad cycle will be broken.

Baby Tess, you are my hope. With your eyes that show such surprise and rage at the world – and your starfish hands that take me in memory to the rock-pools of Charmouth, and to Tess's unformed breasts as they lie exposed on the stones of Chesil Beach on that late summer day so long ago – you lead me to hope, to believe in a different future, in the ending of the endlessly repeating chain.

You will return us to the ancient cycle, when we lived and were transmuted – and we could hear the pain of a stone.

For Lamarck had a fabulous bestiary, and it is to this that we must look for the recovery of the old way of seeing and knowing.

Lamarck's beasts, like the beasts of La Fontaine (so said that great poet-martyr, Osip Mandelstam):

> adapted themselves to the condition of life. The legs of the heron, the neck of the duck and swan, the tongue of the anteater, the asymmetrical and symmetrical position of the eyes in certain fish.
>
> La Fontaine's philosophizing, moralizing, reasoning beasts were a splendid living material for evolution. They had already apportioned its mandates among themselves.
>
> The artiodactylous reason of the mammals clothes their fingers with rounded horn.
>
> The kangaroo moves with the leaps of logic.

As described by Lamarck, this marsupial consists of weak forelimbs, that is, limbs that have reconciled themselves to being useless; strongly developed hind extremities, that is, convinced of their importance; and a powerful thesis, called the tail.

So, in our landscape of fluids and fossiliferous limestone and clay, in our passages and outlets of water where the swans nest each spring and fly off across the Fleet in September, where the solitary flamingo, like some too obvious reminder of an evolutionary past in Africa, stands on long-adapted legs to scan the movements of the fish; let us learn to save the world from extinction, to believe that we are all one in the unity of Nature.

Perhaps it is some preconscious memory of this that has led to the fact of Tess's body on Chesil Beach, only her head sticking out like an odd piece of flotsam blown onto the shingle in the equinoctial gales, and the rest of her covered in stones.

*

And now, Ella, comes a history lesson – on the mothers and fathers of these stones. Learn it well. I'll take you to the little shop in Lyme that you'd think was an antiquarian bookshop – until you see the real story of the world is written in stone.

In the Beginning

The coast of south Dorset is famous for its fossils. You can buy them from a cart by the side of the ice-cream kiosk on the beach at Charmouth. You see them heaped in junk shops in Lyme Regis, where the elaborate spiral of the ammonite looks, in the gloom, like a broken-off claw of a Regency table. People set the fossils in earth either side of garden steps, so the hard snail-like protuberances flank a bed of petunias or salvia. But they're out of place like this, these wallfish, and belong on cliffs and shores.

The ammonite is the fossil most commonly found in our sandstone cliffs. Children from all over the country have visited the Natural History Museum and peered at the hollow, coiled shell, whose nearest living relative is the pearly nautilus. The main difference between the nautiloid and ammonoid shell lies in the partitions that separate the chambers: the ammonoid is the more highly crenellated of the two, and so more complex.

Ammonoids became extinct near the end of the Cretaceous age – that is, seventy billion years ago. We can therefore know them only from their shells. The soft parts of the body must be inferred: one may imagine an ammonoid as a coiled shell with a protruding head, similar to a squid.

Two antithetical concepts concerning the evolution of the *Ammonoidea* have been actively debated: recapitulation and caenogenesis. Many lineages of *Ammonoidea* were set up in the last century on the assumption that the juvenile or young forms were similar in suture and/or shell morphology to the adult ancestors. In other words, the young stages of the descendant recapitulate the adult stage of the progenitor. The second idea, that of caenogenesis, suggests that new characters appear in the young stage as a result of special adaptations to the environment occupied by the young, and that these special characters, if of survival value to adults, gradually spread through time to the adult stage.

A further complication, long known, but recently re-studied in considerable detail, is the effect of sexual dimorphism in the *Ammonoidea* on extant taxonomy, nomenclature and evolutionary concepts.

The first protozoic atom of the life-slime was female, reproducing itself, as always, parthenogenetically. But when, as a precedent, it brought forth a new sex, male, the first fatal step was taken in the undermining of its own authority.

Instead of retaining her power of reproducing life on her own, the female had now delegated half of that power to the male. As far as Man was concerned, neither sex was fully capable of creating life, and the female primeval urge to give birth would, in its need for fulfilment, eventually lead the sex to surrender to the male.

From that day, millions of years ago, the myth of male superiority has grown and flourished.

Now is the time for the new characters to appear in the young stage as a result of special adaptations to the environment.

I am telling you, we must adapt and change. Before the seas and lakes are thoroughly poisoned. Before the sky cracks open for good like an egg.

Outside the closed village school, Ella stands with me, and with Baby Tess in her pram, waiting for the queue in the little shop to disperse, for prying eyes to go away (who is that baby? Like her mother before her, and, so they say, her mother's grandmother too, left on the doorstep, found in a river bed, there's a curse on the family, everyone knows that), and Ella asks:

– Where do babies come from, Liza-Lu?

*

Ella doesn't mean the question as once she might, when the gooseberry bush or the crude details of the biology lesson were the only answers to the first essential question a child will ask.

It's not like nearly half a century ago, when Alec Field explored Tess as she lay coiled as a fossil shell on the beach at Chesil Bank, her soft body in the shallow chamber she had made for herself in the stones, her head protruding like a squid.

By the time it was my turn it had come on to rain again and I was spared. But Retty Priddle, down on the coarse sand the colour of a lion's mane, which is only visible at low tide, had her knickers down in the waves and her left hand on a part of Victor that protruded, too, from his grey shorts like the soft head of an ammonite from its shell.

No, it's not like then. Men 'got you pregnant' and you had to 'catch' them or suffer the stigma of illegitimacy and shame.

Was the primeval urge to give birth the reason Tess allowed the stone to be pushed into her – a reverse, you might say, from the condition of her progenitors, seventy billion years ago, where the stone carapace was a place to breed alone. Did she have this urge, so strongly even at the age of seven, that she would countenance Victor's preposterous 'game' in the hope it would lead to the real thing?

Tess didn't know. Nor could anyone know. Something about the 'game' led them back all those millions of years to the first appearance of the male.

And, like the first male, Victor strides and struts on the beach to attract the desire and attention of Tess. Without him, she cannot give birth.

It's different now, and Ella knows it. Ella's question comes after seeing – whether she understands them or not – countless news stories on TV: surrogacy, artificial insemination, test-tube babies, drug fertility scandals with six or eight in a litter. Sperm banks, anonymous donors. Genetic engineering. Where do babies come from, Liza-Lu?

We're back in the Cretaceous age. With modern science we can reproduce by ourselves.

But men are more powerful than we, and they will stop us – sooner or later. Very likely, sooner.

Our power is now that we can do without them. Sperm can be frozen a thousand years. In a millennium's time, it will be as if you, today, were the child of a silk weaver or a Saxon farmer – or a royal prince. In the here and now, we don't need men any more.

Not for physical strength: we protect ourselves against danger with electronic alarms and all-female services. Not for manufacturing and heavy engineering: the Industrial Revolution is over.

But they won't let us get away with it. Certainly not.

It is they who must change and adapt.

And us along with them, if we and the planet are to survive.

So I say to Ella: Babies come from Love.

And she looks up at me with that uncomfortably accusing squint – and sticks her tongue right out at me, in front of the vicar and assorted worthies as they leave the village shop.

It could be true, I think, if the chain of desolation could be broken, with the coming of the new Baby Tess.

Crime and Punishment

It looked at first like a bundle of old clothes, lying in the eelgrass by the edge of the lagoon.

The swans had crossed the Fleet a few days before, and their deserted nests were higher than the body, which, in its coiled, uncomfortable position, was like one of those men found in a peat bog – unreal somehow, although obviously human.

And my mother Mary Hewitt was poking at it with a stick – one of those long twigs, to be precise, that the swanherd brings in to help the birds build their nests. It was six in the morning and barely light: we'd just passed the equinox, and the gales had brought the sea right up to the height of Chesil Beach.

Had the body been washed out to sea and then come in again with the equinoctial gales?

Or had it been dumped there the night before, in the sand-fringed grass at the edge of the water?

One thing was certain. There had been a thick fog earlier that night and no one could swear they'd heard the outboard engine of a small boat as it made its way up the coast to West Bay. Not Tess, or our mother, or me.

So that was September 1969 – September the twenty-second – and my mother's expression is something I'll never forget. Even though I hadn't been there at the time – even, as I knew but couldn't bear to know, she wanted most of all to punish herself. It was as if she wanted so badly to punish someone for this unthinkable – unbearably foul – impossible – act, that she'd thrash the daylights out of me for want of anyone else in the vicinity.

And she nearly did. She held the stick high above her head. No, I won't forget. Nothing compares with the anger of a mother. (Even if, as I was to discover later, the anger was really turned against herself.)

The crime of your grandmother – my sister – has reverberated, as it must until the chain is sundered. The chain of passion, betrayal and revenge goes on – and your mother has abandoned you here, as unthinking as any mother who has had no mother of her own to teach her how to care for you. If she comes for you, she won't stay long. She's restless, your poor mother, and she can't settle, as the swans do, year after year in the same place.

After all, her mother was a murderess.

*

25

But this is a sad lullaby, for a newcomer to the world. So, while I tell you that my mother poked the body again, and I went right up to it and saw the blood ooze up under the shirt, I'll tell you as well about the swannery, and how my father loved it so much that he spent all his time there, away from the ship's chandler's office in Bridport, and how my mother came to hate the place, almost as if she were jealous of the swans and thought my father loved them more than he loved her (which he did, of course).

Abbotsbury Swannery is unique in that it concentrates on mute swans: nowhere else do they breed colonially, as they do here in Dorset.

A colony was first recorded here in 1393. The swans nest on the northern side of the saline Fleet, which is a seven-and-a-quarter-mile stretch of water – as you know, between the mainland and Chesil Bank, and itself unique in the British Isles.

Ella walks up to me. It's a warm, late summer day that I've chosen to sit on the shingle bank and tell my sister Tess's baby granddaughter how her history goes, and Ella, still refusing school – the cut bus service only aiding and abetting her in her wish to have nothing to do with lessons which have themselves been brutally cut and oversimplified – cares little for Nature. She likes crime, romance, treachery – like you see it on TV. She says:

– What happened to that man you were telling us about, Liza-Lu? The man you said they'd find buried under the stones one fine day?

– Let me finish, I say. The main oddness, in a place as steeped in the unusual as Abbotsbury Swannery, is the colonial persistence of the swans. Most of this species nest apart from others of their kind, whereas those at Abbotsbury, nesting close to each other, then proceed to drown each other's cygnets as soon as they take to the water. So, while there would normally be strong selective pressure to nest further apart and prevent such internecine slaughter, this pressure is mysteriously missing from our colony of mutes at the Fleet.

Our world is overcrowded and dying.

If you interfere with Nature, my great-great-grandmother (she who ran a School of Witches, at Rodden) would say, Nature will come one day and strike back at you.

– So, Ella says, interested at last (probably by the tale of drowning cygnets), are the swans meant by Nature to die like that?

And if they are, why?

And what is the body of a man doing there, anyway?

I'll try to explain, Ella, but first I must tell you that a man does – and did – interfere with Nature. He was my father, John Hewitt, and he and his forefathers have been swanherds at Abbotsbury for as long as our foremothers were going on their knees up to St Catherine's Chapel on the hill and praying to the patron saint of spinsters.

He interferes from motives of kindness – and economy, of course.

The procedure is to save a certain number of cygnets each year (about one hundred, just as they did at the time of the first count, in 1591), and to keep them in seven pens until they are old enough and strong enough not to be drowned.

They will then be further protected by the best pairs of swans who will acquire most young.

This rearing is the only unnatural event in the swans' lives. They are fed at this time but thereafter are free to feed as they please (zostera and sea lettuce). They aren't pinioned: the good, natural food of the Fleet keeps them there. In summer there are about five hundred – and double that in December, when the swannery is closed to visitors.

And – I say – as Baby Tess sleeps at last in the carry-cot at my feet and I pick up a shell and hold it near her blue-white ear – the gales from the north blow over snow geese, sometimes, and ospreys too.

– Ospreys are extinct, Ella says in the cross voice of a child who, in truth, is missing school.

Going all the Way

The Mill has a great room at first-floor level, with the millwheel in the centre and all the old beams in the roof, which at the southern end of the room are so low they can give you a bad knock on the head if you aren't careful.

On the morning of 21st September, 1963, at nine o'clock, that's exactly what my father did: he hit his head on a beam and he wept – but whether it was from real pain or from the knowledge that his daughter Tess had got pregnant by a man, it would be hard to say.

I stood there staring at him.

I couldn't for the life of me understand why my mother had told him, at all. It was a secret between us.

Pity the daughter who can have no secrets with her mother.

The child of happy parents is an orphan. And, although my father loved the swans, and sometimes hardly saw my mother in daylight for months on end, she told him everything.

So I stood there gaping, as my father wept. I didn't know until much later that my mother, just for this once, hadn't told him everything. Not by any means.

Like the boat trip she knew she would take with Tess when it all became too much to bear, down the coast and against the ferocious current of Chesil Beach, all the way to West Bay.

For now, though:

– Where *is* Tess? says my father in a full voice when he has finished crying.

His pain and disappointment were terrible to see. But it wasn't the first time I'd seen them. For my father, while struggling to join the modern world, had all his life been firmly rooted as any Victorian in the old values.

I don't think he once noticed the chemical calendar on the wall

28

of the bathroom in our creaking old house: the Pill, pinned in its plastic space bubble to the wall, for Tess to take (not me, not yet, even in 1963).

I don't think my father, either, had accepted Tess's life since she had startled him by growing breasts and slamming the door of her room in his face, and playing 'Mr Tangerine Man' until the sound came out of the walls and seeped right into the quiet valley by the walls of the Old Barn at Abbotsbury.

And after, he'd know, of course, that Tess had had a baby by Alec, and Alec had buggered off.

But he'd only know it in some intellectual way, not really, right down inside himself. Tess was still his little girl, who lived in the shadow of the chapel of St Catherine, patron saint of spinsters.

He used to tease both his daughters about that, my poor father.

No wonder Tess was fucking Alec right from the age of fourteen and sometimes in the Old Mill itself, at dead of night, when my father was asleep, dreaming of his swans and their big, ungainly bodies which he handled so carefully you'd think he was carrying his own children instead of birds.

Tess wouldn't let him touch her any more.

And, as she grew into a more and more beautiful swan, I stayed the ugly duckling. I was glad of my father's attentions – but as Tess grew away from him, and the invisible (to him) Pill Diary on the bathroom wall kept cyclically repeating itself, he became more distracted and absent-minded, so I sometimes wondered if he saw me at all.

Tess was living by now in a council flat in East Coker. Alec was still around, then.

My mother went to see her and said she was well. And my father's lip turned down, as if he were going to burst out crying in front of us all.

He couldn't say it, but he knew his daughter had been seduced by a bounder.

There was no language any more to say that kind of thing.

The Pill had taken away innocence, and so seduction was dead.

But, as I'm telling this poor baby, granddaughter of Tess, all that is completely untrue.

29

You remember I told you about the invention of machines?

And how the washing machine, and the tumble dryer, and the dishwasher, and the automatic timer on the oven, were supposed to liberate women? Along with the Pill, of course. Give them choice?

Yes. This freedom, this sudden 'choice' only succeeded in removing any possible moral reasons for men to take the consequences for their actions.

Tess had made her own choice, right?

OK. Maybe she forgot to take the Pill one night. But how can Alec be to blame, when, seeing a pal who has a buddy who knows a guy in . . . yes, in Detroit of all places, he decides, before the baby is even born, to go off there?

It was her decision, wasn't it?

So Tess is now in that new and flourishing category, the single parent.

And maybe the worst of the whole shameful situation is that my father just can't bear her any more. He spends more and more time at the seven pens at the swannery, trying not to look at those unselected cygnets that drown in the Fleet because there just isn't room in the world for them. And Tess's baby – a funny little thing, as Mrs Hands, the schoolteacher, said when it was time for her to go to school – a funny little thing with none of her mother Tess's looks – that was your mother, my poor child. We called her Mary, after our own mother, Mary Hewitt – maybe we hoped some of our mother's new power would come down to her. But there wasn't much sign of it, I'm sorry to say. She was just a baby – with all the crying-through-the-night and teething problems you could possibly wish for.

So you can imagine how pleased my mother was when a new man turned up; and, wonder of wonders, Tess fell in love with him!

So how did we come to accept it all so easily: the 'seduction', the abandonment and Tess stuck with an infant when she should have been out learning about the world, learning how to save it from greed, exploitation, abandonment?

We shall have to go back again – but to people this time, not to stones.

First Rites, Lost Love

❧❧❧

The earliest people to make a mark on the Dorset landscape were the Mesolithic hunters and fishers, who seem to have had almost five thousand years – from 8000 to 3500 B.C. – in which to pursue their nomadic way of life. Being nomadic, they can't have made much of a difference to the countryside; but they had fire, at least, and axes: there was a settlement, for some parts of the year, just behind Chesil Bank, southwest of Weymouth.

How did they live, the women of these migratory tribes?

Were they as fleet of foot as the men? It's probable; but they were weighed down by their babies; and, anyway, how can you wield an axe with a screaming bundle attached to your front or back?

Were they, on the contrary, still powerful, the ruling matriarchs of communities like the Eastern Mediterranean tribes where, ever since earliest antiquity, it was expected that women would shape society? Where the wife, taking more than one husband, ensured that succession in property and authority passed from mother to daughter?

In this natural state of affairs, which arises from a primitive ignorance of the part played in procreation by the fertilizing male, the Earth Mother was worshipped – the Great Goddess, under a variety of names – and the Great Goddess (unlike the Indo-European Sky Father, with his patriarchal pattern of worshippers and his wife somewhere in the background) had her own 'family'.

But the family of the Great Goddess was also unlike that of the Sky Father because it had a duration of only a season. The young lover – or son – or brother – who lived blissfully with the Goddess for just the spring and summer, was killed with the ripening of the fruit and the falling of the leaves: another came with the bursting of buds after the dreary winter.

Possibly, our Mesolithic foremothers lived like this. But, here in the north, things were more complicated again – for only the Mediterranean Earth Mother had established herself alone above male supremacy. When she appears among the descendants of the Indo-Europeans in Europe she is confronted not only with a rather pale northern Earth Mother, but also with a powerful Sky Father. The tendency is for the two Earth Mothers to fall together, although to the end of the pagan period they cause confusion by maintaining half-separate existences both among Northmen and Old English as Frigg and Freya. But to reconcile the supreme Mediterranean Earth Mother and the supreme northern Sky Father was a more difficult matter, particularly as there was a cuckoo in the nest in the person of the Earth Mother's lover, brother or son. When the divine father and mother came together in the north one might expect the lover, son or brother quietly to disappear, leaving little trace. But the lover was too strong and too important to go, and so the mythographers explain the *ménage à trois* in various ways.

We shall see what traces there remain in the north of the young lover or son so closely associated with the Earth Mother. The story is told in detail by the old Scandinavian poets and historians. According to the *Verse* and *Prose Edda*, the goddess Frigg extracted a promise from everything in creation not to harm her son Balder the Beautiful; everything, that is to say, except the mistletoe which seemed to her to be too young to swear oaths. So – Balder led a charmed life and the gods in sport used to cast all manner of weapons at him without his ever taking any harm. But Loki, the mischiefmaker of the gods, discovered Frigg's secret and taking a shaft of mistletoe he thrust it into the hands of the blind god Hoder, who in turn threw it at Balder and brought him to bloody death. Balder went down into the underworld ruled by the goddess Hel . . .

Is that where Alec – Balder the Beautiful – Alec of the purple shirt and the psychedelic rising sun like a stab wound under his heart, should lie now, under the stones . . . punished by the goddess Hel for his crime of seduction, betrayal, abandonment . . . ?

How can we answer these questions, child?

We can say that there is no doubt of the existence of the Earth Mother, the Great Goddess, and her gradual loss of power to the patriarchal god, the Indo-European Sky Father.

And that that primitive ignorance of the fertilizing power of the male had been the cause of this original state of affairs. So when – and how – did men catch on, as Tess, always wise and witty and irreverent, would have said?

(She loved jokes about sex, did Tess. I was the solemn one, learning of the initiation rites at the temple of Eleusis from my mother's old book of Greek myths and legends: Demeter's vain search, in the guise of a nurse, for her disappeared Persephone; Ishtar, deep in the dark temple passageway, in the step-by-step removal of earrings, bracelets, robe. Her eventual ritual deflowering, impaled on a stick.)

– The first striptease, Tess would say. And sounds like some sort of gang-bang afterwards. Can't have been too good in those days, can it, Liza-Lu?

And, as my mother looked up, shocked, from the book, couldn't I hear her thinking, fearing for Tess who was so fearless, so sure she belonged to an age as far from those barbaric days as the earth is from Saturn: be careful, child. For just as bad can happen to you.

And, of course, it did. The question I can't answer is whether the chain we are all caught up in is a direct result of that first loss of women's power.

When men first saw that the moon, considered in the ancient way to be the fertilizing principle – so a woman had only to lie in the moonlight to conceive – when all women, as was recorded, menstruated at the New Moon and crops were planted then, leaving the waning moon for the dark side, the realm of Hecate and corpses and evil spells – when men saw that women didn't conceive in this

33

way, then they assumed power and the Earth Mother began to die.

And the Ancient Greeks, with their nymphs and nereids, made pregnant by rivers and winds: they too have goddesses whose suffixes turned masculine when the source of conception became clear.

Penelope, wife of Odysseus, is a prime example of the end of female succession and the rise of male inheritance and power. Never, until the time of the Odyssey – possibly about the time our Mesolithic foremothers are gathering firewood in Marshwood Vale and hunting the red deer and the otter on the shores of the Fleet – would a woman, once married, have to leave her father's land and come to live in her husband's territory.

Up until the time of the slow, but inevitable eradication of the old goddesses, Penelope would most certainly have kept her name and her entitlement to her land. Odysseus would have come and lived with *her*.

Is this what has been wrong, since those early and almost unguessable days? That the balance was always, by nature, intended to be the other way round – from what we have all lived under, endured, survived through love and struggle: that men should always have been subservient to women, and the old ballad, sung since the ending of that natural way – the ballad of love, seduction, betrayal . . . and, just sometimes, revenge – is a record of that reversal in the natural order of things?

If Alec Field had been as Balder the Beautiful to Tess's Great Goddess, her son, her brother, her lover instead of her mini-patriarch and casual seducer, would there be a greater harmony in the world?

The Very Near and Distant Past

❖❖❖

The nomadic hunters and fishers were succeeded, before 3000 B.C., by a larger and more advanced group of settlers, arriving from the continent of Europe through the southwest of England. Neolithic people – the end of the nomadic way of life and the establishing of domesticated animals and pottery, the setting up of farming and trade. And gradually, as the animal bones on the sites of these people show, the chalk downlands of Dorset lost their light fringing of woodland and began to be covered by expanses of turf – which remained the basis of agriculture in these areas until the nineteenth century.

Huge barrows and burial mounds give evidence of a new way of life – on Hambledon Hill near Blandford Forum and at Maiden Castle near Dorchester.

The amount of labour involved in erecting tomb and enclosure was considerable. Together, these monuments stand testimony both to the effectiveness of the farming, which must now have been capable of producing a considerable surplus to allow so much labour to be devoted to tasks other than food production, and to the ability of the farmers to undertake large-scale communal tasks. But by the middle of the millennium there are signs that the structure of society was changing. As the farming community had expanded, its need to establish rights to herds and land use must have begun to press. That these rights had on occasion to be defended is shown by the massive defences constructed round the Hambledon Hill enclosure.

At Hambledon, the scale of these defences is quite astonishing. An entire hill with attendant spurs was defended by a ditch and timber-framed rampart system enclosing an area of some one hundred and sixty acres. Parts of the ramparts have been destroyed by fire and there is a density of arrowheads around the entrance to the site. By the central gate the body of a young man has been discovered, with an arrow lodged in his chest.

We can only wonder at the new life for women with the advent of surplus and domesticity.

Was it the hearth which finally subjugated them? – four thousand years after the Neolithic tribes made their settlements near Dorchester (behind where we sit, my child, on Chesil Beach, as the sun lengthens and it comes to be time to go back to the Mill). Is the danger for women that to 'settle down', to stay in one place is, still, like the female sea-urchin, to have a stone placed on you?

And that stone was duty, subservience, childbearing, self-sacrifice. The hearth needs an angel, you could say.

It may well be. From the ramparts of Hambledon did a girl walk one dark night, having planted an arrow in her lover's chest?

We can never know.

The time is coming for our departure from the beach. Ella, cold suddenly, and hungry, has run back to her mother's house (her mother has too many cares to make ends meet to worry overmuch that Ella doesn't attend school) and I'll stop my history lesson now. The coming of the Wessex elite, with the Bronze Age, will mean nothing to you, Baby Tess, as you lie in an even earlier age yourself: reptilian almost, with your tiny sloping chin and lidless eyes that blink up at me sometimes when I speak.

You'll know one day what those Bronze Age ancestors of ours did . . . You'll have the stones of Stonehenge as long in your mind as your poor foremother did – the Tess who went to the Stones with the man she really loved and gave herself up to the gallows.

They built Stonehenge, these Bronze Age people who – at least in Wessex – placed most of their acquired wealth with the dead.

They liked rare commodities. Jet and amber from the shores of the North Sea, shale from Dorset, Irish gold and man-made faience.

They liked to bury all these treasures with the dead. And they liked the annual sacrifice at the Stones at the midsummer solstice, too: the bright red of the life-blood as it trickled from the altar.

The place smells of sacrifice. It's where Tess sacrificed herself, on the altar of love.

Part Two

When We Were Very Young

✦⟩⟩⟩⟨⟨⟨✦

Tess is up in a tree.

It's the big ash tree, at the far end of our garden, and Retty and I – and just for this once, Maud, the little girl we're not really allowed to play with – are standing under the tree and looking up at Tess. It's a steamy day, with a gold-coloured mist coming off Chesil Beach; and the figs on the old fig tree that pokes up onto our first-floor terrace are swelling, pale and veined – like, Victor says, those things under there. And he pinches poor Retty until she bursts into tears. Maud, who is Victor's sister, is another of the children from the caravan site at Charmouth who is on the list of proscribed playmates. Which makes them both, of course, as desirable as the latest fad from America (for we're in the fifties now, and the war has left its scar, its feeling of emptiness here). Victor and his sister with knobbly knees and a pigtail that looks as if it had never been undone and combed out, are as tempting as bubble gum or a visit to the pictures at Weymouth, where our mother says there's nothing 'suitable' on for us at all.

Except for *Snow White and the Seven Dwarfs* – but how many times have we seen that? We want something with grown-ups, even if it's Doris Day in a bright, girlish frock; or Bette Davis, smoking a cigarette as if she had chosen it specially to get sucked between her lips, her legs in sheer silk stockings, rubbing against each other with a sound like the hiss of the sea on the stones.

Victor and Maud, who missed out on childhood somehow, are as near to that grown-up world as we can get. Their father was in prison once, I heard my mother say to Retty's mother, Mrs Priddle. He went to Scotland for a job, but he's Welsh really, and they caught him even though he thought he'd got that far away. When he came out the whole family moved to the caravan site near Charmouth.

Now we're going to walk over to Charmouth. There's an ice-cream parlour there, run by a man called Mr Rossini. We know Mr Rossini well, because he short-changed me once (always the youngest: the easily fooled: the idea of a person instead of the real thing. That's how I felt then, at least, and I suppose, to tell the truth, I feel much the same today). We never entirely recover from our early position in the family – eldest, middle one, youngest – like Goldilocks, in search of her identity in the house of the three bears.

Tess's position is unmistakable, particularly just now as she looks out from her safe saddle in the tree and tells us just when she'll be ready to go to Charmouth. We wait, looking up, our mouths open. We will do exactly as Tess tells us to do. In all our games, Tess is Queen and we are her train-bearers, slaves and messengers. Up in the ash, Tess is unassailable.

So how, how did the Queen come to fall out of the tree?

When she seemed about to fly into the skies on her branch? Tess, Queen of both Night and Day.

– I'll catch you up, Tess says. I want a cone with that raspberry stuff.

Now Charmouth is a long way off. We all know we have no chance at all of getting there on foot, and that Tess is the only one with the know-how to hitch us a lift once we're on the main coast road from Abbotsbury to Lyme. The rest of us are too young: we'd just get thrown back at our parents like a catch of sprats. Tess has authority: once she flagged down a whole army convoy and the soldiers laughed and whistled as we climbed aboard. (This, needless to say, is strictly forbidden too.)

– Come on, Tess, Retty Priddle says. Please!

Tess moves regally in the tree, settling herself with apple and book as if she had all day to make up her mind. We see her in the lacing of the branches, as if she grew in the ash herself, and could never be detached from it. In our short silence we hear the little stream as it runs, a few feet away, along the boundary of the garden and the steep green hill. Somehow, the stream seems to belong to

Tess as well, and she to it, as if its noisy clatter could be stopped every time she waved her wand cut from the willow on its bank.

We all believed in that kind of thing. And our mother believed in magic, too, but she was too far ahead of her time – or rather, she had the courage to try and return to her own true time – and she paid a heavy price for it.

So this is the story of the day of the tree and the water and the mother and the daughter – and if we had learnt from it then we might not have ended up, as my father inevitably put it, in the pickle we're in today.

Maud, probably because she has that wicked, old-beyond-her-years thing about her, is the first to notice that Tess's attitude to coming down out of the tree alters suddenly when Victor and Alec climb up through the hedge and into the garden. (It's the only way up, from the public footpath to Abbotsbury, other than walking through the Mill; and they would have been most urgently requested to get out by either one of our parents if they'd tried that way.)

Maud sniggers as Tess climbs down. And Tess, knowing why, turns on her in sudden rage. Long before they're women, they understand each other as well as the birds that swoop in from the Fleet, never colliding with each other, as they pick their cliff nesting place, calling out in what sounds like spite as the other dives and rides the waves. It's as if the Queen needs the maidservant to plot against her, bring her to ridicule, put an end to her reign. To collude, in some way, with the male: for Maud, as Victor's sister, is as keen to re-establish her own superiority as Tess is to maintain her power over us all. And, as Maud goggles in that maddening way, she runs in under the hoop of the willow tree and looks out through a fringe of twigs. One to her: Tess should never have climbed down.

Now we are all turning anxiously in the direction of Alec. He, again, is the only one of us of an age and stature to be able to thumb a ride along that interminable straight road that goes past West Bay and the end of Chesil Beach and on to the soft sands of Charmouth

41

and Lyme Regis. Without him, the prospect of the ice-cream cone with that new, bright, artificial raspberry splash, as hallucinogenic in its desirability as the fruits of Goblin Market, will never be ours. Already dreading the soft drip of the bottled liquid down the side of the cone and onto my hand while – as Tess told me to – I count my change properly this time, and don't eat a mouthful until I've done so – I am still near to tears at the thought that our forbidden journey may be called off.

For Alec, despite the fact of Tess dropping to the ground from the ash tree and strolling over to him as if she and only she had the right to approach him at all, is apparently pretty cool on the idea of going to Charmouth. He says he'd rather go fishing.

It's Alec – who's the one Tess really likes, we all know; she just takes Victor over when she feels like it to keep poor Retty in her place – who mentioned, just casually and before we have time to hear him properly, that there's a funfair at West Bay.

– What? What? Retty and Maud circle the bigger boys.

With the exception of Tess, who was taken on a big dipper when I was too young to go, none of us has any clear idea of what a funfair can be.

But it sounds like everything we are looking for. And we know, without having to be particularly clever, that our mother and father wouldn't like the idea of us going there. So, when our mother comes out onto the flagged terrace that shows the top of the fig tree and houses the tubs of winter-flowering plants and herbs she keeps shielded from the southwesterly gales, we move, again in silent accord, into a pretend game of hopscotch.

– I'm going to the shops. You all stay here playing.

If we'd listened, we'd have guessed that our mother – mine and Tess's, that is – wasn't convinced at all that we'd stay there playing.

And we should have guessed that if she'd been really worried about us, she wouldn't have chosen that moment to say she was going to the shops. At the very least, she'd have popped over to Retty's mother and asked her to keep an eye on us while she was away.

We should have guessed that our mother's hardly seeming to care at all was the first sign of an illness described as such because

42

at that time there was no place or freedom for such as our mother in the world.

But here we are, hopping and skipping and jumping. To make the game a little more interesting, we're jumping the stream. Retty gets her feet wet, of course. But even at its deepest, the stream never gets dangerously deep in our garden. It has to fall down the sides of the steep incline at the far end of the terrace before it reaches and supplies the millpond, and there it gets really deep. That part's fenced off, right along the terrace from the upper branches of the fig tree to the first alders and pines of the little copse on the near side of the hill. You'd have to be a grown-up to get over a fence that high and fall, fall into the whirling water below.

Fairy Tales Replayed

Here you must leave us for a while, on the road to Oz: it's 1958 and eleven-year-old Tess is strutting along just a few paces ahead as she always does, pigeon chest stuck out, the top of her Aertex vest showing above the collar of the 'little-girl' gingham dress.

Liza-Lu – two years younger and destined to stay that way until Tess becomes a non-person, that is, a woman suspected of murder, and then Liza-Lu becomes respectable, the elder of the two – Liza-Lu is humming to herself and making up stories as she goes along. (No one looks at Liza-Lu, not even the man she eventually marries, who was meant for Tess, and she is forced to look at the world instead, and make up stories about it.)

Maudie, also nine years old and with a squint that makes people say she's taking after her father, she'll come to no good: didn't she take a Mars bar from old Mrs Bailey's shop only last week and the old lady was too kind to report her? But watch out next time! And that pigtail . . . you could see a bird's nest in there if you looked closer. But Maudie doesn't care. In her mind's eye is candyfloss, a great magic spun ball of sweet heaven, like they eat in the pictures you can see in the one-and-ninepennies at the Bridport Majestic for nothing if the usherette happens to think she's seen a mouse scurrying across the foyer floor . . .

Victor. Nearly as tall – and as old – as Alec. That is, about twelve years of age and as swarthy as his sister. They're gypsies, there's no harm in them, our mother says when neighbours complain of the Charmouth caravan people and say they're missing money from the drawers of Welsh dressers, they can't leave the back door open like they used to. And wasn't one of the Nasebury girls nearly pulled off the road and into a lane by one of the Charmouth campers?

Alec. Walking in the middle of the road just as it curves round at its most dangerous, jumps out of the way when the cars come. (Tess can beat him at playing chicken but she wouldn't dream of it while we're still in view of the Mill. Our swan-loving father, when it comes to punishing his daughters for some peccadillo, thinks nothing of administering a good beating, or, worst of all for the communicative, gregarious Tess, a whole day of solitary confine-ment.) So Alec, taller than Victor, blond-haired but with the greasy blond turning already to that sleek Brylcreemed look all the boys hanker after – a satiny quiff, a face like Elvis's on the record covers – swerves alone in the empty country road, desperate to create a drama of the Midwest or urban wastelands of a longed-for, distant America. (He'll get there one day. But by then, without knowing it, he truly is a marked man.)

Retty Priddle. Oh, Retty! How can you forgive me? You're the only one of us, on that brick road to the West Bay funfair, who actually has some thought for others. You're eleven years old and you're holding my hand on one side and Maudie's on the other in case a big lorry comes too close and we cry out, frightened. When Maudie's sandal comes undone – it would; those shoes, as our Nasebury good neighbours would say, are rightly a disgrace – you're the one who calls for everyone to stop and wait unless she gets left behind.

Retty, who knew how to love, and fell in love with the wrong man, a man who was himself marked out for an extraordinary fate: lover of a murderess, prophet of a new age disgraced. Poor Retty, who drowned for her love. But I will make it up to you, Retty, for all the unhappiness you suffered. I will tell Ella and Tess's baby granddaughter all there is to know.

I see Ella now as she runs in the fast, end-September dusk between our houses, eager already to get away from the lessons of the past. Ella, who must go to school and yet refuses to. Who asks, why should I learn this history and maths and English, Liza-Lu? It's so *boring*. And to whom I must teach the Living History; and the Maths that will make a different equation of the world; and English as it first came out of the mouths of women, as they passed their secrets – precisely – by word of mouth.

In the beginning of our lesson, Ella –

For here you are now, holding up a book at me, frowning at the task your mother has set for you.

– Mum says can you go into Dorchester for her tomorrow and get some more of these?

As we go into the Mill, Ella holds out the guidebook. In the kiosk by the swannery where her mother sits all day, selling postcards, and lobelias in pots from the tropical gardens, and entrance tickets, these guides go like hot cakes. And this year, for no reason that anyone can give, the swannery will be open beyond the equinox, right to the end of October. (Putting profit before safety, say the Nasebury folk; when the seas come up and threaten to spill over Chesil Beach at the time of the autumn gales, children have been known to get trapped on the high ridge of shingle and, every few years, one drowns. So the enclosure is securely locked and the birds left to their migration across the Fleet in private. Not this year, though. Tourism, the Heritage business, is big business in west Dorset these days, and the late sun brings coachloads to see the wooden pens abutting the Fleet, and to catch a glimpse of the swanherd, in his post held down the generations for over six hundred years at Abbotsbury Swannery.)

I almost tell Ella that it's not worth giving visitors the guidebooks they put out. For if anything's an example of dead history, it's what

45

they write. But there's no sense in upsetting her poor mother; and I say I will. (If I can, I add under my breath. If I'm still here. But I must still be here, to tell the tale.)

And, as Ella goes up to take Baby Tess and lay her down in her cot – and as she looks round the familiar room and adds the new baby – miraculously arrived as she had always somehow known they did – to the faded old sofa by the fire, and the kitchen table at the far end by the door out into the night garden, the table laid with a lino cloth and a fresh egg for her tea – and as she looks round the long room again, with its low beams and its collection of bric-à-brac and flotsam that no one moved away when one after another my parents departed, I see her begin to try and make sense of history.

She sees my parents' history: the piece of driftwood that looks like a leg broken off at the knee, or an arm and fist, so gnarled and veined it could be painted by Dürer – it lies on the sill and my father brought it in one day; it was washed up on Chesil Bank and for some reason it caught his fancy.

The lump of stone from the River Brit, in the Marshwood Vale where all your foremothers come from, little Tess, that my mother found and said had gold in it. My father laughed; but when you pour water on it the gold gleams – the stone is as veined as the wood, but with a living ore from millions of years ago. My father's wood is a dead thing.

I see her looking at the quilt my mother made, that was on her bed and is now covering Baby Tess; and I see her frown again, in the effort to understand generation, continuity, the nameless beauty of women's work down the centuries: embroidery, tapestry, patchwork, samplers, homilies, stitches of prayer. She sees, in this room, the labours of my poor mother – as she waited for my father, out to all hours, up to the thighs in waders, on shores dotted with sleeping white birds; and in the quilt she sees the gold my mother wove from her pile of worthless straw.

For the moment, Ella, you're happy as you walk to the table and lift from the brown egg the cosy my mother knitted when she was in hospital having Tess – and she'd gone in in such a hurry she'd picked up the wrong bag of wool and there was only enough for an

46

egg cosy (a bad omen some of the nurses said). You slice the top off with a knife. You're smiling now – and something in the sudden lifting in the atmosphere makes Baby Tess open her eyes.

Can she see you? In the blurred blue of her eyes she can see you, perhaps – lifting a spoon to eat egg and 'soldiers' of bread and butter (made by me to tempt you here, Ella, for your next story or lesson).

You're awake, little Tess, in this room with the low ceiling at the end with the log fire, and the millwheel in the middle, and the great white stone keeping the door into the garden securely closed against the beginning of the equinoctial gales.

And as you're awake, and history lessons must start as fairy tales – as you will discover in your time – I'll tell you of my mother, your great-grandmother – and about the foremother of Ella, too: the first Tess.

Stay with me, as those runaway children dance down the road to the swings and the roundabouts of West Bay. Hear how the beliefs of an extraordinary and brave woman – and the punishment she received for them – led her to end this particular day. But be grateful for her. As I have said, our mother went to the beginning of time, to the roots of women's poetry and myth, to the origins of the lies they had for so long been told; and she was before her time in doing so. But without her – and without other pioneers like her – we would still be as unfocused in our way of seeing things as an infant – as Baby Tess.

On the Art of the Spinster

I didn't know then – indeed I couldn't know until much later – that the stories told by my mother were warnings really: coded messages passed from the lips of one woman to another down the generations and in need of constant repetition in case the old stories were forgotten.

But the worst of it was that two men – the Brothers Grimm – listened to these old tales told by mothers to their daughters; and they decided to record them for posterity.

For a male posterity, of course. How could we have a posterity when we have no past?

Like the tapestries, embroideries and patchworks which carried the message of our anonymous love or suffering, the oral tradition of telling stories was our great, unsigned charter.

And, like the earth before the balance was thrown out by the rise of the phallocentric culture, the stories we told were equally about the bravery, and the hardships, and the love and growing up of female and male children alike.

But the Brothers Grimm could understand only the tales of courage and manliness and chivalry on the part of the boys. The girls were relegated to virtues – Patient Griselda; or sheer physical beauty – Sleeping Beauty; Beauty and the Beast. Always we must read that our heroine is a Beauty.

Would it have been better for my mother to have left these tales in their patriarchal form – frightening, but somehow not quite real, or convincing (to little girls and women, at least)? Good for interpretation by Freudian male analysts – but not for us?

No, she would not have done better, definitely not.

But the truth, like the truth about women, is far from reassuring or anodyne.

Men have professed through the centuries that they are 'terrified of women'. They have clothed us in fragrance and exquisite gentleness and pink and white colouring to hide the primeval truth they know very well lies in us. The blood and the birth-pain and the milk and the sex-juice that in Eastern cultures is called 'chi', giver of energy, and the tears. They are afraid of us – and so were the Brothers Grimm. They preferred us to remain silent on the subject of ourselves. Yet my mother did try to present a balanced picture: to read one story from the coloured picture books and to tell the next from the store of words that lies in all women: and, as all women know, the story won't end well.

My mother tried to teach us that the story can end well, if we see the way and we keep our strength and courage. It was immensely hard for her to do: and I can understand her suffering – and the retribution of the shocked and angry world – only years after she has died.

At the same time, she has no more died than the first Tess who lived on this western shore. The Tess who, too, lived by telling and hearing and not by the male structure of the written word. Like that first Tess, of the Celtic people, who lived and fought here as brave as any warrior, my mother believed that death was only the midpoint way of life.

And so do I believe that. And next time, I say to the infant Tess as Ella half leans, half sits on my lap (she's too old for a fairy tale, she thinks: but none of us ever are), is now: your time has come and the cycle of unhappiness and imbalance must finally be broken.

Like the sea, I will say the same song over and over, until your unformed mind shapes like a rock worn by the rising and falling of my tales.

– You see, my mother says.

And I do see her, as I sit here on this wild night, with the wind whistling already higher in the chimney than it has dared to go all summer, and the first of the leaves of the fig tree blown off and scampering the length of the stone-flagged terrace.

I see her, Ella, as we sit on this lip of worn stone, some four hundred years old, that juts into the room of the Old Mill.

She encouraged Tess to see herself as a free spirit. And then put all that blame she carried around with her straight onto Tess when we were 'naughty'.

Our poor mother. She was only trying.

I see her there, at the end of the room where the very last part of it goes under the oak staircase – when our father opened out the first floor of the Mill it just came to be there: it was a broom cupboard once, I suppose. It's dark there and the light goes in strands like silk – or wool – as it comes down through the open slats of the old staircase.

She's spinning, I say to Ella. She told us about the loom.

And I tell Ella that it was my mother who said we must recoup

49

our powers, that we were spinsters all, that the female side of the family tree is known as the distaff side because spinning was the work of women; and that we must spin a new tapestry on our looms.

Our mother tells us this on a snowy, cold night in January – when we are very young, when we haven't even yet danced away to the freedom of the fair – and our father is out somewhere in the flat salty marshes of the Fleet, trying to help swans frozen to icy lumps under the mantle of snow.

Did I see then that my mother was a spinster, whether she was married or not?

Did I see that her exclusion from my father's life only mirrored the situation of a million wives, living on the periphery of their husbands' lives, jobs, 'hobbies'?

Perhaps I did, for when my mother sighed and stood up and went to take down the decorations from the little Christmas tree by the fireplace, I knew somehow that another year was starting for her: another year almost impossibly difficult to bear, with the days of the Lord of Misrule done with for another twelvemonth and the normal structures of daily life returned.

– Tomorrow is the sixth of January, St Distaff's Day, she said. The distaff is the staff from which the flax is drawn in spinning. And spinning is women's work. So it means that holiday-time is over.

Did I understand? Tess pretended she did. She glanced upwards and said in a tone of mock prayer: St Catherine, grant us our wish. And she recited the spell to get a husband:

> St Catherine, St Catherine, oh lend me thine aid
> And grant that I niver may die an eld maid.
> Send me a husband, answer my plea,
> A *good* one, St Catherine,
> But arn-a-one better than
> Narn-a-one, St Catherine.

But my mother frowned. The ruins of the little chapel on the hill above us were too important to her, I think, to be taken lightly. The saint, patron saint of spinsters, had, she said, often visited her in her dreams and told her to be brave and stay young.

Even then, my mother was beginning to show symptoms of what we would now call a 'female malady' – female because it has been induced by no virus or ascertainable indisposition of the mind, but by the imbalance of living in a world where a woman's rights and true expression are denied to her.

Today, those suffering from my mother's disease are given lithium, learning at least that a mineral, a part of living rock, can help the wild mood swings of a being denied her own humanity.

Like a pendulum broken loose from the stifling confines of a grandfather clock, your great-grandmother, Baby Tess, in the last years of the mid-century – while the world built itself up from the last war, and exploded its nuclear devices in 'trials' that killed and maimed – our mother Mary Hewitt told us her strange stories.

The good people of Nasebury thought her mad.

But it was the truth she told that they couldn't bear. Only Retty Priddle's mother didn't mind her little girl coming to tea with us.

Maybe, to understand my mother, you had to know what it was to be born in that most remote and tucked-away of places – and even now it's as easy to lose yourself there as in the days of Thomas Hardy. (Hardy loved the Marshwood Vale. On his way there he walked Tess down the hill from Toller Down to Beaminster, and had her walk back in thin pumps when her boots were stolen. He found the dying mistletoe that marked her tragic wedding night at the station at Evershot.)

So, Ella and little Tess, I'll tell you, as the history books tell it, about the land my mother came from – as well as your foremothers who first settled here.

The Marshwood Vale is a wide, rather thinly populated area, which always appears to be set entirely apart from the rest of Dorset. One crosses it briefly from Crewkerne to Axminster, with a branch-off to Lyme Regis, but otherwise it is not on the way to anywhere and many of its corners are unvisited by tourists. It is all the better for that, and certainly its beauties are unspectacular and lie largely in its secretiveness, and the more unobvious charms of quiet and occasionally real wild country. It has, however, its main attractions, among them the twin giants of Lewesdon and Pilsdon Pen, the two highest points in the county. There is a local saying, 'As alike as Pilsdon and Lewesdon', which means not alike at all and is a lovely piece of rural irony. Pilsdon is a bald, promontory fort, Lewesdon a wooded hump. The Vale also contains the two beautiful earthworks of Lambert's and Coney's Castle, but strictly speaking this is not one single vale at all. It is a large, irregular stretch of broken country bounded by the Devon Blackdowns to the west, the Axe Valley to the north, the Dorset chalk downs to the east and south and the coastal hills on the extreme south. All these natural features have the effect of cutting off this part of Dorset from the rest of the world.

Pilsdon Pen

This hilltop, the highest in the country, is crowned by an oval fort of some three hectares. The defence consists of two lines of rampart and ditch with a counterscarp, broken by entrances at the northern corner and halfway along the southwest side. There are pillow mounds and possible barrows inside the hill fort.

Excavations between 1964 and 1971 revealed a number of circular wooden-hut foundations in the centre of the fort. One of the huts may have been a gold-worker's shop, since a crucible with traces of gold on it was found. These huts were replaced during the first century B.C. by an unusual large rectangular wooden building with an open courtyard at the centre. It was at least thirty-two metres long and each wing was not less than two metres wide. From the footing trenches it was impossible to decide how the building had looked or what its function had been, but one might suggest a cult centre as a possibility. When the building had ceased to function, its foundations were covered with a low mound of earth, traces of which can still be seen on the surface today. Cobblestones were laid at the centre of the enclosure and there the excavators found the head of a Roman ballista bolt.

From Pilsdon Pen, a walk can be made down to the sea to join the coast path from Lyme Regis or Bridport, the walk taking in the rim of the vale, then descending into and crossing it to reach its chief village, Whitchurch Canonicorum. The first village passed is Bettiscombe.

At Bettiscombe Manor lived the last members of the Pinney family, who had rented their other house nearby to Wordsworth. The wealth of the family was based on West Indian plantations set up by an early member, Azariah Pinney, who escaped to Nevis when being sought as a rebel follower of the Duke of Monmouth. It was a descendant of Azariah who resettled here in Dorset. With him from Nevis he brought the skull of a Negro slave, a man who had been called Bettiscombe when he worked on the plantation. The skull was not thought to be the most pleasant of furniture by other owners of the manor and was buried in the churchyard. From the grave came frightening screams, and the house was filled with strange and terrifying sounds. The skull was retrieved and several other graves were tried, but always with the same result. Finally it was thrown into a pond in the hope that the water would lay the spirit. But the noises in the house continued and the owners had to borrow a boat and rake the pond to retrieve the skull. It was replaced in the house and the spirit silenced again. The skull is still there, as it always was, but the legends that have grown up around it have multiplied . . . the less romantic maintain that it was retrieved from a burial mound on Pilsdon Pen and is of a young woman from the Bronze or Iron Age. If it was a woman, then she was confined here, perhaps even walled up, until her death. There is no adequate way finally to silence the screaming skull of Bettiscombe.

(NOTE: a Professor of Human and Comparative Anatomy, Royal College of Surgeons, confirmed recently that it was indeed the skull of a female aged between twenty-five and thirty years 'probably dug from some barrow on a west Dorset hill'.)

From Pilsdon Pen you can look nine hundred and seven feet down – and across the Marshwood Vale to the sea.

As my mother told the story, I saw Tess (it was always Tess, as

53

I've said, who was the Beauty of these tales) stride across the hills from wooded Lewesdon to our bald, heather-covered fort. And on, over the flat-topped hills to the sea.

How could we care about the story of Beauty and the Beast, read to us in a polite voice by my mother from the Walter Crane book in the Mill, when we knew Tess could go in her iron shoes along all the southern coastal hills as far as Maiden Castle, the most famous and impregnable of the hill forts, and wake her prince with a resounding kiss?

Tess could walk over seven hills to find her love, woman, man, or the wide sky she could keep to herself, as the Celt women had done, before the fall of Maiden Castle (which, as you know, is just to the north of us here, Ella, at Abbotsbury; to the west of Dorchester), and before the fall of the temple of my mother's country, Pilsdon Pen.

I think she honestly believed it.

Yet Tess – of course – had no idea of how love had shaped the country where she walked; and how the love and longing of one man would shape her future too.

It is time, my children, to show you the procreator, lover and murderer of his very own Tess in these west Dorset hills – in this case, Mr Thomas Hardy at home.

Tess's Mouth

❦

It's unbearably dull at Max Gate, the cold, ugly house where Thomas Hardy brought such unhappiness – and where, after her death, in a fever of remorse, he fell in love with and wrote all his best poems – to Emma. It's a 'structure at once mean and pretentious, with no grace of design or detail, and with two hideous low-flanking turrets with pointed roofs of blue slate', according to one observer at the time of building. And, worst of all, the stairs up to Emma's bedroom go past the walls of Hardy's study. In the last months of her illness, he will hear her mount those stairs – often in agony – and he won't go even as far as the landing to offer her assistance.

No wonder, after Emma's death, he feels remorse!

But at the time, nothing matters to Thomas Hardy except himself – and his new love, of course.

For Hardy has fallen in love – with the young Florence Dugdale – she who sent him a posy of flowers in her ecstasy of admiration; she who, invited to Max Gate with Hardy's old friend Florence Henniker, stood at the front door as she was leaving and drew the great man's attention to the flowers in his own front garden.

'Until then the faint scent/Of the bordering flowers swam unheeded away', penned Hardy lovingly.

But in the autumn of 1888, the meeting with Florence Dugdale is seventeen years away into the future.

And Thomas Hardy longs for love. He dreams of a young woman he sees sometimes in London, Agatha Thornycroft.

He dreams, too, of Augusta Way, whom he sees when he visits his mother at Bockhampton.

Most of all, he dreams of Augusta Way. And, in his dreams, he word-paints Tess.

The old ballad begins to be sung through Hardy, in that grim house where Emma, increasingly absent-minded, makes the running of the house and the management of servants an impossible burden to them all.

Hardy's best companion is his dog Moss, a brindled-looking animal, half-Labrador. They walk together, in the Valley of the Little Dairies and the Valley of the Great Dairies (Blackmoor and Frome) and on Egdon Heath, where Moss starts up a hare.

And, as the hare dances away, Hardy sees his love disappearing too: his taste for love, his ability to love, his own capability of inspiring love in others. After all, he is nearing fifty.

Hardy stands alone with Moss, on the outcropping of green hill that was once an Iron Age settlement and looks down at the sea and Chesil Beach.

He bends to pick up a stone.

With its worn, rough curvature and an indentation at the centre under two stripes and a knobbly protuberance that is like a nose under eyebrows, he could be holding an early love goddess: a Neolithic Venus: a totem for the fertility he feels draining away on all sides – from his loveless, childless marriage, from his own powers as a fertilizing male.

Hardy looks at the stone and it seems to look back at him.

Anonymous were the representations of the individual in antiquity. All-important was the shape below the casual dash of features, of eyes and brows and nose.

The mouth. The vulva. So shrunk were these goddesses of copulation and procreation that the one stood for the other, and the figurine – round, squatting under its outsize baby head – was only a receptacle for a receptacle. The bearer of a hole.

Hardy dreams of Tess's love. He sees in his creation (for already Tess is more alive than the original, the pretty dairymaid Augusta Way – and, to this day, remains so) the mouth of his dreams. Perhaps it's Agatha Thornycroft's mouth, seen and conceivably tasted on those metropolitan visits so necessary to an unhappily married genius who lives in the depths of Dorset. But, unquestionably, first and foremost, it's the mouth of Augusta Way.

And as Hardy walks back – a long walk that will take him through Powerstock and Toller Porcorum – up onto the ridge of the hill that leads down to Beaminster via Evershot – he fills his Tess with love and hope and dreams – and as surely takes them away again, like the sea dragging and pushing on the stones.

Hardy blows life into Tess. Of course, she's a fictional character when all is said and done, and he has to give her the kiss of life – that is, artificial respiration.

When he has brought her back to life – when he has blown his own breath into her mouth – he will fill that mouth with stones.

*

56

Of Tess's mouth, the erotic symbol which infatuated both Alec D'Urberville and Angel Clare, Hardy wrote:

'her mobile peony mouth'
'the pouted-up deep red mouth'
'the red and ivory of her mouth'
'her flower-like mouth'
'those holmberry lips'
'surely there was never such a maddening mouth since Eve's'

and

'she was yawning, and he saw the red interior of her mouth as if it had been a snake's . . . The brimfulness of her nature breathed from her. It was a moment when a woman's soul is more incarnate than at any other time'

and Angel

'had never before seen a woman's lips and teeth which forced upon his mind with such persistent iteration the old Elizabethan simile of roses filled with snow'.

Poor Tess. He shaped her ready for the bloody sacrifice to come.

The Beginning of Tess

Love. 'The ferocious comedy of England, with its peculiar mark of violence'. Thus Thomas Stearns Eliot; and Thomas Hardy, with his predisposition for women and the gallows, preceded him as a transcriber of the old ballad. Love, betrayal, revenge: raped Philomela to Lucrezia Borgia: Hardy hears the strains as he walks the lanes and streets of Dorset; and as memories come stronger and clearer when they're of childhood, he revisits Bockhampton, where he grew up, and finds his Tess.

In 1888 Thomas Hardy is nearing fifty. His marriage to Emma Gifford is one of constant illness (on Emma's part) and heavy colds (on Hardy's). He dreams of the village beauties of his youth; in London, in an omnibus, he sees a girl with 'one of those faces of marvellous beauty which are seen casually in the streets but never among one's friends . . . Where do these women come from? Who marries them? Who knows them?' And at Bockhampton, where his mother still lives, he sees the beauty of Augusta Way.

Nothing in Thomas Hardy's life at this point holds any beauty. Three years have passed since he and Emma moved into a house remarkable for its ugliness, Max Gate, at Dorchester, where, due to its elevated position, it is exposed to the full rigour of winds from every direction. True, to the south and southwest it has magnificent views across to Came Wood and the monument to Admiral Hardy; and the downs which overlook Weymouth and the sea. And from the upper windows of Max Gate it is possible to look northwards over the Frome valley to Stinsford church, Kingston Maurward House, and the heath and woodlands surrounding his mother's Bockhampton cottage. But the landscape is empty and hollow, to the eyes of a man without love. Obsessively, he studies the murder trials of the time and of earlier in the century; he sees, under the quiet, peace and domesticity which is the smiling face of England, its recurring theme of cruelty, murder, reprisal and revenge. In the seedy, new-genteel suburbs, which Hardy, with his great desire to find himself in company as elevated as the position of his new house, Max Gate, would never dream of inhabiting, are the protagonists of the old ballad come back again: Adelaide Barrett, the 'Platonic Wife' who slowly administers chloroform to her voyeur-husband who has encouraged her to make love to the young, soulful rever-end, George Dyson; Madeleine Smith in Glasgow, of a refined and strait-laced family who force her to announce her engagement to a man she does not love, Mr Minnoch, and her measured adminis-tering of arsenic to the lover who couldn't marry and support her, L'Angelier.

Love. Thomas Hardy goes to Bockhampton, where as a child he went up to the barn at Kingston Maurward House to hear the old carols sung at Christmas; and from there he walks across to the manor of Kingston Maurward. He sees a milkmaid, a beauty who in 1888 is eighteen and who works in the dairy of her father, sharing in the milking and other chores. Her name is Augusta Way; and she will be his Tess, just as her father, Thomas Way, will be Dairyman Crick in the great novel that is forming in his mind. (NOTE: no shabby-genteel rendering of the old ballad will come from this. *Tess* is a rural drama in a landscape as old as myth, and, to Hardy's great sorrow and sense of loss, turning before his eyes to the new world and away from the old calendar of the countryside: the first cuckoo, the last swallow, harvest, Easter and Christmas, christening, marriage and burial coming round as they always had done and until now had shown no sign of changing.)

No, *Tess* will have none of the sordidness of these contemporary murders. *Tess* will be pure incandescence, the picture of woman wronged, the murderess as saint.

Love and melodrama. If a seedy note does creep in, it's at the lodgings in Sandbourne (Bournemouth, as we know) where Tess and Alec spend their second, unloving honeymoon. In these cut-price plush surroundings – as fake as the impostor Alec himself – Tess will be driven to the ultimate act of violence. And by killing him, she inevitably sentences herself.

By killing him, she doubly kills – for it is the terrible betrayal of Angel Clare – the refusal to accept her when she confesses her lovemaking with Alec, her baby – that she avenges while immolating herself as well.

Tess hangs.

And Angel Clare, after standing under that prison wall with Tess's young sister Liza-Lu, takes the girl's hand and they go off into the future together.

It's no way, really, for a young girl to start out in life. In the shadow of the gallows of her sister. What can have become of them? – as the Victorians used to say.

But I'll tell you the rest of the story, as far as I can. Which means, as you know, that we have to go as far back as we can.

For now, remember this: Hardy has found Augusta Way. They stand talking in the meadow. (How lovely she is. What a mouth! Hardy is driven insane by women's mouths.) They go indoors (for in those days there was no marked distinction, in old rural communities, between gentry and dairyman farmer: Thomas Way and his family live in part of Kingston Maurward Manor, a delicate and grand eighteenth-century house that is used just as any house would be, by a large family busy with a farm).

Do they kiss?

Kissing is very much on the poet's mind. At Evershot station on the way here, he has discovered some mistletoe that had been there 'ever since last Christmas (given by a lass?), of a yellow, saffron parchment colour'. This mistletoe will come to him again, when he writes of Tess's disastrous honeymoon with Angel Clare and her return to Wool Manor, where they had sworn to be so happy – before she told him of her past – to find it, mocking, discoloured, still hanging as a meaningless symbol above the bed.

Thomas Hardy kisses the beautiful milkmaid, Augusta Way.

And so begins the story, both literal and figurative, of your life.

When You Were Free

The owl hoots and the old black-and-white TV 'snows' so you can't see the face of the presenter, and to my eyes all those dots and whirling grains could be the piles of shale they're shifting at West Bay – expecting? – half-expecting? – to find the body of a man buried under there and thirty years dead.

So let me tell you, little Tess, before we go to the funfair that plays all day and all night in my memory – the fair where Tess lost her sense of freedom and happiness and adventure, if not, at least, her maidenhood (but what does that matter when freedom had gone?), and Alec became for once and all the champion, the chief and overlord of us all.

Let me tell you of the days when women strode and fought and were priestesses, druidic votaries with wreaths of the pink summer-flowering vervain about their necks.

Let me tell you

About the Celts

Up until about 400 B.C. the inhabitants of this island were Indo-European, a sophisticated race who managed to get through from Iron Age to Bronze Age without indulging in so much conflict that they wiped themselves out. (They were small and dark: Maud and Victor are pure Indo-European, Alec is pure Celt. Tess, with her dark beauty, is a mixture of the two.)

When the Celts came, everything changed. Their religion was of an otherworld, where Dis ruled, and a goddess who sounds closely allied to Demeter. They went in for bloody human sacrifices – to Earth Mother, the Great Goddess – and they told their history orally. The secrets of their power were passed down by word of mouth.

In Dorset their tribe was known as the Dwr-trigs (dwellers by water). And, like the water, they were ruled by the moon. Their time was cyclical time.

Does that sound familiar to you, Ella, as you wriggle there and want to get out of the history lesson altogether?

Listen, I'll tell you something – you see, you sat up already because you knew that if you were told something that way, it would mean something to *you*.

It wouldn't just be a piece of dead writing, as dead as that old piece of driftwood over there, important only to men of thousands of years ago.

What you heard would be like the streak of gold in the white stone my mother brought from Pilsdon Pen when she married my father, to remind her of the Marshwood Vale that was her real mother country.

You understand now, Ella.

And, Baby Tess, you are the soul of the first Tess – for the Celts believed that death is only a midpoint way in life. You have returned for your next half of life, as free and bracing (if you help to make it so) as the life of those Celtic women warriors, who lived in tribes and along with the men dyed their gold hair golder still. And worshipped trees and water. Lakes and bogs and streams and springs. And oaks and hazel. And mistletoe.

The druids taught that there was transmigration of souls. And, knowing they would live on in another body, the women and men of the children of Danau had an extraordinary courage.

Tall, golden-haired, they loved to wear high torques of gold at their necks and to fashion bronze mirrors where they could see their beauty.

They celebrated the dying and returning of the year.

They had a cult of the head; and severed heads abound in their forts and roundhouses.

They cut mistletoe with a gold knife – for it was 'all-healing' and must on no account fall from the oak or apple tree to the ground. As you did, Tess.

They worshipped water, and the women were free. To live in their own time, the waxing and waning of the moon. From the Celts comes the word fortnight, for it was in the two phases of the moon that they lived, endlessly dying and reborn.

Well, I told you this was a story about a tree and water, and a mother and daughter. And, as all women know, it won't end well. Baby Tess, it is for you to end it well after all.

Before the Fall . . .

✦≫≪✦

Even then, in the days of the druids, the end of the matrilineal age was in sight.

The brave Celtic women warriors – and many were as prepared as Boudicca, Queen of the Iceni in the east of England, when the Romans came and raped her daughters and threatened her with vassaldom – had already seen the beginning of the end spelt out for them.

The gods became male gods. The severed heads, like that of the screaming prisoner, 'confined and penned', of Bettiscombe, were more frequently female. Bound, gagged and blindfolded, women lay dead and naked in shallow graves for the crime of adultery.

Women were becoming expendable.

And on the side of the hill at Cerne Abbas a Giant appears. His triumphant phallus is as long as a field and rears up on the side of the hill towards the Dorset sky. His club twirls in thin grassland over chalk soil.

Barren couples, still, in the month of May, go and sit astride the Giant's cock, symbol of the overwhelming new power of Celtic man. They pray to conceive a child; and they have forgotten entirely the powers of fertility of the Great Goddess Earth.

So now it is that summer afternoon at West Bay, where the noise from the hurdy-gurdy makes Retty's eyes smart with tears – and Maudie, who is used to noise of all sorts from the caravan site at Charmouth, takes advantage of Retty's confusion to nick a sixpence from her purse and run off to buy a candyfloss.

Tess clings to the wall of death, taller and braver than Alec or Victor – just as the Celtic women, defending Maiden Castle against

63

the cruel and invincible attack of the Romans, came out with slings – and stones from Chesil Beach – to break the heads of their adversaries.

The boys in the wall of death all look longingly at Tess. She is so brave, and so beautiful.

As the wall spins, there isn't a boy who doesn't worship her.

So why, only a little while later, has Tess somehow conceded defeat? After all, she's still a child: and she's bigger than Alec at this stage, and much brainier at school.

You want to know, Ella, why there isn't a fair on at present at Bridport or West Bay, and I tell you because the summer is over now. And, too, they're shifting that pea-gravel, aren't they, because they'd sooner make a profit from putting a row of bungalows by the side of the sea than allow children to have fun there with the fairs and the itinerant gypsies and the sales where you can buy any type of livestock, from a mongrel with yellow eyes to a fine horse.

But I'll tell you again about the big dipper if you like. And the ghost train. And the fortune-teller who said something to Tess that made her come out of the tent all white, like the time she was sick on the picnic at Torquay.

The dipper – maybe that's where she – Tess, I mean – had her fatal lack of nerve.

Because she'd shown nothing – except amused contempt – in the ghost train, although Retty grasped that it was the screaming skull that had come to get her, and even Maudie thought the woman in chains and rags was the ghost of that horrible motor accident on the Lyme road the week before.

As for the fortune-teller, Tess got her colour back all right after a few minutes – especially when Alec and Victor started teasing her about the serious expression she had on. ('What was it, Tess?' I asked as we went over to the queue for the big dipper – nearly everyone in the queue a good few years older than us, I have to say – and she pretended to bend down to do up her shoe so she could speak to me really softly.)

– Liza-Lu, don't be a silly girl, Tess says in that patronizing tone I can't stomach; and don't like to think about to this day. But I knew she wanted to tell me all the same.

– The old bat says I'll kill a man and marry two, says Tess. And she breaks out in a fit of giggling so loud I should have guessed there was something wrong. But, of course, I'm too overawed by my elder sister to add up anything at all at the time.

Like if you're told at so tender an age of an unusual and violent fortune in store for you, then maybe you do panic and try to climb down off the big dipper like she did that day.

All I remember is the slow haul in those little painted cars up to the top – the very top of the world, it seemed. Retty and Maudie were standing on the ground scowling up at us: they hadn't been allowed on.

And Tess in the car at the very top – just behind where I sat with Victor (Tess was with Alec, of course).

When the machine juddered and the cars stopped, there was a hush and then a lot of screaming, like air being let out of balloons or the shrieks girls give off when they catch sight of themselves in the funny mirrors of the fair.

I remember thinking, it was like being caught in the branches of a great big tree, like the tree on the map in Mrs Moores' school-house, a Traveller's Tree from Australia or somewhere – and you would never, never be able to get down.

I suppose the truth is that if Alec hadn't grabbed her in time, Tess would have been killed.

I heard the sound of her trying to climb over the side of the little, flimsy carriage. I turned round, to see her face at a level with the low-slung door.

Then the engine of the dipper started up again.

Tess would have been caught in the spokes, in the metallic branches of that great, looping tree. If Alec hadn't risked his life by climbing out onto the dashboard of the little car – just as we paused trembling like a flock of birds on the edge of the rush down the rails to the pool of water at the bottom. Tess would have fallen to her death or been minced by the machine.

He hauled her back in. And we swooped down, as if that minute of precarious motionlessness had never been.

But Tess wasn't at all pleased.

We all walked back in silence, along that road from the fair; and we didn't care how many lifts we thumbed, to get home.

The trouble was, it was no day for either mother or daughter. As you shall hear.

We didn't understand then that Tess had somehow lost an important part of herself. Well, why should we? She must have been grateful for Alec's help.

Perhaps it was the strength of his arm when he pulled her back into the car that made her thoughtful and sad.

And here, Ella, your last history lesson before I put you to bed, is the fall of Maiden Castle.

Try and see the past, and you will be able to conquer the present – and the future, too.

The Rape of Maiden Castle

The Romans landed in southeast England in 43 A.D. probably in Kent, and pushed westward, overcoming some fierce opposition. They crossed the River Frome at the ford, a spot we now call Dorchester, and must have been astonished to see before them the huge ramparts of the castle. Vespasian was a good general and would have recognized from his experiences in North Europe that the multiple ditches and ramparts meant slingers. He would have seen the western gate, recognizing the strength that the maze of alleyways between the ramparts gave it. He would have noticed that the peace which had fallen on the countryside had allowed a few huts to be built very close to the eastern gate. A man destined to be emperor would most definitely not have missed such a tactical blunder.

The defenders of Maiden Castle must have known that the Romans were coming and would have been prepared. All the farmers from outlying crofts would have gone inside for safety. The water containers would have been ready, the piles of sling pebbles placed at points along the walls. When the Romans approached they would have kept their distance, wary of the sling, perhaps marching a small reconnaissance band around the castle. The Celts, in the time-honoured fashion, would have hurled the odd pebble and a vast quantity of abuse at the band of men in their body armour and uniforms. The Romans, battle-hardened by their march across northern Europe and southern England, would have ignored the defenders. They had seen all that before. If there were, among the defenders, any from the mainland or survivors of battles to the east, this would have been no surprise. If not, then to the roughly clad farmers the sight of disciplined, unperturbed, uniformed troops must have been sobering.

Away in the distance a corps of Roman soldiers busy themselves assembling the invading army's artillery, the ballistae – stone- or spear-throwing engines. The defenders are not aware of the potential of these machines, nor of Vespasian's evolved tactic of softening up the enemy. The twang and thud of the machines is fascinating, the crash of stones among the huts less so, the shrieks of speared men much less so. A confused panic grips the defenders who do not know how best to defend themselves against the death raining down on them as they stand in their impregnable fortress, scientifically constructed to be out of reach of the invaders' weaponry. By the time they recover their wits, the Romans have started to advance, not towards the west gate, but towards the east. The defenders load their slings, whirl them around their heads and release a mass of pebbles, but the Romans have been this way before. Each man raises his shield, and the whole group takes on the appearance of a metal square, so well drilled that the stones rain down with much noise but little hope of penetrating the armour plating. The defenders aim at the uncovered legs of the first row. Some Romans fall, some defenders are shattered by ballista missiles. The metal square reaches the outer rampart of the gateway and starts a desperate surge forward and upward towards the castle. The untidy group of huts near the gate is fired, the smoke causing enough confusion to allow the attackers to make progress, out-flanking the defenders. The gate is forced, the Romans form a bridgehead in the village itself. Reinforcements pour in, start to fire the huts inside and to hack at women and children. There is panic among the defenders and they fall back in disarray, pursued by, at first, the disciplined might of Rome, at last, by a blood-lusted mob of victorious soldiery.

It is unlikely that the action lasted very long, or that the legion suffered great casualties. But at the end, the Romans, incensed either by the unexpectedly bold resistance, the difficulty of the capture of the castle, or the frightening and damaging bombard-ment of the slingers, went wild, attacking women and children, until they were called off by their officers. The legion withdrew to a camp below the castle after having closed the two gates and left the villagers to the night and to their dead.

The villagers who were still alive buried their menfolk and families in shallow graves. Fearful of the soldiers still camped so close, perhaps able to hear the wild victory party, they worked hurriedly. There could have been no great ceremony but no one was interred without the food and drink they needed on their journey to the afterworld. In some graves a small gift was added, a family heirloom, the present from a young widow or an orphaned child.

Fifty years ago the war cemetery was discovered and the graves were opened. The opening of a recent war grave would, today, be met by a storm of protest. But it was all so long ago, the people are not even a memory; the archaeologist wins out. The report of the excavation includes photographs of the remains. Each grave was identified by a letter and number. Each skeleton was examined for damage. A woman had her hands tied behind her back and three sword slashes to the head. A man was hit ten times across the head. Another skull was shattered by a ballista arrow. Many skeletons show no evidence of violence – the sword-thrust to the heart leaves no trace on the bones. The photographic record is, at first, interesting, enlightening. Finally it is sad, sickening. No one ties the hands of a dead person. The woman was tied first, slashed after. No one, in battle, has the time to strike an opponent ten times across the head.

The museum in Dorchester has the remains, as excavated, of one grave. The skeleton is famous and much photographed. Embedded in the spine is the metal head of a Roman ballista arrow. The spine and spinal cord were probably severed. As I stand beside the glass case, a group of schoolchildren arrive beside me. They are delighted by the exhibit. The arrow, they decide, would 'come tight', and *hurt*. They depart for the next case. They are right, it would have hurt. And this is no abstract pile of bones, but the remains of a real man who, though he lived many years ago, lived none the less, and was afraid, and hurt, and died.

Maiden Castle – from Mai Dun, the big hill – is a pleasant place to be on a sunny afternoon in late summer. The grass is lush, with wild flowers poking through. You must watch your step or nature in the raw, a cowpat, forces itself on you. The ditches and ramparts are alive with the noise of children; what were defences are now an adventure playground. It was like this in the days before the invasion when the scene was equally pastoral and filled with the same happy, excited noises. But beneath your feet as you walk still lie the unexcavated remains of the warriors who fought and died that day in a failed effort to maintain their liberty.

Following the Roman conquest the castle was still occupied for a decade or two by the survivors of the slaughter. Then, as the Roman presence became less aggressive and the army no longer an army of occupation as the country became absorbed into Romanism, the people moved out and north to the new town of Dorchester. The windblown soil filled the ditches, and grass regained the ramparts. Three hundred years later a group of heretics to the authorized religion, Christianity, built a small temple near the old east gate. There was a two-roomed house for a priest; four of them lie buried near the spot. Relics unearthed near the temple indicate a return to paganism – Minerva, Diana or Mars, or perhaps all of them, the old pantheon of gods. The site was abandoned again. Then, a century later, near the temple, a strong Saxon was buried with his short sword and knife. Who or why is a mystery.

When Thomas Hardy wrote of the castle he described it as 'an enormous, many-limbed organism of an antediluvian time substance, while revealing its contour'. It is not a particularly enlightening description, though much quoted. He also wrote that the castle had 'an obtrusive personality that compels the sense to regard it and consider'.

When Tess and I got our last lift home from the fair at West Bay, we heard that our mother had taken a fall – somehow she had slipped into the millrace below the house. Just by chance a couple of farm labourers happened to be passing and fished her out.

We knew – at least Tess and I both knew – that you can't just slip over the high fence in our garden into the water below.

Our mother had lost her sanity because no one believed in the way she saw the world.

Tess had lost her sense of freedom – and of fun.

A tale of a tree and a tale of water, as I said, no longer sacred to the gods.

A mechanical fairground tree and an artificially contrived rush of whirling, obliterating water.

A tale of a mother and a daughter, as I said.

The Summer of Dis

✦✦✦✦

In ancient times once a god's secret name had been discovered, the enemies of his people could do destructive
magic against them with it ... the tribes of Amathaon
and Gwydion were intent on keeping the secret of Achren
– presumably the trees, or letters, that spelt out the secret
name of their own deity ...

The Tuatha de Danaan were a confederacy of tribes
in which the kingship went by matrilinear succession ...
the goddess Danu was eventually masculinised into Don,
or Donnus ...

The mother of Danae was Belili, the Sumerian white
goddess, who was a goddess of trees as well as a moon
goddess, love goddess and underworld goddess ... above
all, she was a willow goddess and goddess of wells and
springs.   ROBERT GRAVES, *The White Goddess*

In the summer of 1954, the summer of the game of Stones, we
played for the last time in the old space reserved for children and
the primitive, moon-worshipping mind.

The Celtic year began in July (Pliny said they bragged of two
harvests a year and this would make sense: the hay harvest fell
before the end of their year and the corn harvest after); and it was
the new year for us too, the end of school and the beginning of
the endless, hay-scented, corn-ripening summer holidays, when
Retty and Victor, truants both, climbed in the bales of old Fred
Bowditch's hay.

It was the summer of the fair, 1958, and the woman who looked
into a crystal ball in the tent by the hot-dog stand and sent Tess

out quite different – pale in the face, a woman all at once, showing the first signs of dignity, patience, fear, all the attributes our mother had shown us for so long – and it was the summer of playing by the stream, by the old shrines we had set up when we were very young.

It was as if all those stages in our life together co-existed just that summer. Before, we were children. After, we had stepped over the boundary into a secret knowledge, which seemed to drop down on us like the mistletoe our father gathered in the copse on the hill the other side of the garden, every Advent: white berries of a knowing-of-life that seemed to come from nowhere and had certainly not grown up in us from seeds planted prosaically in the ground.

And it wasn't as if any specific change – recognizable to us, at least – took place in us.

Retty and I still jumped the stream, by the hidden place where we had said our secret names and made a blood sisterhood by scratching and holding wrists together, the wound made by Victor's penknife, itself a secret, satiny-sheathed thing we were never allowed to borrow and had to steal for the purpose.

The gash on the bark of the silver birch tree, made by Tess in rage when our father had ordered her to come in by ten in the late hay-making nights of midsummer and stop her night trips with Alec, across downs and under hedges, in pursuit of hare and rabbit, ghostly in the gloaming light of forbidden after-supper evenings, still grinned at us as it was growing dark, a malevolent black mouth midway up the trunk of the tree.

And our mother seemed to see us less and less, as if the changes taking place in us had rendered us most of the time invisible – though she, as we didn't know then, was changing too, drawn to the last stage of the Triple Muse, the stage of the Hag, as surely as Tess and I (not Retty, who stayed, as if bewitched, a young girl, a 'maid' all her short life) were budding into the wild rose of mid-summer, Beautiful Woman.

But all these things were unseen by us, too.

As for us, all the time we were being invaded – by blood that sang out suddenly for union with another, for a bound into the future like the hare that Alec chased after with a sling and stones from Chesil Beach – we still played at hopscotch or begged for a ride on Farmer Beazer's pony, or knitted little strips of scarves for our teddies and then left them out in the dew to rot and lose colour by the summer's end.

The invasion wasn't so sudden. It crept up on us, took us insidiously, gradually – until, like the game of 'scientists' on the shingle bank that late summer day, we had joined forces both: child, woman, man. Our game was one of the magical, secret games of childhood – but it was also rape.

I shall tell you, Ella – you who sleep now in the downstairs study in the truckle bed my father would lie on, when, increasingly, my mother refused him her bed (she wanted, I see now, to confront her loneliness and fear of insanity with a stoicism that was her downfall, for we must all join together at all times) – I shall tell you, Ella, of the waves of conquering peoples as they came to these shores like the waves of the sea, of

Invasions, War and Peace

and their effect on women. Especially here: in England; and especially in Dorset, where Maiden Castle and Pilsdon Pen, as you have heard tell, were invaded by the Romans and the women raped and murdered like so many sheep by the invading troops.

First – as you have seen – the Celts were overcome by Caesar's army. And not without a great struggle and extraordinary courage on the part of the women. Boudicca, eager for instructions as to which direction to go in search of her enemy, released a hare from her skirts as augury.

As you, Tess, my sister Tess, did one evening after ratting in the barn at Fred Bowditch's until the very last light – and then running across the fields – to find Alec had stoned a hare and captured it and it sat blind and bleeding on the ground beside him.

You gathered it up in your arms – I was there with you, Tess – and it seemed to lean back on you for a moment like a baby.

Then, suddenly, as you knelt and the hare was lifted tenderly into the folds of your skirt, the creature darted off. Right across the field until you couldn't see it in the shadows made by the night sky at the edge of our little wood.

Mended – magically healed. You did that, Tess.

You killed only after the extreme provocation you had to suffer.

As I say, invasions must not be seen as sudden happenings, complete in themselves and bearing their own successive history within them.

Like with Tess and Alec and Liza-Lu and Retty and Victor that summer, the changes were gradual.

The goddesses of the Celts changed slowly into the deities of the Romans.

The power of the women, already on the wane since the stencilling of the Giant and his acre-high phallus on the downs above Cerne Abbas, fell steeply, to concur with the absolute patriarchy of the Latin world.

Women became no more than possessions – of the father, the brothers, the husband.

On the straight roads the Romans built, women looked out from litters or chariots in bewilderment at deathly order where once there had been the living landscape of their ancestors.

Their wells and springs were taken over – most notably the well of the Celtic goddess Sul became the Roman Aquae Sulis at Bath.

When an invading people wishes to impose itself utterly, it brings clock, calendar and language.

All of these the Romans brought. Along with their architecture:

magnificent villas and temples to replace the simple, round, thatched huts of the country-loving Celts.

Yet, even after four hundred years – for this was how long they stayed here – they could never get the Celts to accept any of their innovations entirely.

Like women driven into an unwanted marriage, the Celts kept a part of themselves completely separate from their conquerors.

Yet how many have studied the effects of four hundred years of Roman law on the women of pre-Christian England?

Can we not see the effects on Tess?

For the end of that summer of '58 came – as it was bound to, though we, whose own calendar and body-clocks were changing just as rapidly as had the Celts' when their fortnight – and then their seven-day week, whose god was Dis – were overruled by the Roman pendulum – could hardly imagine it ever would.

We had to go back to school – we, who had passed the great barrier in life – and we had to rule straight lines in copy-books marked out in exact blue squares.

Our clocks – Tess's and mine, at least, were now diametrically opposed to those of Alec and Victor and the other boys at Weymouth High.

We lived in the old druidic calendar of the moon, while they had moved on to the Roman tables.

Five days after starting secondary school – which meant going into Weymouth on the bus – Tess entered menarche.

And I, as if I knew it would be the only part I would play in life, exactly two years later followed suit.

Tess's Sex

The Mill has two bedrooms on the ground floor, and the big long room with the millstone on the first floor, which opens out onto the garden that's hidden from the road. A long garden, with the fast brown stream running alongside and St Catherine's Chapel, like a broken-off tooth, standing high above it.

There's one more room – high up in the Mill – and from there you can see the sea on one side and the flank of the green hill with the chapel on the other.

It was there, on a Saturday in winter – the winter of 1961 – that Alec made me watch him and Tess doing it.

Retty and Victor were there, too. We'd climbed the creaking wooden steps to the room where my mother used to go to read – to escape from both of us and from my father with his endless talk of the Fleet and the rare tasselweed the birds come all the way up from the south to eat.

But today my mother is away, 'visiting friends'. And my father has had to go to Bridport, to see a sick friend.

So we're alone, at the top of the Mill.

There's a round window in the room, which is on two levels; and the round window, as we reach the first level, seems to look down on us like a disapproving eye. The sea, which is its own special property (you can't see it from anywhere else in the house), floats like the grey iris of the eye, observing us – but uncaring really, as the sea always is.

Perhaps it's because of that marine, cold eye that Alec and Tess don't care either what they do, or who sees it.

Alec is pulling off Tess's pants on the bed as we climb the attic ladder to the second level of my mother's room.

Tess's legs swing upward and go round Alec's neck, like a pair of nutcrackers.

Retty and I draw in a breath; and as we do so the sweet, soft smell of the sea creeps in through the oriel window and slows the action, in the eye of the mind.

Retty starts to giggle. Alec's head, caught like that between Tess's legs, looks like the head of an infant to which she has just given birth. (Horribly prophetic, that. But it seemed funny at the time.) With her hand Tess pushes that surprised-looking head, with its red face and popping eyes, down and then down again until it seems to vanish inside her cunt.

Alec is sucking and lapping at Tess's sea.

Retty gets excited and puts a hand up my skirt, to where my pants are wet, too.

Then Tess pulls Alec's head away. She's holding it by a tuft of hair and for a moment it looks as if she's bitten the head off (*vagina dentata*, as the woman-haters, monks and misogynists, envisaged the fearful saw-toothed cunt of the forbidden woman) – or that, like Judith with the head of Holofernes, she is holding aloft the magnificent trophy of her revenge.

But then Alec is up and astride her. His cock is swollen and purple and Retty slides her hand right into my knickers. Slyly she enters me as Alec goes into Tess; and Tess's long shudder – of pleasure, of pain – seems in our half-drugged state to reverberate like the cry of a priestess in a sex initiation ceremony, in a sacred grove, deep under the ground.

For the shudder – the moan – is something we have never heard before and yet is instantly recognizable to us. The cry of woman – in ecstasy, in the agony of giving birth – one and the same, terrifying, strange and yet familiar to us.

Tess's moan, which stopped us entirely from hearing my father back from Bridport early, as he climbed those creaking stairs and came in to see us there.

Maybe it's because I'm laying you in that very bed now – in the Mill where my mother died after my father left, and where I stay as caretaker to the rich film people from London and LA who never find time to come down – that I remember that scene so vividly.

Was it really half a lifetime ago that Tess's legs rose like pale blades and imprisoned Alec's willing head?

Part Three

Bad Women

Punishment. We're standing, Baby Tess, in the church of St Mary in Beaminster – or just outside, to be accurate, one foot in the porch and the other on the flagstones that cover the sinners of the past eight centuries – the men who sinned and the women who led them into temptation, that is. This is why I've brought you here – daughter and granddaughter and great-granddaughter of a Ruined Maid, to show you one of Dorset's finest shrines to Christendie – as your forebear Thomas Hardy fancifully called the punishment machine wherein we stand.

Your eyes, innocent of evil and good alike, strain in perplexity at the gargoyles, the monsters, the leering griffons that rise in a frozen elevator of stone on the exterior of the western tower. Where are they going, these vile-cheeked, puff-tongued beasts? Why have they got it in for you? Whatever, in the name of whichever god was the god of your distant homeland, have you done to deserve their rage and retribution? You have been born, and you haven't yet the power to choose between one course of action and another. You are as innocent as the day you were born. But you are not – as the presence of this fine perpendicular church, late twelfth-century, aisled and austere, will testify – you are not pure. You are the daughter of Eve – and she is the mother of us all, the reason for the need to punish Tess, and every Tess before her.

Until the concept of original sin is washed from the consciousness of man, woman will be eternally blamed for all the ills and malefactions of the world.

Before Eve was chosen from Adam's rib, his first wife Lilith exploded in a chaos of disobedience and the stars no longer knew how to follow the path of God.

Eve would submit – but she, too, went against the orders from the Creator. She tempted Adam – she was cursed, along with him – and they fled from Eden to the barren rocks, the shingle beaches, the swampy marshland with which every country in the world is cursed (and we have our fair share of them here, too). She remains on earth to tempt men (remember Hardy's Tess, who is told strictly by the apparently reformed New Man and preacher Alec D'Urberville after her abandonment by Angel, the only man she could love, that she must on no account 'tempt' him: this after his seduction and subsequent refusal to take responsibility for the baby that was the consequence of it!). For all Hardy's apparent compassion for Tess – and his description of her on the title page of the book that became him, overcame him and stayed more in the imagination of the world than anything else of him – as a 'Pure Woman', he was as guilty as the next man. His compassion was an exquisite cruelty. Hardy used the execution of Tess for the crime of murdering her first and hateful lover as a final, tender way of killing the woman he loves; he shaped her, through all the ages of history that woman has toiled, died in the agony of labour, stood at the stake, fallen gagging on black water in the duckponds of witch persecution – through all the centuries of slavery and non-belonging, without even a name or a woman priest to turn to in the hours of worst desolation, Hardy led Tess to the last, inevitable punishment, the price she must pay as daughter of Eve. For her prime disobedience to man, her ruler, her father, her seducer, Tess must swing.

As a child in Dorchester, Thomas Hardy attended public executions and was haunted ever after by those murderesses with their billowing skirts ... urine and faeces trickling down on yellow-stockinged legs swollen from labour and penury, faces grim and blackened, lips that could not even form letters when confronted with their own death warrant to read. Hardy's compassion stirred ... but Tess must end as they did. (It was a scandal, of course: Hardy never really recovered from the storm of protest and loathing his love affair with Tess provoked. He never fell out of love with Tess either, as we shall see.)

Woman is bad. You remember the way we came, Baby Tess, to this smug, pretty little market town, this minster that took its name from a Saxon saint, Bega?

Your eyes stared around you. You'd never been inland before. Washed up on Chesil Beach, all you'd heard was the (Saxon) murmur of the pebbles – for that's what the word for shingle was in the tongue of the next invaders and conquerors of Dorset – Chesil, Chesil . . . the lull of the pebbly word had you sleeping as we left the Mill, and I looked once more round the garden to make sure I hadn't left the washing out to get soaked in the sudden downpours that fall through the tropical forest at Abbotsbury, as they do in Dominica or one of those high, green islands where your dad's ancestors toiled on the plantations, very probably.

I looked round the garden, with you in a sling tied under my breast, and I wondered what Hardy's Tess would think of my sister Tess, if she saw us here together. And I could hear the voice of our father as he came back into the Mill that time, when we were up in the room with the round eye . . . and Tess was only fourteen and Alec knew he could go to gaol for it . . .

Yes, I stood there with you quite innocent, sleeping on my ribs and your breath coming in and out as quiet as the sea in the shell, when it pauses to listen to you – and I saw us all as we ran for it – Retty and Victor and me, that is – for how could Tess when she had Alec still inside her? Did it feel like the first stone, that was pushed in her and weighed her down, anchored her there, a helpless sea-urchin, with the spiky hair of the sixties and a half-burned fag in a saucer on the floor and the new pop music belting out as our dad mounted the stairs to find his under-age daughter fucking?

Did Tess feel the weight of the blame she, like all women, would always have to take, with Alec heavy as that great boulder of stone by the door of the Mill, lying on top of her?

No, of course she didn't. Not then; Nature looks after it that way, you see. Tess thought she was making a choice – if she thought anything at all. And she laughed right in our father's face. I can see it now – for all our running away we only got as far as the stairs out of the loft. And I was the first to catch it. Punishment.

Our father, you see, was born in the last great age of punishment for women – he was a Victorian, pulled from the flanks of his sickly mother just as the old Queen was dying – coming into a world reeking of ether fumes and corrective braces and camphor oil. He saw his mother waste away from too much child-bearing; and he saw the men of his elder brother's generation slaughtered on the Somme while dreaming of their saintly mothers, their lily-white fiancées. He saw what happened to a woman if she stopped smelling of roses and lilies and sank into the mire: he saw the iron discipline needed, the pulling in of the stays that held the body and the will in check; he knew the Ruined Maid as well as our great poet, Hardy, who wrote of her and dreamed of her, incarnated as Tess. And to our father there was no change, since the days when ruin, the burden for the whole family, of the bastard – brought unending shame. He was going to stamp it all out, now – and no amount of little round pills and rock and roll were going to deflect him. (I don't think he ever really heard the guitars and drums that sounded from our room. Like the swans he tended at Abbotsbury, our father liked to think of women as silent, mute.)

The strap was kept in the dark, grey room on the ground floor of the Mill where my father's sister Tibby sometimes stayed on a rare visit from Scotland. In an oak cupboard with a bottle of brandy and an old pair of binoculars my father had inherited from *his* father – and which he'd confiscated when my mother took to gazing at the sky through them. (All day, at a milky-white sky where she saw stars, she said, speaking to her as they danced away with her happiness. But that was before our mother Mary fell into the millrace that day we went to the funfair, and was fished out and sent to the big house on the other side of Bridport, where they filled her with drugs and the stars couldn't get through to her any more.)

I wasn't surprised that I was the one to get the strap, not Tess. And, looking back on it, I'm glad it was that way round. Rather that than get locked, as Tess was, like a moping bird, bedraggled and unwashed, for three whole days down in the Mill storeroom, where iron bars on a tiny window looked out on dark water rushing, tirelessly, desperately, down into the pool and out through the sluice at last. My punishment, though it brought rage and an unbearable sense of humiliation at the time – well, at least it was over quickly and I could run to Retty for comfort and a dab of calamine lotion for the smarting weal. Mrs Priddle, Retty's mother, was as shocked as any of the women in Abbotsbury when the news spread, told eagerly by Retty, of how my father had pulled down my knickers and beaten me with the strap over the sofa-bed that used to get folded out for Aunt Tibby – and with Victor watching as well, his eyes round as sixpences. He shouldn't do that now Liza-Lu is twelve, the women of Abbotsbury said as they went into the general store and stood for pension books or stamps or washing powder . . . no, Mr Hewitt shouldn't, not now she's . . . and, I can tell you now, Baby Tess, that the look on Mrs Priddle's face as she dabbed on the lotion – her pursed lips and her knowing look – well I knew then that I was no longer in the blessed state of belonging fully to neither sex – I was no longer a child, I was a woman. And it was for this that my father had punished me. Somehow I knew all this.

We walked away from the Mill and you seemed to look back – at the iron bars grown even more rusty since that punishment for the sin of carnal knowing, of temptation – and you seemed to look in astonishment, with those agate eyes of yours, in their cloudy saucers of pale blue – in amazement at the centuries of blame that came to rest on your grandmother, my sister Tess, all those years ago, at the very beginning of the so-called Sexual Revolution. You strained to see back in time to your grandmother's pale face at the low window by the racing water – and maybe you did, for you burst out crying suddenly, you cried so heart-rendingly that it was as if you'd seen her wraith appear there, begging you to set her free. But we walked on all the same, and we struck inland, and we hitched a ride all the way to Powerstock. Then we walked on, and we came to Batcombe Down. For I had to walk you down the most punishing walk the first Tess was ever to take – a walk where she lost hope and found the Devil – and I stood with you a while at Crossy Hand before we went down to the little town where our mother, born in the surrounding Marshpool Vale, was taken to be christened (as were her mother and her mother before her). I had to bring you here to make you understand the final, all-important component of Tess – of Tess before Hardy could breathe life into her, and of Tess my sister and all women too, brought up under the auspices of the faith of the land – I had to show you here, in the portals of the magnificent (perpendicular) church of St Mary at Beaminster – how Christianity came to us, and how it changed our foremothers – and then how Christian perceptions of women, too, changed – so we would forever take the blame. (And I told you, as we stood by the squat stone pillar known as Crossy Hand, for it bears the small imprint of a palm, the stone shadow of a killer's hand nailed there, so the story goes – I told you that while Tess pined in the Mill dungeon, and I squirmed under my father's strap, Alec went off free as air, roaring up to Amesbury on the old Harley Davidson his pal Brian'd rehabbed a few weeks earlier – roared up to Amesbury to deal in motorcycle parts and swagger about at the bar of the George – while Tess and I both bled, she from losing her virginity, as our father would, and did, denounce it, and I from the leather thong, and then, later that day, as Mrs Priddle had foreseen, from my first period.)

And I'll tell you about Alec and Tess and how they met again. But first, as I began to say as we walked from the stone hand that Alec D'Urberville made Tess swear on that she wouldn't 'tempt' him any more – there is the story of the Making of Tess, from the wild freedom of Celts and the constrictions of Roman life to the teachings of St Augustine.

The first four centuries of Christianity held that men and women were responsible for their actions: that they had the choice to sin or to gain salvation through obedience to the teachings of Christ. Our foremother Tess would have known nothing of this. For, as the Saxon conquerors came and were repelled and came again like the waves of the sea at Chesil Beach (and in Dorset, especially there, they were successfully kept at bay far longer than anywhere else in Britain), so also came the monotonous dirge of the monks as they made their way across Europe. Original sin was on its way; and for all the crystal ball on its long, fine pendant chain of silver could tell the first Tess of her continuing power, another, more powerful and more destructive prophecy was about to take over. The creed of

St Augustine was the real conqueror – of women. Here are his words:

> The entire human race that was to pass through women into offspring was contained in the first man when that married couple received the divine sentence condemning them to punishment, and *humanity produced what humanity became, not what it was when created, but when, having sinned, it was punished.*

The punishment itself, Augustine adds, 'effected in their original nature a change for the worse'.

And Augustine, the fourth-century libertine-turned-saint, the man who fought against the 'raging lust that exercised its supreme dominion over me' and, from his exorcism of the terrible bondage to the flesh, changed the Christian view of human nature, brought the blame fair and square down on the woman, gave as proof of this new definition of sin a highly idiosyncratic reading of Romans 5:12.

The Greek text reads: 'Through one man [or 'because of one man'] sin entered the world, and through sin, death; and thus death came upon all men, *in that* all sinned.' John Chrysostom, as did most Christians, translated this as meaning that the sin of Adam introduced sin to the world and death came upon all because *all* sinned. But Augustine read the passage in Latin, and so either ignored or didn't realize the meaning of the Greek original – so he misread the last phrase as referring to Adam alone. Augustine proclaimed that it meant that 'death came upon all men, *in whom* all sinned' – that the sin of one man, Adam, brought upon humanity not only universal death, but also universal, and inevitable, sin. Augustine uses the passage to deny that human beings have free moral choice, which Jews and Christians had traditionally regarded as the birthright of humanity made 'in God's image'. Augustine declares, on the contrary, that the whole human race inherited from Adam a nature irreversibly damaged by sin. 'For we all were in that one man, since all of us were that *one man who fell into sin through the woman who was made from him.*'

When he describes the onset of original sin Augustine chooses political language – and specifically the language of sexual politics. It's not long before he can 'prove' that – just as soul and body must co-exist, with the soul in a position of authority – Adam and Eve must have been created to live together in a harmonious order of authority and obedience, superiority and subordination. 'We must conclude', says Augustine, 'that a husband is meant to rule over his wife as the spirit rules the flesh.' But once each member of the primal couple had experienced that first internal revolt in which the bodily passions arose against the soul, they experienced analogous disruption in their relationship with one another. Although originally created equal with man in regard to her rational soul, woman's formation from Adam's rib established her as 'the weaker part of the human couple'. Being closely connected with bodily passion, woman, although created to be man's helper, became his temptress and led him into disaster. The Genesis account describes the result: God himself reinforced the husband's authority over his wife, placing divine sanction upon the social, legal and economic machinery of male domination.

This, Baby Tess – as we walk into the church of St Mary at Beaminster and stand by the (Norman) font, thrown out in a period of restoration in 1863 (when Thomas Hardy was twenty-three years old) and found in a stonemason's yard in 1927 – this, my poor child, is the litany of the sins into which you have been born.

This is the song that came, louder each year, across Europe: the sad, monotonous chant of the monks, the song of punishment and blame.

As luck would have it, the day Alec and Tess were caught in the room with the round eye was the day our mother came home. She'd been 'visiting friends', I said – and so we all pretended to believe at the time: after all, we knew our mother's family was from the 'other side' of Bridport, and we knew there were cousins in Whitchurch Canonicorum, with a cider orchard and geese besides. We knew our mother's elder brother – who she said she never liked much but she felt sorry for his poor wife Sally – lived high up in the Marshwood Vale – where she'd grown up too, up above the village called Wootton Fitzpaine, nearly up at Lambert's Castle where you could look out over the whole of west Dorset to the sea. We pretended that was what our mother had done. She'd felt like a change – that was how Mrs Priddle put it, when she 'came in' with a face as sour as a crab apple, to fix our father's shirts and socks, and put breakfast on the table for us too, drag a comb through Tess's dark, thick, knotty hair in the struggle to get us to school.

We knew really that our mother hadn't been well since the day we went to the funfair and Tess lost her nerve – at just about the same time as our mother Mary lost her wits, you could say. We sensed that the tall, grim building on the road out of Bridport towards Charmouth was where she'd been taken, to have the voices drummed out of her – or shocked by lightning streaks that would judder her whole body – or simply numbed by poisons she (and her female ancestors) would never have concocted, even for the deadliest enemy. There was nothing we could do about it – except hear her plaintive voice in the water of the millrace at night, begging us, her daughters, to come and set her free. We didn't know how to act against authority then; and if we did, it was, as in the case of Tess, with whole-hearted selfishness. As if the race, with the decline of our mother, must be propagated as soon as physically possible: as soon as Tess bled, her body took action to multiply and bring forth. It was brutal; we couldn't help knowing what went on even though we could never admit it to each other. We let our mother and her warning voices fade away from our memory, and the urgency of the present and the future took us over. We played truant from school, we hung about on the corner in Weymouth where the ships come in by the harbour front, and the tarts and the dope dealers stand bunched and lonely at the same time: outcasts thrown together, dregs brought in on the oily scum of the port. Tess picked up a Russian sailor, and then ran away from him when he'd taken a room at the Bellevue down the other end of Weymouth, by the pier. Egged on by Maud and Victor, I took a job behind the bar at the posh hotel built and named after mad King George, who liked to come down to Weymouth and lower his trembling extremities into the sea. I said I was eighteen (couldn't possibly have been) and they overlooked the lie to get an extra hand with pouring gins and tonics, bending low with tits hardly bigger than a pair of nuts, eyed greedily by the men down from Birmingham. Once we decided to go away to London – after all, what would our father care? – and we took the little train from Weymouth to Westbury – but Fred Henchard, with the bristling moustache and the dairy acres down at Kimmeridge, Fred who used to call at the Mill and ask if he could have a pair of swans for the new ornamental lake he was building (he was always told No, they were the property of the monarch, and we used to joke old Fred Henchard'd go to the Tower if he slipped up the Fleet one night and pinched them) – he saw us on Westbury station and asked ever-so-strict what we thought we were doing there, on a weekday in term. Fred Henchard was a magistrate, a JP, and we went back meek as mice with him in the stuffy little van that smelt of toffee papers and cattle mix. He dropped us at the school and we said nothing: his look told us that he wouldn't either, if we behaved ourselves. But we couldn't for long, of course. Alec was waiting – like a shabby, hand-me-down piece of our destiny, that's the way I see it now. I know we couldn't duck out of it – we'd heard Mrs Priddle say girls without a mother didn't stand a chance of staying on the straight and narrow – only our father, oblivious to everything except the nesting habit of the rare Abbotsbury swans, had to have a scene pushed up right under his eyes to believe it was happening at all.

For days after she was brought back, our mother was as silent and white as a ghost – that's what we heard Mrs Priddle say, who stopped letting Retty in to play with us; she was afraid something was going to happen. Of course I realize with hindsight that she wouldn't want her daughter involved in our mother's second suicide attempt – but it was hurtful at the time. Our mother's return made us pariahs again. The school gave us afternoons off, 'to help at home'. We felt more trapped and unhappy than ever, at that time – and I really don't think we gave a damn what happened to our mother then. We'd been so much freer when she was shut up, you see!

What did happen, though, was – as so often happens – just the opposite of what we secretly dreaded and everyone else openly expected. Our mother came down to breakfast one chilly winter morning – about five weeks or so since Tess had been locked up for trying to fly, with Alec between her legs like a witch's broom-stick (that's how little Maud drew the scene, at school, and the visiting art teacher scrumpled up the paper with its crude, Saxon-looking representation of Alec's big penis and Tess's grinning face, stick legs gripping his shoulders – and threw it away in the bin, which is how we all came to see it later, of course, crowding round Maud as she proudly smoothed it out). Our mother Mary told us she had decided to go and live on her own. She was leaving our father. She had a friend down at Langton Herring, a village down the far end of Chesil Beach with a smugglers' inn and an old white-washed house where her friend Betsy Dowle of the fishing fleet folk did B & B. 'And that's where I'll be working,' our mother announced to us, plain as that. 'I'll be looking after the fishery side.'

I remember it was a dark, end-of-the-world-feeling morning because as soon as she spoke, our father John Hewitt turned on the light in the kitchen – I suppose we'd all been sitting in the gloom for so long, since the 'disgrace' of Tess, at least, that we'd come to take dark for granted – and for the first time for what seemed like years I took a good look at my mother's face. And I felt proud and afraid, together.

Mary's face had become the face of a martyr – or an ascetic – a face that was lined with suffering and had grown longer, more thin-nosed, more pensive: you thought of the faces on the old Celtic crosses, or on Anglo-Saxon tombs, where Mary Magdalene, kneeling submissive but full of joy, wipes the feet of Our Lord with her hair. You glimpsed only intermittently now the old pagan features, the eye with a glint, the lips that muttered runes and magic, the full-shaped arms that pulled down thick brambles to get at hanging mistletoe, healing vervain. The lineaments of pain, an ecstasy in self-abasement, denial of earthly pleasure, were strong in that face, and had converted it from madwoman to votary. But the voice of self-determination fitted the new face, the Saxon, free-woman face Mary Hewitt now presented to the world. Like her ancestors in the female line before her, Mary would prosper with her own stall selling the fish the Dowles' boats brought in, rough or calm. She would serve all-comers, and in all weathers, when the men went home to wives and wet oilskins drying in the front room. After a while she'd have her own shop, in Bridport where her mother and grandmothers had lived and worked the hemp for nets for the fishing; later still she'd employ a staff, a young man with a van who'd supply all the posh new hotels along the coast and inland as far as Evershot. Crab; mussels; red mullet caught in Devon along with lobsters; Lyme Bay plaice that melted in the mouth, you didn't need the batter. Mary would be independent, financially and emotionally. But it took all of us a long time to take that in.

– So how long are you planning to stay? John said.

Silence fell. I looked next at Tess, deep in her obscure punishment, retribution for her sin being the slow, painful regaining of our father's trust and affection. This was worse than chains and whipping: how could she know when the father, the lord, the head of the family, would consider her sentence done, her forgiveness complete? Standing in for the Christian deity, might he decide to withhold grace from the fornicating woman until such time as she offered her whole life to him, serving him as nuns serve God in a nunnery, dedicating every moment of her life to his comfort and happiness? It was possible: look at Lily Tither down at Rodden, who'd been caught with the young lord of the manor, the heir to red-walled, yew-planted Parnham – no, there was no shotgun wedding, not to young Master Thomas, anyway; more a wedding to old Frank, her father, a giving, like a bride of Christ, a celibate union that was nonetheless to the death and far beyond. Lily's get-thee-to-a-nunnery was a marching order to Tesco's every day except Sunday, to buy the pilchards and the toilet paper and all the other needs of old Frank Tither; her stations of the Cross were Monday washday, Wednesday baking, Saturday Women's Institute with other daughters and wives of the parish. And as the years shrivelled, and she counted them out like pips or plum stones on the side of the plate – no tinker husband, no tailor, not even a beggarman or thief to take between the sheets, so Lily turned yellow and sere herself, her menopause taking her suddenly and bringing fits of weeping like winter storms. And a fat lot her lord and master, the head of the family as Christ is the Head of the Church, cared for that.

Things would be different now, of course: it was 1961, wasn't it, and there was the Pill, and the technology we were all promised, and a future where the wasted, sacrificed life of Lily Tither wouldn't be possible. Or so we thought. But it was hard, watching Tess as she shrank at our father's step, turned to smile at him where once she had been so high-handed, went for milk down to Mrs Warren and asked for all the best brown eggs from her too – her dad did like a brown egg for breakfast – it was hard to watch the frown she received in return, the high-domed head hidden by a newspaper when Tess tried to speak, the heavy, dank smell of disapproval at the Mill. Could Tess, at fourteen, really hope to escape from the generations of moral superiority on the part of her forefathers, the centuries of chastisement (of which the most cruel-minded disciple, Thomas Hardy, was the most delicate practitioner)? Of course she couldn't. We were foolish enough to believe in instant change as reported by shallow-minded journalists: first wave of liberation with the new music, first rash of birth-control clinics promising a return to Celtic freedom and power, Saxon independence, property-owning and business for women. We believed it, so we suffered more at the ache of the old pains, the bonds of love and tenderness we had felt for a distant, patriarchal father who nevertheless told us he had always loved and cared for us. As for our mother – it's only now that I can see the courage with which she confronted her husband. It's only now that I see a woman, driven mad by the constrictions of her life and 'put away' for the crime of trying to point out the connections and correspondences between every living and inanimate thing on the globe – face up to her legal wedded spouse and say, penniless as she was, that she wanted no maintenance for herself and her children, thank you, because she was going off on her own, to make a living on the hard shingle at West Bay, where the sea spray in winter comes in in white lumps the size of snowballs and your hands get red raw handling frozen cod as it's thrown in off the trawler.

I see it now. But then I simply felt abandoned. And Tess, perhaps sensing that she would have to fill some gap – that her most severe punishment would be to stand as wife to this strange, reserved and probably bitter man – made her new womanly face at our father and asked if he'd like a fresh cup of tea.

– It's not a question of how long I'm planning to stay, Mary said in reply to her husband John's question, I'm going for good.

– For good, John repeated, as if he had no idea what the words meant. He cleared his throat, picked up the newspaper, glanced at the tide table and rose, assuming a practical, businesslike air.

We all watched our father as he went to the door of the kitchen, pulled at his oilskin – which fell to the floor, bringing a clutter of Mary's old hats down with it. John left them there – almost with jubilation. The hats, big, floppy things Mary used to paint in in the days she did water-colours and showed them at the village show, were like dusty haloes, straw collapsing and fraying as the years passed. Our father shrugged on the bright yellow waterproof and left for the swannery.

But it was Mary who left properly, later that day.

The Transformations of Mary

I shall tell you, while we stand by the font chiselled from Purbeck marble by the conquering Normans and we think of my mother as she was dipped in there to undergo the waves of her future woman-hood: her ages as maiden, fruit-bearing woman and hag spilt out over her with the cup of holy water, all her previous incarnations swallowed up in the great might of the lords across the sea (for that is how it always was, in the story of women, a time of freedom and power, like the Celts, extinguished by the Romans: a period of independence and material prosperity such as the Saxon reign, trampled and overcome by the next wave of conquerors) – I shall tell you that the day my mother left the Mill and Tess took up her years of penance (two of them altogether) was the day our mother became a hag, a witch, a prophetess.

Never mind the windblown hut on West Bay where she scraped scallops and bearded mussels and pulled the bones from sole and plaice with their mournful eyes looking up above the orange mottle of their skin. Don't be taken in by family photographs which show our mother smiling, kerchief on her head, long, daily sharpened knife in her hand, door of the Dowles' beach shop open behind her and trays of fish in misty coats of ice. And don't listen to Betsy Dowle, when she says Mary was the perfect lodger, in the white-washed B & B in Langton Herring, down the coast – always the first up in the morning, helping with the visitors' teas, putting a skillet on the big stove Betsy fed with fuel each night rather than go for the modern inventions.

Or if you do listen to her – or to Retty's memories of our mother as filtered down to the younger women in the village, remember there's more to life than what meets the eye. The life you are living is not the life you lead, as that great persecuted wit Oscar Wilde put it. In other words, look below the surface of any life and you see another running deeper and parallel, like a big fish under the waves. Look down into the life of Mary and you see the hag she was destined to become, as soon as she left the protection of hus-band and home. But don't be afraid – she is only one of a long line of such women, themselves persecuted because they saw the truth – and what lay ahead, sometimes, too.

We must go back to the very beginning. And then perhaps we shall begin to understand – how Mary knew of the fatal split man-kind and womankind had inherited, from the thinking of Augustine – and Plato – and Marcus Aurelius, whose thinking makes for the foundation of the world in which we live: a world for white males, to be obeyed and respected by women, the ethnically 'inferior' groups and the poor and dispossessed. We shall see how our mother, daughter of a long line of Ruined Maids, mother of another, 'saw' the other life that runs under the surface constructed by the ruling culture. She 'saw' as her foremothers had seen, since the first poets gave words to the special powers, the powers over life and death, no less, that were the preserve of women. So here we go.

The classical Fates may be old women but they are immortal old

95

women. When Adhelm, early Christian author in Saxon times of *De Virginitate*, uses the word 'pythonissa', he is referring not to the priestess of Apollo's oracle at Delphi, but to the woman in Acts who 'possessed a spirit of divination', *puellam habentem spiritum pythonem*, but was presumably mortal. Furies are as immortal as fiends. King Aelfred (a Saxon king who would have given happier conditions to our poor mother in that incarnation than the one she knew in the middle years of our fast-receding century) may not be sure in his translation of Boethius whether *Parcae* are Fates or Furies, but knows nevertheless that they are *gydene*, goddesses. And the two Old English words *wicce* and *haegtesse* which give us the modern derivatives 'witch' and 'hag' are both used by Anglo-Saxon scribes to translate on the one hand the mortal *pythonissa* and on the other the immortal Fates, the *Parcae*. The words cannot have meant anything as trivial and superficial as their modern equivalents.

Charms were used against elf-shot and *haegtesse*-shot –

> Out, spear; not in, spear
> If there be in here any bit of iron,
> The work of a *haegtesse*, it must melt.
> If you were pierced in skin or pierced in flesh
> Or pierced in blood or pierced in limb
> May your life not be torn away . . .

In both Norse and Old English texts the idea occurs that to have power over runes may include some form of supernatural power. Tacitus records in his *Germania* that the *Germani* believed 'there is in women an element of holiness and a gift of prophecy' . . . and the precarious survival in Anglo-Saxon of the word *Heahrune*, and that this is used of the biblical character possessing a spirit of divination – suggests that the concept of women who prophesy did come to these shores from Germany.

So when our mother met us for fish and chips at West Bay, and before leaving the shop wiped her long knife on the side of the wooden block where she gutted and filleted fish; when she gave us an odd look and said she thought the land behind the West Bay Hotel would flood up one of these days soon, with the tides running so high, we should have read the signs, we should have seen the pictures she was showing us.

A spear – the long knife old Mr Dowle gave to Mary. A body pierced in flesh . . . in blood . . . in limb . . .

Mary foresaw the murder. The Old English word for mother is *modor*. If we had been attuned to our mother once she became a *haegtesse*, living alone and seeing the future, we would have known to run away from our destiny as fast as our legs could carry us.

But we were in a dead world – a world that had been dead for millennia, and which the human race is fast making uninhabitable for humans. Bishop Aelfric, long after Bede's writings on Anglo-Saxon paganism (where pagan priests are mentioned, but never priestesses or prophetesses), writes in his homily 'On Auguries' that people are such fools they will bring offerings to 'earth-fast stone or tree or well-spring' and he jeers at the practice. These parts of our world have no attendant spirits, he says, they are 'the dead stone and the dumb tree'. He scoffed at the various charms and amulets that were the grave-goods of an earlier period: the single beads, boars' tusks worn as pendants, crystal balls and cowrie shells found in the graves of women, who were healers, using the rock-crystal ball in particular to guard the family's health.

The belief that our trees and well-springs and earth-stones are no more than inanimate objects is with us today, and supports the violence and destruction with which we are cursed. We must return to save the healing and seeing powers of the *haegtesse* and give the world a chance to breathe and live.

As it was, we saw nothing on that windy day, Tess and I, when we went to visit our mother after school, in the time before the equinoctial tides brought all the water she saw in her dreams – and still more. We should have seen the spear she held up for a moment in front of us, as she asked Tess in a quiet, matter-of-fact voice whether she was still seeing Alec or not. A cloud may have thickened overhead and a drop, an augury of the water that was to sheet down, may have fallen on Tess's head and caused her to shiver, to pull up the collar of her coat.

97

No, she wasn't seeing Alec any more. He'd buggered off somewhere. And she couldn't care less, anyway.

We walked down past the little harbour and crossed the slatted wooden bridge to the fish and chip place. Tess was angry and withdrawn. She knew the world was punishing her – she knew the rules had been written for someone else, long ago; and, obscurely, she knew there wasn't much she could do about it.

Except, perhaps, what she did do a few years later, on the night the bunting was out along the streets at Bridport and the funfair was whooshing and whirling . . . What our mother showed us, but we didn't see . . .

– I'll have the egg and chips and peas, our mother Mary said to the waitress when she came up and we were sitting at the little plastic-topped table. I get sick of fish, working with it all day.

Our Mother's Country

As it happened, the battle for Tess was fought out on two high ridges of land, grassy escarpments on either side of the deep hollow of land where we stand, in Beaminster. On one side, our mother's country, the Marshwood Vale, with its three high points – Lambert's Castle, Pilsdon Pen and Lewesdon, the two latter known as the cow and her calf, but the calf covered in a thick pelt of beech, red and rust in autumn, while Pilsdon is hairless, just a tonsure of bell heather on the crest and a great pile of cracked earth below, white from sun in that summer when the fight for Tess really began.

It must have been the summer of 1963 – but already I've forgotten to explain to you where the other side lies – because already my eyes are fixed on our mother's country and its three high points, and the ramparts, if you can so call the ditches that fall steeply from the sides of Lambert's Castle – again a castle only in name, in fact an Iron Age fort but ship-shaped and nearly as high as its neighbour

Pilsdon, at eight hundred and forty-two feet. My thoughts are there. Tess fell there for the last time. Or that's how our father saw it. But there was a good deal of strength on the other side, too – and rumour has it that he'll come back one day – Ralph Morgan, that is – and however old Tess may be, and him too, he's going to claim her for his own.

Fat chance, I say! Wherever Tess may be, it's no place for a gentleman like Sir Ralph – as he must have been since the death of his father several decades now – to go courting.

For Tess is either in a madhouse, like the house where our mother heard the voices and dreamt the dreams of all her past lives and incarnations – or she's in gaol for the murder of a man they never could find. And I don't see Ralph Morgan, for all the polite manners he doubtless still displays, going to a lunatic asylum or a prison to find a wife. He wanted Tess, to show off her spectacular beauty – he wanted to take her to London and show off those dark looks – and he liked to tease her that she had no Anglo-Saxon blood in her at all.

– You'd have been known as a Welshwoman, Ralph said, when he came to the Mill and took Tess down to Dorchester for a bite of lunch and then back along the coast, to turn inland and go to his estates high up at Mapperton. We'd have used you as a slave.

Of course, he was only joking. Our father, who was never there when Ralph threw out these jests – and he called me the little Goose Girl, too – Watch out, Tess, she'll take your lover off you one day, he used to say, which only made me feel all the plainer and made Tess lower her eyes in embarrassment – our father looked with cautious approval on this courtship. And why shouldn't he? What a relief after Alec, you might say.

But Alec lay in wait in the little market town where we now stand outside the church (it's growing late and Evensong has just begun and I must carry you home, to Chesil Beach and Ella who'll be wanting her tea). Alec lay in the shadow of Mapperton – of Sir Joseph Morgan's estates, on a high ridge of land above Beaminster. These were the contestants in the battle for Tess: the land of our mother's Marshwood Vale, rich, deep-laned, wooded dairy land with the three giants slumbering over it – and the high, windswept land of his rival, Ralph Morgan. Mapperton versus Lambert's Castle. And even during that time of Tess going out with the young man from the Big House, the Jacobean manor house with its dramatic vertical garden that drops a sheer hundred feet to stone pools where water-lilies float in fetid water, I knew somehow that the real battle in Tess's life would be between our mother's need for her to find herself (as our mother had done so tragically late in life, sacrificing all her beauty years to our father and to 'madness') – and Tess's own urgent rush towards self-destruction, violence, self-immolation and all the other treats in store for young women in a world where the natural balance of things has not been restored.

Our mother knew that Ralph Morgan, dull though he might be, was still preferable to Alec, whose wild ways would only bring Tess to her knees and leave her there, wiping the floor, mopping up the mess of broken home, screaming baby, money taken from the Co-op and off he's flown. Neither of our parents was worldly – but they knew that the icy indifference a man of Ralph's class will show his wife (for he will always love his dogs and horses more) was at least a form of freedom. Life with Alec would be slavery.

If Tess had been a Welsh slave girl, as Ralph, with his stuck-up voice and his terrible tweed jacket with leather patches at the elbows and his E-type Jaguar liked to tease her – she would, paradoxically, have been less enslaved by marriage to the lord of Mapperton than to Alec, whose father was an engine driver and his mother a char-lady at Parnham House a mile outside Beaminster, getting a lift there and back from the lady of the house. Tess would be 'freer' with Ralph.

But what a choice! When you're older, Baby Tess, you'll ask why Tess couldn't have got an interesting job, looked out for herself in the big world.

Well, you saw her neglect her education – and you saw that our father never really had any expectations for daughters to make good in a man's world. They were there to marry the right man, pro-create, bake. And our mother fell into the millrace, remember, and they took her away as the other lives came up out of that dark, swirling water to claim her . . . So what chance did we have? And how many other girls' lives have been, and still are, dictated by such circumstances, one way or another?

Countless millions, is the answer. Just look at the stone memorial here, on the wall outside St Mary's Church in Beaminster – and see how many families had children that died in infancy. Look at the suffering, the endless struggle of life. Of so many families – all sons and daughters lost before the age of thirty. Just because people live longer now, don't think that everything is solved, for us and maybe even our mothers. It isn't . . . we have to fight to make the earth whole for all of us together.

But now I'll take you up to Mapperton. From there you can see right across to Lambert's Castle – where Tess went that fateful evening – and I'll tell you how the battle was won, by cunning and stealth, by a foot soldier from the valley, who didn't even have a motorbike, let alone a white E-type with a cassette player that blared the Everly Brothers in the high, quiet lanes that run down to Powerstock and West Milton.

I'll tell you how you came to have a mother, and how all the defences of our mother country, and all the aggression of the ancient Morgan territory could do nothing to combat the force that drove Tess up to the high, open promontory that night.

It's not a pretty story.

The Rape of Lambert's Castle

From here – from the hundred acres of stubby coarse grass and heather that form the top of this Iron Age fort, not a castle at all really and still unexcavated – we can see all of Marshwood Vale and the sea beyond, pale blue and thin as the shell of a robin's egg, waiting for the September storms to come and blow it to smithereens. We see Whitchurch Canonicorum, where our mother Mary lived some of the time, by the church of St Wite, the martyred Saxon saint who became St Candida – and we can tell, as we look down on the spire of that peaceful church, dedicated to the memory of that healing woman, and containing her bones and a shrine where people to this day place pleas for recovery, wholeness, balm – that there was nothing she could do to stop the rape and pregnancy of her daughter. The soft, green air of Marshwood, with its feminine promise of acceptance and healing, was poisoned by the fumes – the stench of petrol from the old, unmended exhaust pipe on Morgan's E-type (he liked to keep it that way, so the male roar of him preceded his coming, in the twisting lanes of dairy farms and high hedges) – and the wild flowers crushed by his wheels could never find the strength to stand upright again. He was stronger than any woman, you see – and, as we know, Morgan and Alec and all the men, whether Celt or Angle, had been the stronger and more powerful sex for as many centuries as most of this landscape can remember. Stronger than St Wite, St Candida – for all that the wild periwinkles that come up every year here on Stonebarrow Hill are still called St Candida's Eyes and the well at neighbouring Morcombelake is said to have water that has curative properties – particularly for sore eyes. The power and aggression – what St Augustine recognized as 'the blight of male domination' had ruled since time immemorial by then. (Yes, we're looking back to 1963, two years after the scene in the attic at the Mill, when our father caught us at our games. It was Tess's misfortune to be caught, too, in history, and to fall for what seemed to be the answer to the terrible imbalance, when her Angel came along. But each incarnation of Tess has been caught in history, you might say – and no fall has been better or worse than another.)

Tess was sixteen years old and she was just coming out of that time when guilt and shame at incurring our father's anger mixed in with a determination to 'behave badly' – as shown by our truancy and general wildness, our escape on a train that brought us straight back to Weymouth, where the ferries left each night for Cherbourg or St Malo and we never quite had the nerve to stow away, boarding on a frosty autumn evening amongst the freight and lying in the hold until dawn on the French coast. Tess was just coming out of that time, as I say, and the attentions of Ralph Morgan had brought her into a sudden new phase of her womanhood.

What I remember of Tess in those days was that she looked like a Spanish girl, a young infanta, perhaps, who had come to live in Dorset, stepping gently ashore on Chesil Beach, marriage in mind, dark hair piled high with a Spanish comb fixed at the back. Her mouth all at once grew fuller and her lips red without putting anything on them at all. When we went out that summer, and tourists in Burton Bradstock saw us on the beach, she was once or twice taken for a gypsy and young mothers down with their families from Birmingham would push their husbands off to the kiosk for ice cream, beach balls, rubber shoes, rather than let them meet Tess's eye. Once a man who owned the travelling circus that came every summer to Dorchester came up to Tess and asked if she'd like to learn to fly the trapeze, to ride bareback in the sawdusty ring, crack a whip and wear a scarlet satin top hat, live in a caravan with the rest of them.

Tess said yes, of course – but by the time we got home there was another phone message from Ralph: he'd like her to come up to Mapperton tomorrow; there was a big dance for his twenty-first. And bring Liza-Lu, the message said. The circus was forgotten.

So that was the night it happened, Baby Tess. And as I carry you down from here and we make our way back to Abbotsbury, to Ella who needs us now, I'll tell you the rest. But look once more at this high escarpment, at Lambert's Castle, where the crime on that late summer night took place, and imagine the days of the power of moon and water. For this great fort, with its immense natural ramparts, was once the fiefdom of Canute – he who commanded the sea to retreat, he who tried in vain to turn the tide. (When he was Christianized, Canute took the name Lambert.)

Then, the sea conquered. Canute retired here, high above the disobedient waves, to a mountain kingdom where pine and fir and stunted oak thrive amongst the gorse and bramble.

Now, what you see are the heights of his castle and the eminence of Mapperton, across the fields and valleys. Whichever way Tess turned, she found herself in a stronghold from which there was no escaping. And it probably didn't occur to her at all (although it did,

103

perhaps, to me) that the worst danger came from the peaceful, sheltered valley itself: the cry of battle a screech of a garage door by the petrol pumps at the bend on the Beaminster–Yeovil road.

Local folk talk of the stone griffins on the gateposts when they talk of Mapperton. I'd been up there, of course, when it was fête day and the toffs from the manor house at Four Ashes brought picnic hampers and pretended to praise the crude pottery Meg Keech (the first hippie, I suppose, but we wouldn't have known the word then) had for sale in the old stables, while the rest of us licked ice cream from the tub and then ran down those very steep grassy paths to the stone-rimmed pools, slimy with green water, below.

The griffins were said to fly down to the water to drink, every midsummer night. Or maybe it was the sea they were seen flying to – out over the lagoon, stone wings flapping above the heads of the swans and my father looking up sleepily at them as they went over. (So I imagined, anyway: I had no way of knowing what route the birds would take.) But one night, I'm sure, I heard them. There was a rush of cold air in my room and I opened my eyes to see them outlined against the moon, blackened with grime and lichen accumulated over the centuries on the gateposts at Mapperton but flying grimly on, heraldic, slightly chipped.

So on the day of the fête, while crowds collected by the plants stall to buy cuttings from the famous Mapperton garden – fuchsia, marigold, phlox, shrubs like daphne and the spring-flowering cistus bush – and the few jumble stalls and children's games drew grannies and whining pin-a-tail-on-a-donkey kids to the apron of flat lawn by the side of the old house, I would go and stand by the gates and stare up at the stone birds. They wore a harassed, determined air. Perhaps they would fly straight out over us, with half the people not even looking up until it was too late and the gateposts were empty, stone stumps with the guardians of the old Jacobean house gone. Perhaps only the child on the little piebald pony – who every year wandered off out of bounds into the woodland and down the dangerous gorge, slipping and slithering until at last they both fell and the gardener had to be called for, perhaps only that little girl, in the moment of her dizzying tumble, saw the stone birds flying low over beech and oak trees, showing their dark underfeathers, harbingers of the ill fortune that some said had been since the time of King Charles the fate of Mapperton. (But the child was always rescued; there was a scolding, in the gravelly courtyard where the birds sat silent and disapproving on their plinths, a threat of no ice cream for the rest of the holidays and then the fête was over, cars edged politely in the driveway, while Sir Joseph, hoarse from showing the public his gaunt, sparsely furnished rooms, sat down to tea and scones.)

Every year the fête was the same at Mapperton – and always for that reason flat, disappointing. The drama promised by the house and the ravine where it stood perched, as if about to dive headlong into its own Italianate terraced garden, and sink in the stagnant water of the stone-rimmed pools – was never to be enacted. There was a calm, sad air to the place – which I later learnt was the air of death, for the Plague road had wound down by the side of Mapperton House and thousands of dead were carried along there from Beaminster to the burial grounds at Netherbury. There was – and it still stands – a hollow tree, the Posy Tree, which marks the sinister crossroads, just a short way along from the house our father John saw in his mind's eye already as the future home of his Tess (he'd a plan to breed peacocks, I know: where better than at Mapperton, where the fans of the blue and green iridescent birds would fall like exotic suns below the horizon, as they strutted down from one level of the garden to the next?). This tree, an oak without a centre, a husk that sprouts leaves and acorns but is heartless, dead, was the tree for which the area was best known. Death and bad luck, the locals said – though nothing could be pinned on it since the Plague days, at least, and the old box hedges, planted as a prophylactic against the tell-tale Ring o' Roses of the fatal malady, were creaking with age now and no help to anybody, should the swellings, the dizziness, the fever come again. Nothing bad – but something waiting in the wings – that's what you felt up there, windy, sunny or rain.

As far as we were concerned, the one worst thing that can happen to any foolish girl came to Tess as a result of her engagement to the heir of Mapperton. The night of young Ralph's birthday party – that night (but whether it was a prank played by some of his fast friends down from Oxford or whether it was the old story coming true, we'll never know) the stone griffins left their gateposts, never to return. And Alec Field came up to Mapperton.

It was a dark night, no moon. The house was strung out like an ocean liner with lights glimmering and twinkling on every deck – over the great black swell of the valley beneath, with the tops of the trees in Sir Joseph's fancy arboretum catching the light from the servants' quarters, and from the pantries where all the rich food was being laid out.

I was too shy to go in, at first. Tess was in a short, black dress – our father had looked angrily at her for a split second, as if one of his cygnets had been dragged in covered in tar or mud – before pretending to smile, and congratulating Tess on the way she looked.

– You look lovely, dear, John Hewitt said.

And Tess smiled at him, pityingly.

Because, of course, the balance of power had changed completely since the day our mother left. The days of penance, and rebellion, were over. Tess had young Ralph Morgan eating out of her hand; and even if she hadn't had that, she was just too sheer beautiful to stand any nonsense from a shabby, eccentric man like our father. (John grew a moustache after Mary went and it was grey, sparse, as if it were there by mistake: it gave him a constantly apologetic air.)

– You look nice, too, Lizzie, my father went on, after one glance at me in the white dress with the pink roses I'd got in Weymouth with the money earned working part-time at Mrs Sturgess's chemist's shop. Now, don't be too late, will you, girls?

Even as he spoke, the power drained out of John Hewitt's voice. He saw the night, perhaps, the fatal night that was so dark and would end only in disgrace and violence. Or maybe he saw Tess, at the end of a night thousands of nights hence, walking the dark, panelled halls at Mapperton House with her husband and children, while the portraits of the Morgan family, the blade-nosed proprietors of the old forts and terraced vineland of this part of west Dorset, looked complacently down at her.

Whatever it was, our father knew there was something momentous about that night.

He went to the oak sideboard in the musty-smelling and never-used dining room and took out a box.

– These are for you, John Hewitt said to his daughter Tess.

So it was that we drove up to Mapperton, in young Tommy Crick's van (Tommy was the son of the best butcher in Beaminster, then, and he shot his pheasants with Ralph, went duck-flighting with Ralph and his Oxford friends on winter afternoons when the last glow in the sky above the water in the ponds at Pymore showed the birds flying high towards the sea) – we went up to Mapperton, as I say, in Tommy's little van that smelt of dogs and blood, with Tess hanging the sky from her earlobes and the deep blue shine of the stones beaming out to me in the back every time we passed a lighted house or a pub with an electric sign outside.

The sapphires had been Mary's, our father said, and she'd left them behind when she went, for Tess to wear one day. Somehow, John Hewitt knew that this was the day.

Tess was patient with me, at first. She could have been daunted, too, by the lines of expensive cars all incongruously parked in a field where earlier there had been a herd of sitting cows, their supine posture warning of coming rain. And the people! We'd never seen anything like them. All the women looked like fairy-tale creatures, half-human, half-beast – in mink stoles and short fox jackets, faces peeping over the top of the fur like cunning vixens: their hair was bouffant and hard. They wore long gowns, mostly light colours, with satin slippers that gave out a creak of surprise on encountering muddy grass and little hillocks of thistles. The men, invisible in the darkness in their tuxedos, showed only patrician faces and blinding white shirtfronts. Like an army of ghosts, these gentry from Loders and Uploders and as far west as Lyme (Jane Austen's Lyme Regis, of course), advanced on the house, their voices as sharp and sly as arrows. We stood back, for a while, to let them pass. Then Tess started to get impatient. 'Come *on*, Liza-Lu,' she said. 'Do you want to stay out here all night?'

The answer was, I suppose, that I'd far rather run all the way down the road outside Mapperton and hide in the hollow trunk of the Posy Tree, shelter from an evening of agony, dancing with no one, passed over by Ralph's smoking-jacketed friends and taffeta-ballgowned debutantes, than go in after Tess, past the stone griffins at the gates. I hung back. Tess gave me one of those looks only a younger sister can know, that elder-sister, shrivelling look that sends you back to the nursery, however old you are (and, don't forget, I was only fourteen, to Tess's sixteen). And she walked off! She left me there, by the side of a long, sleek car with a chauffeur inside, who snapped awake when Tess walked off and grinned and winked at me. I ran, in turn – but away from the main entrance, down the slope of the garden, over a hedge that tore my stockings – and then, there I was, down in the gunwales of the great house, in the courtyard, like a prison courtyard that opened out onto a sheer drop of grass.

There must be something about me that asks to serve – or there was then, perhaps – because I was no sooner in the first door leading off that courtyard than a tray laden with goodies: smoked salmon twisted in little rolls, glazed pastries, fake caviar, like the jet beads our mother's mother used to wear, piled on boats fashioned as miniature swans and gleaming under tiny wedges of lemon, was in the act of being carried at breakneck speed by a young waiter to the door of the Great Hall and handed over to me without so much as a by-your-leave. No one questioned my dress, hardly a maid's uniform with apron, clearly a 'young girl's dress' bought for the occasion, scoop-necked, embarrassingly tight around the bust, three-quarter length and coming down to show a stretch of leg and white satin pumps already stained green from the night field. Yet I was a servant. It was as simple as that. The head chef shouted at me to get a move on – and I did, as if I'd been brought into the world to take orders. A passing waiter held the great, iron-studded door open for me and I went through, carrying the tray of food just under chin-level. Without a flicker of surprise, guests started to help themselves, talking across me as if I had no meaning other than as tray-bearer, replenisher of the Oxford appetites of young Sir Ralph's friends.

It didn't take me long to spot Tess. I must say that if I appeared a born maid, obedient, subservient, invisible, then Tess seemed a queen that night. For all the darkness of her looks, and the dazzling fairness of most of the young women (after discarding their animal-skin coats they showed very white, puffed-up breasts, held high by whalebone wiring infinitely more sophisticated than anything the little shop in Weymouth could produce) – Tess was as immediately and wordlessly recognized as the giver of orders, the decider of the action of the party, as I was seen as a waitress, a temporary hired help.

Tess's short black dress stood out in that hall, where people milled and jostled and called out in high, meaningless phrases the latest piece of foolishness that came into their heads. Tess stood there with her dark, near-black hair tumbling down to the neck of the simple black dress and a solid wall of young men stood round her. Some were in hunting jackets, I remember – and there was a sad, over-excited stench in that hall where the Morgans of three or four hundred years looked down in their ruffs or velvets: it was a stench I'd come to know when the hunt came over our land, our little piece of garden at the Mill, clattering over stones in the brown water, flattening Mary's favourite magnolia tree that came out early each year and made her think, when her madness was growing inside her, that she was the Madonna, with the magnolia-white skin.

It was the stench of the need to overpower, to kill, to pursue that I recognized, trapped as I was there with my tray of ancestral silver jutting out from just below my face, cutting me off from any possibility of joining the party or getting near to Tess. She was cornered. They bayed at her – and Ralph called for another tray of champagne. They caught my eye and I was sent for it. And what could

I do but go – signalling as I went to Tess, whose faintly flushed face showed she'd had too much already, signalling that she should wait for me, she wasn't to go off and leave me alone here, waiting on the toffs until my feet fell off. Surely I deserved some fun?

And Tess did see me, she did wave at me – though as soon as she raised her arm a bundle of young masters of hounds grabbed it, made fun as if they were going to jive with it, to bring Tess whirling, falling . . . down.

– Come back! she mouthed over the crowd at me.

Ralph saw me, his forehead creased. I could see him ask Tess if that wasn't Liza-Lu, the little sister . . . likes handing round the drink and food, eh? Good for her.

Ralph, in his dark wine velvet smoking jacket, with a face so handsome and so stupid it could have belonged to a ventriloquist's doll, stared baffled at me across the sea of people. His blue eyes were blocked out by a tall, old man with white whiskers, who could have been asleep upstairs in the famous Mapperton library for a few centuries and strolled down to join the party. And when the old man had passed I was halfway through the big door to the kitchens, to fetch the champagne . . . and Ralph was no longer to be seen. But who could blame me for failing to fight my way back there and then and grab hold of my sister, stop her in the course of the night that changed her destiny? Not I . . . I can't blame myself: I had the wine to fetch for Master Ralph. I was only doing what I was told. Though something else half-told me that when I came back, struggling with the little shallow glasses filled with sparkling wine the more stuck-up young guests twirled in the glass with gold swizzle sticks, so the bubbles went flat . . . they laughed and swilled it down and bayed for more – something at least whispered to me, as I say, that I wouldn't find Tess and Ralph there, when I came back, at all.

I don't know who was the most to blame, Alec Field, or Ralph Morgan, with his fancy waistcoat, gold filigree on plum satin that made him look twice the age he was; or me, for letting things get so wildly out of control that night. After all, I was the first to see Alec, hiding there in the pantry where Sir Joseph's gamekeeper hung the game – coming up against him suddenly when the cook sent me in (the deepfreeze was in there too) for a side of the salmon caught by Ralph on the Scottish estates and smoked on oak chips in preparation for the glorious twenty-firster. I could have yelled out – and Alec could have been marched from the great stone pantries and cellars and out across the cobbles of the courtyard, on to the north-facing drop of Mapperton and away down the drive before anyone was any the wiser for it. But I didn't. I came right up against a furry, still-warm thing – a rabbit or a brace of hares, I don't know – and I choked my scream on its flank, with Alec's face staring at me not two inches away and with a kind of mad glee in his eyes. I coughed, and I spluttered . . . and 'Hurry, girl!' came from the kitchen before I could think, and 'What's keeping her, in the name of God?' from an Irish footman who'd had it in for me all evening. (Yes, that was how quickly they'd assumed I was the servant girl, even if my sister was on the brink of becoming the Lady of Mapperton. And don't tell me that social manners had changed and a new freedom for the erstwhile 'lower' classes was in operation by then. Because it wasn't – and it isn't now, and it never will be. So you'd better look sharp to your own future, my poor baby.)

Well, I stumbled to the deepfreeze and pulled out the hard, pink side of salmon, and all the while Alec was laughing in a nasty, snickering kind of way that reminded me of those games he made us play on Chesil Beach when we were no more than little children. He was rolling an Old Holborn too – I'll never forget to my dying day the horrible acrid smell of the tobacco and the beating of my own heart at the knowledge that I must warn Tess somehow – warn Tess to escape before it was too late. Instead, as I say, I did nothing. I stood there with that stiff board of a rich man's fish in my hand as if I'd gone deepfrozen too and there was no use in thinking of thawing me.

– Well, well, Liza-Lu, says Alec. After all these years! Now – and he leant right forward so the vile tobacco was puffed right in my eyes – you'll take me to the garage, won't you, love?

– The garage? I knew Alec worked in the Beaminster garage, at the foot of the hill, on the road that winds in so sharply, still as narrow and sad as the day the first Tess was sent down it by her maker Thomas Hardy to search in vain for the love she had lost. I knew Alec worked there; selling Polos and Mars bars and inflatable balls to the kids in summer when they stopped there on the way to West Bay, the great shingle beach that shows sand only at lowest tide. Alec was a mechanic, otherwise: it was said that he was good with his hands; he liked to lie under a car all day, radio playing, his view of feet, or of the vicar's gown as he made his way to the church of St Mary for Evensong. But Alec was up here now. Why should I be expected to take him back down there? And how could I, a fourteen-year-old girl, do so anyway?

– He must have told you where it is, Alec jeered. C'mon, Liza-Lu!

Of course, I suddenly knew what he meant. Ralph Morgan's white E-type was famous in the neighbourhood. Alec would go home quietly if he was allowed a look at the car. And I *did* know where it was kept – or where it 'lived', as you might say, so much greater a character than most ordinary people on the estate did that white, streamlined wonder possess. I'd been taken on a ride in the Jag, as Ralph fondly called it, perched in the back with Tess's dark hair streaming out in front of me. I'd come all the way back to Mapperton and felt the intense satisfaction Ralph had known when guiding the gleaming white thighs and black hot nose of his car into the garage. And the garage was only a few steps away! The other side of the court-yard! No one need ever know – I'd plop the salmon in the kitchen, excuse myself and climb with Alec out the scullery window and over the cobbles, in the dark. I nodded at Alec, and thus sealed all of our fates.

You may ask me, did Tess still have a fondness for Alec, after the time we were all found in the attic at the Mill, and Tess fell into a kind of apathy, broken by rebellious acts, that made up the extent of the punishment her father and the world visited upon her?

I would say the answer is no. We played games when we were young; the illicit sex with Alec had been as much of a game as the stones on Chesil Beach – and when the games were over she never thought more of him. (I still don't know if this is entirely true, but Tess certainly never gave away to me, in those years we were at the Mill, those nights we sat with damp hair in heated rollers, sitting and smoking and turning the pages of the women's magazines that told us how to 'get' an eligible young man like Ralph, or a film star, or Adam Faith, that she had regressed about Alec; that she still wanted to see him.)

The tragedy, I suppose, was that Alec didn't feel that way at all.

The car travelled with a low roar. It ate the sides of hedges in lanes that were no more than lost needles, trails of silver-grey in a tangle of late summer hay and over-green leaf; it grazed the tiny grassy islands that stand for roundabouts in the Marshwood Vale. Powerful headlights brought a dance of moths and night creatures, caught fatally in the glare. A strong wind, made by the speed at which we raced, banked and accelerated as soon as a small stretch of straight road showed itself, stung our faces and lifted hair like a drawing of a child confronted by the supernatural. And the first drops of rain came straight down on us – for the Jag never had a hood up, not if young Ralph could help it, that is.

I looked from time to time at the floor by the back seat (a space so small and cramped that both of Ralph's golden Labradors couldn't fit in together). I looked down at the bundle, covered with an old oilskin (Ralph went out fishing from time to time, from West Bay; our mother would laugh at the small catch he brought back, the line of mackerel she said would bring him in less than half the cost of fuel for the boat he rented from old Dowle), and I prayed, against the stinging wind and the spatters of rain that jumped into my eyes and rolled down my cheeks as if I were crying already for the crime that was about to be committed, I prayed the oilskin would never move, that we would come back from our joyride and park the car in the stables and no one would be any the wiser.

Of course, the oilskin hid Alec. He'd been crawling about under the car when Ralph and Tess appeared – just like that – and for a moment we all heard the music in the house, and (a door must have been left open) we saw light from the chandeliers and young girls in misty balldresses strolling out to take the night air with their escorts, most of them half-drunk. Ralph was saying to Tess that a ride would be fun – 'up to your part of the world' – he was teasing her, I know, for our mother's life in the dairy land, as a child, of Marshwood: her life as a humble farmgirl, milking cows on the big Bowditch estate. Tess always bridled up when he did this. But he leant towards her – they kissed – he said they might even leave the 'bloody party' for an hour or two and go to that stupid nightclub on the road out of Bridport.

By this time Alec had crawled into the back seat of the Jag and sunk down on the floor. I stepped forward (why did I always seem to be spying on my elder sister? Is it part of being the younger that you always think you are?) and Ralph saw me first. He was surprised, then seemed to take my presence there quite for granted.

– Liza-Lu can come along too, Ralph said. He had a kind of patrician kindness, I have to hand him that: like one of those lords or landowners who're accustomed to have a court round them at all times, whether a cluster of gamekeepers, beaters, estate workers or whatever – so the actual wooing of a prospective wife is a pretty public affair. There's no mean desire for privacy with those people, you can say that at least.

Before I knew what was happening, Ralph had opened the door of the car and I was pushing my way past the thick black leather seats into the little ledge at the rear. I even stepped on Alec – it was impossible not to – but the oilskin bundle made no grunt or move. Tess, who'd thrown me rather an odd look at first, now seemed perfectly happy with the arrangement and climbed in next to Ralph. And with a terrible roar we were off.

The car stopped under a clump of pine trees that looked as if they'd been sawn off by the wind, on that high promontory of land that is Lambert's Castle. And we must have looked an odd sight – the Jag at a ninety-degree angle to the land, front bumper up against the trunk of a conifer that released a shower of pine cones onto us, Alec and me thrown sideways out of the car at the back and Tess and

Ralph noticing nothing, lips glued in a kiss. The sky had cleared. A moon that looked as if it too had been sawn in half by an amateur woodsman glinted coldly down at us.

It could all be described as a mistake. If Alec hadn't chosen that moment to grab Ralph's hair from the back and twist his head round – and Ralph, horrified and shouting with pain, hadn't wrenched the car free and jammed his foot down on the accelerator so the Jag shot forward, no lights, only the moon showing in the clear air the precipice that is the wall of Lambert's Castle – and if Tess, twisting in her seat, screaming too, seeing Alec and trying to pound him with her fists – and if the car hadn't gone slam into an oak tree, wrecking itself this time, crumpling metal, a first lick of flame bursting from the engine – then I wouldn't be telling you, Baby Tess, the story of your mother and grandmother's life. It would all be different. You might be at Mapperton Hall today, and going when you're older to the posh girls' school near Shaftesbury, where they wear little blue and white cotton dresses in summer and carry hockey sticks in winter, not allowed to knock holly berries off the trees as they go, like we did as kids. I wouldn't be holding you like this – a refugee baby, wrapped in a shawl and nowhere to go. You'd have a pram, a nanny most likely. But the dice fell another way – just as surely as Alec, who had hurtled from the car at the first impact with the pine tree, had rolled, right to the edge of the cliff, and hung there, gripping the unsettled stones and the unfriendly bracken shoots of that high-up terrain.

Tess was out of the car and running, Ralph behind her. I don't know which one of them saw Alec's head first, peering like a badger's over the side of the cliff – as he desperately edged along, finding a crevice for his poor hands, hiding as much as he could of himself in the gorse and overhanging bracken – but it doesn't matter which of them it was, because Ralph's words, loud and carrying in the thin night air, are as strong in my memory now as they ever have been. 'God,' Ralph shouted, at Tess maybe, at no one in particular, 'it's that ghastly little pleb from the garage.'

And, as he walked to the Jag, pulled open the boot and brought out his .22, Ralph said, 'That's bad.' Then – you could feel the venom that came from his polite, clipped accents: 'I always think it's better to shoot vermin straight away and get it over with, don't you, Tess?'

I don't know – and I never will know – whether Ralph would actually have taken a shot at Alec. It may seem incredible even to imagine that he might – that a man could kill another on a quiet Dorset hill in 1963 – but I dare say it could have been passed off as an accident or self-defence or whatever, and with Ralph's word against ours in Bridport County Court I wouldn't like to say for sure we'd have been the ones to be believed.

Anyway, you could say it might have been better if Alec had been shot there and then – like vermin, as Ralph said. Our mother certainly would have thought so. It's hard, when you look back on times like that – when things could have gone one way or the other – to decide what you think in retrospect. It all happened so quickly, you see –

No! A shrill, raucous cry – a swan in the last throes of battle, that was how Tess sounded, her No! No! to the casual, arrogant disposal of Alec by the man in smoking-jacket velvet, the owner of all the acres of Mapperton and the land Alec's garage stood on, too. That cry, that cut a swath between the men, as the gun went higher and Alec dropped down as far as he could go without losing his hold on the stones, made Ralph turn to her for one fatal, electrifying second.

By the time he swung round again, Tess and Alec had both gone.

Don't ask me what I did to help, before Tess made her great leap and took Alec with her, the two of them rolling down, down through pine trees and over leaves and boulders, to safety. I did nothing. Younger sisters so often do just that – they stand and watch and then it's too late. And I don't know whether Ralph knew that Tess and Alec had been lovers. I expect he did – with a girl as beautiful as Tess most of the young landowners in the county would have noticed and asked before she was properly in her teens. No matter. The atmosphere became very strange. It was as if nothing had happened up there at all, on the ramparts of the earthworks that was our mother's territory, her imaginary home passed down through her mother and foremothers since the days of the auto-cratic king who was refused by the sea.

Nothing had happened at all. Ralph had come for an evening trip to break the tedium of the ball given in his honour; there had been what he would doubtless later describe as 'a bit of a prang', and he'd gone home again.

Ralph and I walked all the way down from Lambert's Castle to the village of Wootton Fitzpaine and called up from the call box and a family retainer came, in a Range Rover. I was dropped off first. I didn't say good night, and they drove off without waiting to see if I had a key to the Mill – to see if I was safely in, before they went. There was no mention of Tess. She might never have existed.

My father had been waiting up. He stared at me as I walked in alone and then went back to his records of the swannery – he'd often sit up late working out the figures, the numbers of birds, the casualties and the new nest-building sites. I knew somehow he wasn't surprised to see me come in without Tess. He'd known that night when we set off that she'd never come back – the black swan he never could tame or understand.

When Tess next contacted our mother – and myself – she was living (temporarily; she didn't know how temporarily, poor girl) in Alec's uncle's flat in East Coker – and her pregnancy was three months gone.

Where You Came From: The Ballad of Tess

It's getting late; so late that the first streaks of morning are coming up in the sky over West Bay. There's an odd, grey twilight the colour of the stone facade of St Mary's Church and we pause, Baby Tess, by the gates of the church, on our long way back to the Mill and to the full light of day when the stones in the shallow pit behind the George Hotel at West Bay will finally be shifted and the body will be found.

We look west – to a lightening sky over the sea that stretches to America, where Alec fled and no question of support for Tess or baby. And I'll tell you, when one day you want to know why Tess chose to have that baby – yes, the baby was your mother, Baby Tess – and not go back to the old woman of Langton Herring or to the National Health doctor in Weymouth to plead for a 'termination'. Our mother lost her freedom when Tess's baby, your mother, was born; but she helped us, our newly strong witch-mother, as best she could.

For our father, of course, it was another matter. Tess had 'thrown away her life'. Tess had 'slipped up'. Tess had brought shame on the family. (Yes, in 1963. But our father was born in the last year of Victoria; and even today you'll find that attitude a great deal more prevalent than you might expect.)

Tess's fault. So, as we watch the dawn as it touches the top of St Mary's spire and softens the frowning gargoyles on the porch, I tell you that whatever Tess had chosen to do, it would have been her fault. We are still, whatever the appearances, in the age of Christian punishment, you must remember. If Tess had aborted the baby it would – to many – have been considered a sin, her fault. By deciding to go ahead and have it, she showed her foolish 'wilfulness' to the world. Her fault. Society, built as it is on patriar- chal attitudes that are only just recently beginning to undergo an assault by the oppressed, the pitied, the dispossessed, flinched from Tess just as much in 1963 as it had done a century earlier – the hypocrisies were different, that's all.

Conception. Let me show you, as we watch the sun rise pale and red and turn the world upside down, making an evening glow on the last day of the year (by the Celtic calendar) of the last century of the second millennium since the birth of Christ, let me show you the dark old house that stands by the side of the church and looks out across the valley over the roofs of Beaminster. For it's there that the poetic conception took place that makes up the ballad of Tess. There, Tess was born and reborn, incarnation and reincar- nation of the dominating, controlling imagination of the great Thomas Hardy. Come with me – we'll walk to the end of the short drive and look up at the stumpy, largish cottage with the 'picture' window that looks out over the quaint Beaminster lanes. You must know the more recent past. You must understand the antecedents of Tess's story. So I'll tell it to you as our mother told it to us at the Mill when we were very young, and Tess was fidgeting with her mug of milk and spilt it on the rag rug so my mother had to stop and go to fetch a cloth to wipe it up. Then she told us again, when we were older; and Tess's dark eyes, vague at first, roaming the room in search of some distraction from the 'boring' past, grew darker and wider . . .

As we already know, Thomas Hardy first set eyes on the young woman who was to be the inspiration for Tess when he was on a visit to his mother in 1888. Augusta Way was her name, she was eighteen years old and she worked as a milkmaid on the Kingston Maurward estate. She lived with her family in the old house . . . Hardy saw her in the fields, bringing in the herd of cows . . .

Thomas Hardy falls in love with this dark-eyed beauty. He sees in the humble life she leads in a house that has all the remnants of grandeur a reflection of his own (imagined) decline from an important and distinguished family to the obscure and impoverished Hardys that were his father and grandfather. Sweet Augusta, untroubled by thoughts of this kind, smiles at Hardy as he dallies at the gate, pretends to pick a wild rose from the thorny hedge by the side of the field to present to his mother, the aged Jemima, in her cottage at Bockhampton, a short walk away. Hardy sees Augusta's smile and he smiles back at her. Tess – Tess of a grand old family, the D'Urbervilles, now living in humble circumstances, begins to be born.

Hardy conceives Tess, and Augusta Way starts to cease to exist. Already, perhaps, divining that she will be a footnote in history, an appendage of a great man (of whom at this time she has not even heard), she feels for the first time in her life self-conscious. Why does this man with the angry moustache, this man nearing fifty who carries all his neglect of and dislike for his wife in his small, slanting eyes and questioning, arrogant angle of his head, keep smiling at her? His hands fumble with the latch of the gate, and Augusta turns and flees.

The next time Hardy looks up from the reverie that caught him by the gate with the stile set into the wooden staves of the fence at the side, the stile he could easily have climbed if he had really wanted to come closer to Augusta – to kiss her, perhaps, as could and did happen only too often to milkmaids at haymaking time – Augusta has disappeared and a cloud has come over the sun. The cows that belong to the Kingston Maurward land stare at him before ambling away. Hardy lets the wild rose, crumpled and faded already, drop from his fingers to the ground. He needn't look in on his mother, after all, on the way back to Max Gate. He's in a hurry – although as yet he hardly knows why.

By the time Hardy has arrived at Max Gate, his ugly house high in the hills above Dorchester, and walked past the dismal smell of boiled cabbage and mutton in the hall (Emma is a terrible house-keeper), his wife has the most formidable rival of her life. (Indeed, after she has died and Florence Henniker has succeeded Emma as Hardy's spouse, this rival will outlive her too. But Florence is the one who is destined to suffer most, the unwilling participant in her husband's rites of incarnation, his incestuous obsession with his own creation: Emma by then can count herself lucky to be dead.)

An early autumn evening and Hardy takes the train to Evershot station. He sees there some mistletoe that had been there 'ever since last Christmas (given by a lass?), of a yellow saffron parchment colour' – most likely the 'source' of the mistletoe which Tess finds hanging, like a mockery, over the wedding bed after she has made her fatal confession to Angel Clare: the confession of her 'past': Alec D'Urberville and the poor baby, dead now of course: the confession of her fault.

The rootless plant, the white berries and fine grey-green leaves that entwine oak trees – the kissing plant that cannot touch the ground – hangs faded and spurned on a small country station. Hardy stands and stares at it, before boarding the little puffer to Dorchester.

Augusta Way and mistletoe. The sad fate of Tess has been decided. A beautiful, dark-eyed young woman is born, who will love, and find her love destroyed by the seducer who came first into her life – and in return for this she will murder him.

The cycle of love, betrayal and revenge has been caught again, and will be set down for posterity by Thomas Hardy, progenitor and lover of Tess.

There – over there – in that dumpy old cottage by the side of the churchyard in Beaminster, is the home of the daughter of Tess, the daughter of the beautiful milkmaid Augusta Way. She was also the love of Thomas Hardy's old age. Her acting career – she played Tess in the theatre – was blocked by Hardy's second wife, Florence. Florence came here, to the cottage in the town by the side of Marshwood Vale, our mother's country –

But first I shall show you

The Growth of Tess

It's 1896, a sultry summer. Hardy spends the season in London, in South Kensington, Pelham Crescent, where the stately white houses with their porticoes and long, slender windows have a formal coldness conducive to one of the worst fits of illness and depression the great writer has suffered in years. He has a chill – then rheumatism – his friend Lady Jeune suggests a trip to Brighton to take the air. On his return, refreshed but still lacking, still wanting . . . what? that elusive thing, happiness, a sense of well-being . . . he sets out to enjoy the London season, meets the witty Margot Asquith at a party she gives with her husband who will shortly be Prime

Minister, and even feels well enough to do a few turns of the 'Blue Danube' waltz with his old friend Mrs Grove.

By July, Hardy is back at Max Gate, much invigorated, his depression and illness forgotten. He decides to go and see his mother at Bockhampton. And he finds her perceptibly older (which reminds him again of mortality, of the passing of time). For Hardy, sex and death are inexorably linked, and the fact of Jemima's ageing, her nearness to becoming a part of his carefully hoarded and nurtured past, drives him to walk out in the fields at Kingston Maurward . . . to wonder what became of that lovely milkmaid he saw there eight long years ago, the dark-eyed young woman who inspired the writing of *Tess*. He feels his age, through his mother's shrivelling, and he feels his childlessness, too, his lack of youth and warmth; Hardy stops by the entrance to the drive, walks up the untidy road which Dairyman Crick (as Augusta Way's father has been named and immortalized in *Tess*) has no time to weed, and stops by the front door which is already open, as if expecting him. A bale of hay lies in the hall. A chicken rushes out. Hardy smiles and turns to leave. But as he goes, a young woman walks up the drive – a married woman, Hardy can see from her gait and her slightly more rounded figure. He also sees that she is alone and that she is, at twenty-six, an even more beautiful Augusta Way. This time, she smiles back at the tentative visitor, with his hat and his imposing moustache. She invites him in, for tea . . .

> He was subject to gigantic fantasies still. In spite of himself, the sight of the new moon, as representing one who, by her so-called inconstancy, acted up to his own idea of a migratory Well-beloved, made him feel as if his wraith in a changed sex had suddenly looked over the horizon at him. In a crowd secretly, or in solitude boldly, he had often bowed the knee three times to this sisterly divinity on her first appearance monthly, and directed a kiss towards her shining shape.
>
> THOMAS HARDY, *The Well-Beloved*

Thomas Hardy searches for his 'evasive well-beloved'. He has seen her incarnated in woman after woman – but each time, as he comes nearer, she vanishes like the moon behind clouds.

In other words, when Thomas Hardy falls in love, he falls in love with his own creation. His is the male, controlling imagination that devours women in its lair: Monster eats the Muse.

And on the stifling July day in 1896 when the great writer bows to the beautiful if slightly more mature Augusta Way, he finds he has met another incarnation of his desires.

Augusta, the model for Tess, is both the incarnation of the woman he loves and his own creation. (The second version of *The Well-Beloved* appears in 1897, the year following Hardy's visit to Kingston Maurward – as does Augusta's baby daughter. But more of that later.)

Since writing *Tess*, since receiving the scorn and moral indignation, the fame and blame of the most scandalous book of the age – in which a woman commits *murder*, if you can imagine such a thing, and gives birth to a bastard on the way – Hardy has written his fantasy of a man in love with three generations of women.

Now, whether he knows it or not, he will act out the theme of the novel in real life. And it must be said here that Hardy's novels don't only repeat one another in theme, having as their constant the subjects of betrayal, grotesque incongruity in clashing desires and perpetual dissatisfaction in love, but the suffering love causes is in each case associated with the theme of repetition. For all Hardy's novels in one way or another pose the question: why is it that most human beings go through life somnambulistically, compelled to repeat the same mistakes in love, so inflicting on themselves and others the same suffering, again and again?

Hardy, nearing fifty and with *The Well-Beloved* writing its final version in his head (it will also be his last novel), walks into the bright hall where the dust dances against the long sash windows old 'Dairyman Crick', Augusta's fictional father, has never bothered to cover with the rich Victorian brocades of the age. He feels his own old age settle down around him. He needs fresh blood! He craves the repetition, the greedy cycle of possession which, we know so well, my poor child, springs from the crushing of equality and freedom that took place so long ago. Hardy may believe he seeks the other half to an androgynous whole – but he whistles for the moon, his double 'in a changed sex'. How better than to find her already the inspiration for the most 'living' of his heroines, poor Tess?

Hardy waits in the bare hall while Augusta goes into the pantry and prepares tea. No matter that she doesn't live here any more, that she has married a confectioner named Bugler and lives with him in Dorchester, that she is happy crystallizing the rose and violet petals that decorate her husband's fancy chocolates, that she is happy to have left the hard country life, up at dawn to milk the cows, hoeing turnips in the frost-hard ground. It's of no importance that Augusta likes the town, the staid walk to church on Sundays in a long, deep-green velvet dress with a cloak that has a fur-lined hood. No matter that she wants a family with her husband, a little boy who will look, in her dreams, just like the pleasant *chocolatier* . . .

To Hardy, Augusta is the incarnation of Tess, the woman he loved and brought into the world, only to have her hanged at the end (as we remember, Hardy loved to see the corpses of the hanged women after a public execution in Dorchester, when he was a boy, the long, bunched and soiled skirts swinging in the wind . . .). To Hardy, Augusta is Tess, and Tess is his.

As she comes in from the pantry with a tray, Hardy rises and goes to meet her. He bows low as he relieves her of the cups of chipped Crown Derby, the humble brown teapot used by Dairyman Crick. Tenderly, sighing as if already haunted by nostalgic regret, Hardy leads his Tess over to the fireplace where logs crackle and flare, and takes her in his arms . . . his long moustaches tickle her extremely as he starts his kiss.

From that embrace came the next incarnation, baby Tess – of Hardy's well-beloved, whose home is over there on the edge of the churchyard of St Mary's in Beaminster. Only metaphorically, of course: Gertrude's mother and father were Mr and Mrs Bugler of Dorchester; but the imagination of the great man rules both generations and when Gertrude acts the part of Tess, she suffers the vengeful rage of Hardy's second wife, Florence.

At the time of Hardy's visit to his much-aged mother at Bock-hampton and the surge of erotic fascination and creativity that followed when he went to call on Augusta Way (now Augusta Bugler), Florence was no more than a sweet possibility on the horizon; a sweet possibility that would be soured, as was his marriage to Emma, when the reality of a woman replaced the fantasy.

But for now – and, as it will prove, again later – the bodily incarnation of Tess is what Hardy wants more than anything in the world.

For Hardy, the theme of misalliance and mismating springs from the stories his mother told him – his mother who had grown up in abject poverty, in that part of northwest Dorset well known for its privations to Victorian chroniclers of misery. It was in the rectangle bounded by Sherborne, Yeovil, Holywell and Minterne, in the village of Melbury Osmond, that Hardy's grandmother, Betsy Swetman, made the 'first fatal mistake': she married George Hand and condemned herself to lifelong poverty and parish charity.

Hardy's mother Jemima's fireside tales were of an unhappy charity childhood. The cottage where her own widowed mother had brought up seven children, including Jemima, in shameful poverty was in the east quarter of the Melbury Osmond parish, in the direction of Hermitage and Minterne – Minterne with its grand house belonging to the Digby family, its three-tiered garden where long lakes, smothered under carpets of a vivid green weed, lie in the descending slopes of the valley.

Here, where local women, in an area known for its hardness, knew that to live just above subsistence level was the best that could be hoped for, Hardy set his novel *The Woodlanders*. In this square of coppice, woodland and hedge he wrote out the story – the story he always wrote: faithful suitor, flashy rival and a heroine who makes the fatal choice. (This was to be the first of Hardy's 'darker' works. There had been a sardonic exchange between the author and Leslie Stephen, whose dry comment, 'The heroine married the wrong man,' drew from Hardy the reply that mostly women did just that. 'Not in magazines,' Stephen laughed.)

The heroine is Marty South, the dark-eyed beauty who lives in hardship in that thickly wooded area of northwest Dorset so often described to Hardy by his mother. The rich Mrs Charmond, from a house and estate very like Minterne, buys Marty's lovely long hair, hair that's nearly black but not quite, that dark brown-black that may have come to southwest England from Spain or Morocco, hair that is just like the hair of my sister Tess.

Marty is a low-paid spar-worker. Giles Winterborne, who is a humble coppice-holder and cider-maker (Hardy sings of 'that atmosphere of cider which . . . has such an indescribable fascination for those who have been born and bred among the orchards'), meets Marty South. The tragic, inevitable story is played out.

And seventeen years after Thomas Hardy meets his original Tess, Augusta Way (now Bugler), in the hall at Kingston Maurward, a young actress appears in a presentation of *The Woodlanders* by the Dorchester Debating, Literary and Dramatic Society. The young heroine is so moving and appealing in the part of Marty South that even the London critics are astonished by her. On 20th November 1913 her photograph – a dark-eyed beauty with a cloud of brown-black hair and a mouth that is full and lusciously open – appears in the *Daily Mail*. She is described as 'a natural actress, slender, with expressive eyes'.

Her name? Gertrude Bugler, daughter of Augusta Way. Her father owns a confectioner's shop in South Street, Dorchester. Gertrude Bugler will play a large part in Hardy's last years. She is the final incarnation – in his lifetime, that is.

Look now at the squat, dumpy cottage on the fringes of the graveyard at St Mary's in Beaminster, where Gertrude lived . . .

Gertrude Bugler, daughter of the inspiration for *Tess*. Poetically conceived by Thomas Hardy.

For, by now, the Minotaur wants his victims to be real. No more webs to be spun, no more invented heroines, who become tiring to play with, as they trace and retrace the thread of his ideas in a labyrinth of his own making. Gertrude, the real, actual Gertrude who so resembles her beautiful mother, will be the next Tess.

The year 1913 is a pivotal one for Thomas Hardy. In November 1912, after years of pain – and shockingly, a whole year of agony – Emma, his wife, dies.

No more shuffling, crippled mounting the stairs to bed after another silent dinner with her husband – the stairs that run behind Hardy's study, and where he had heard her so often climbing – unaided, unloved, a prisoner in her own home of his cruelty and the ignorance of the maids. Even on the day before her death, Hardy makes her come down to preside over a ladies' tea party: Emma is weeping with the severe spasms (possibly gallstones, certainly something that could have been operable if there had been anyone in the world to care for her) that tire her heart and wreck her constitution. Hardy, as always, notices nothing.

In the morning he is called to Emma's bed by a frightened maid. There, in the attic room, where the birds, with whom Emma had an almost magical rapport, flock to the window and look in at their ill protector – there, in the bed Hardy has left unvisited for as long as anyone can remember, poor 'mad' Emma dies.

Yes, Thomas Hardy made of his wife that well-known Victorian phenomenon, the madwoman in the attic. His neglect and cold indifference alienated her, she became 'scatty' and the housekeeping got beyond her capabilities. More and more she stayed in the high room with the sloping rafters and called to the birds to fly to her window. Robins, a wren, chaffinches, once even a blue jay, heard the call of the sick, lonely woman. While Hardy boasted of being able to hear the trees he planted sigh as he placed them in the ground, the 'madwoman' of his creation was the one who was able to reach the denizens of the natural world, with her simple love for them.

Emma dies. Of course there's gossip and excitement when a month later Hardy moves Florence Dugdale into the hideous house at Max Gate. The maids swear they're sleeping together. It's a scandal. And poor Mrs Hardy – he never took her to the doctor, you know – that woman was a saint and he was sleeping with the other woman all along, so they say.

Florence Dugdale. The helper, the amanuensis: another very Victorian figure, with her pale, nervous face and haunting eyes.

Poetic, sensitive . . . in her long black skirt and modest white blouse she stands on the edge of the trench of the coming World War, her long, finely honed nose pointing always slightly upwards in the direction of the revered, the world-famous Thomas Hardy.

Florence stands behind a seated Emma on the beach at Worthing. Oh poor, dear, mad Emma, in that huge black hat laden with veils and oddities, like an undertaker's birthday party. Florence stands for the future. She is the worm that feeds already on the corpse of the first wife who will be left to die alone and in pain. Florence, for years before Emma's death, was the owner of Thomas Hardy's heart (though, as we know, both wives would be cheated of it, the ashes going for burial to Westminster Abbey and Hardy's heart sandwiched between the two women he married and destroyed).

Florence is mistaken when she thinks she is the proud possessor of that questionable commodity, Thomas Hardy's heart, of course.

We know where his heart really lies – why, it's simple, it lies in the mirror, in the double he creates and likens to his sister, the moon – in the women he fashions from words and sets to live for ever. (For, if you go to Batcombe Down and you see the sinister Crossy Hand I told you of, where Tess was made to place her hand and swear she would no longer 'tempt' Alec D'Urberville, you'll see the words 'Tess lives' scrawled there, with a penknife most likely, in the rough stone of the crude little dolmen. And you won't see the words 'Florence lives' anywhere, I'll bet you, nor Emma Hardy's name either attached to the immortality granted his famous heroine.)

No wonder Hardy, at the performance of *The Woodlanders* in 1913, just a few months after Emma's death and a few months in advance of his wedding in February 1914 to Florence Dugdale, leans forward in a state of high excitement. The young actress Gertrude Bugler, he has just ascertained, is none other than the daughter of his Tess! After the performance he asks for her to be brought to him. A 'fatherly' man, as seventeen-year-old Gertrude remembers him. He smiles down at her. Seven years will pass before his incarnation is ready for him.

Florence will become the nervous, ignored, 'hysterical' wife.

Indeed, she confides, the very month she moves into Max Gate, in a letter to a friend, that on the day of Emma's death she passed from 'youth to dreary middle age'.

Florence has become the incarnation of the wife. And no sooner was his first wife dead than she became Hardy's early love again: he wrote six or seven of his most moving and lyrical poems in remembrance of her, in November and December 1912, with Florence newly installed.

For Florence, worse was to come.

Autumn 1916. Thomas Hardy and Florence have been married two years. On 3rd October comes the publication of *Selected Poems of Thomas Hardy*, a volume designed to make his verse more readily accessible to a wider public. Some poems were excluded – when Hardy's friend Cockerell complained to Florence that it was a pity 'A Trampwoman's Tragedy' had been omitted (along with a few others considered a possible source of offence), Florence replied that her husband had wanted to make the volume one which could be given 'to a schoolgirl, or the most particular person'.

Of course, there is one particular person – a person with the youthful looks and demure demeanour of a schoolgirl, a dark-eyed beauty who has recently come to the attention of the seventy-six-year-old poet and who has received his most ardent attentions too. From early spring Hardy has been putting together – revising and expanding – a series of *Wessex Scenes* from *The Dynasts*, and these were performed by the Dorchester amateurs in Weymouth in June. Everyone remarks that a man of his age should be willing and able to devote so much energy to a project. Where can it come from, this creative fervour which leads an old man to rewrite, to attend rehearsals, even to write in new scenes? Can it be the young actress, Gertrude Bugler, for whom he writes in 'a little romance thread', involving a young waiting-woman and her soldier husband – the young actress who made such a striking Marty South a few years back?

If it is, Florence is already keen to extinguish the flame. What started as a source of 'pleasurable excitement', she confides to her friend Rebekah Owen in a letter, has become in the end a source of constant worry. 'He is too old for the worry and the responsibility – for of course if it is a failure it will reflect on him. It *has* worried him so.'

Poor Florence. She has seen the 'worry', the sleeplessness of a man obsessed by the incarnation of his own creation. The 'romance thread' lies between the recently wed couple, as they lie in the gloomy marital bedchamber at Max Gate – Florence in knots of despair that will lead to a major illness and then a lifelong fear of its recurrence – and Hardy in a soft spider's web of desire. For the moment, as he worships his new love, he is an innocent fly, caught in the toils of the lovely Gertrude. (But one day they'll wake up together, Hardy and Florence, and in the name of married middle-class respectability break the thread, between them destroy the young actress's prospects.)

Not yet, though. Gertrude must play Tess. The story must, literally, be acted out.

In 1921 Gertrude Bugler marries her cousin, a farmer also by the name of Bugler. They go to live in Beaminster – in the house that stands on its own by the side of the graveyard to the south of the church – one of the most beautiful churches in Dorset, remember – with its fine tower (but the font has been thrown out: it will be found in a stonemason's barn too late for the christening of Gertrude's first child). She has gone far from Max Gate – but not far enough for Florence, as we shall see. (Poor Florence. She has had the very thing all wives with roving-eyed, double-hearted husbands dread: the presence of Gertrude in her house, right at her hearth.) For surely Gertrude is the perfect choice to play Eustacia Vye in the dramatization of *The Return of the Native*, given by the Christmas mummers in the festive season (by now it's 1920).

Dark Gertrude plays Eustacia – a Corfiote, a Greek beauty in the imagination of Thomas Hardy. Her tragedy is played out right there, under the eyes of Florence, as Hardy, eighty years old by now, becomes once again animated. Doesn't he say to the lovely young actress, as the applause still sounds out and he leads her aside, away from Florence's anxious gaze, to the little parlour –

doesn't he ask her then and there if she will consider playing Tess one day?

Of course, Gertrude is so pleased . . . but what does Florence say when she catches up with her in the porch as the mummers, fortified by mulled ale, depart?

'A beautiful creature, only twenty-four,' Florence writes in the last drear days of December to her friend Louisa Yearsley, 'and really nice and refined.' But there's a puzzle somewhere here, she continues: 'she tells everyone she is taking my advice *not* to go on the stage and I am puzzled as to *when* I did give that advice.' Florence concludes that the advice must have been Hardy's and jokes about Hardy's partiality for Miss Bugler, whom she herself greatly likes.

Florence goes out onto the porch at Max Gate. It is dark and a thin fall of snow hisses under her feet as she taps Gertrude's arm and draws her aside. An interruption: the terrier Wessex, feared – and loathed – by the literary world, for its unpardonably uncivilized behaviour, rushes out into the snow and rolls at the feet of the mummers. The young actors laugh – one falls on the ground, ambushed by a snowy Wessex, whose white, wiry coat is now horribly wet and cold – and, taking advantage of the commotion, speaking close into the young actress's ear: 'If you take my advice you won't go on the stage, Miss Bugler,' Florence Hardy says to Gertrude.

But by April of the next year, when Hardy's love is pushing up anew with the sparse scatter of purple and yellow crocuses at Max Gate, Gertrude Bugler has added Bathsheba to her repertoire of Hardyan heroines. In June, the Hardy Players perform the Bathsheba episodes again in the castle ruins at Sturminster Newton. Hardy and Florence are present.

Florence has a depressing day. Sturminster Newton is the scene of Thomas Hardy's old home, with his first wife Emma. And after the performance, Hardy insists that the cast come to tea at Riverside Villa, where he had lived with the now-idolized Emma fifty years earlier.

Hardy invites Gertrude to stay the night.

What can Florence do? Her mouth sets in a gather of fine lines that jump and dart in the nervous movements that are precursors of her speech. She sets out hand towels – Irish linen, pale blue – for the so-much-unwanted guest.

Hardy asks Gertrude to sleep in the room in which he had written *The Return of the Native*. Surprised, flattered, she agrees.

That night, Hardy lies sleepless by the side of Florence (equally sleepless but having to pretend: only the nervous tic that has now swept to her eyelids, causing a continuous fluttering, giving away the fact that she is not enjoying a good night's rest at Riverside Villa).

Hardy has everything, or almost everything, a famous poet of eighty could possibly want. The incarnation of his greatest creation, who has now played Marty, Eustacia and Bathsheba, all the dark heroines of his dreams, lies next door in the room where he invented the tempestuous Eustacia.

All he needs now is for Gertrude to take on the mantle of Tess (beside whom all his other heroines, even Eustacia, pale). Tess, the murderess, the 'Pure Woman, Faithfully Presented'.

And maybe there's something else the childless Hardy wants – and gets. There are, as the novelist in him is so well aware, two ways of looking at it.

Wessex's Tail

It's September and Hardy can feel the usual mixture of death-love (anniversaries will be coming up soon: Emma's birthday and then the day of her death, just three days away from each other in November: how Florence hates having to accompany her husband to the grave, to lay flowers on the body of the woman she taught to die) and of renewal too, for new loves for Hardy bloom on the graves of old ones, as we have seen, and he has ambitious new plans for Gertrude Bugler.

September, and Hardy walks in the mild air with Wessex, the white wire-haired terrier who so terrorizes his literary friends (even going so far as to walk along the trestle table at mealtimes and snatch food as it goes onto the fork); and as man and dog go, they pause on the crest of the hill and look down at the world Hardy has made his own. Wessex! The whole landscape has been re-formed by the imagination of this great man; boundaries have been redrawn and names of towns altered; there are pilgrims already to the famous sites, such as Wool Manor where Tess would have spent her wedding night if she had not confessed to Angel, or the cottage at Higher Bockhampton, where the poet suffered his humble childhood. Hardy's dog is named after the fictional landscape which has seemed to become more 'real' than the portion of Dorset, Wiltshire and Berkshire these straggling counties had been known as before – and it's Hardy's dog Wessex who pricks up his ears suddenly and stands unusually silent in the very still air.

Of course, what Wessex has heard is a hare getting up in a wheatfield below, or a rustle of wood pigeons in the coppice at the edge of the field. But Hardy knows why he and Wessex have taken this walk today – the walk that leads him to the high spot where he can look out across the pale, mottled green and yellow hills to Stinsford, Bockhampton and Kingston Maurward. Wessex barks and Hardy tells him, with unaccustomed gruffness, to shut up.

The sweet sound of bells that floats up from Stinsford church marks the wedding of Gertrude Bugler to her cousin.

Hardy stands and listens. He writes in his mind the description of the little confectioner's shop in South Street, Dorchester, and the family and friends . . . the strong, rich smell of chocolate and marzipan as Gertrude's father stocks the shop, hands over the glass cases with their laden trays of bonbons and ledges of softly puffed profiteroles, to the assistant who will serve while Mr Bugler and his anxious wife are at the church.

The mother of the bride, Augusta Way. Hardy flinches in his mind's eye from the thought of his first Tess grown stout and flushed.

He thinks instead of the bride. How lovely Gertrude must appear today. He sees her as a white sugared almond, from one of the tulle-covered baskets Mr Bugler prepares, complete with miniature stork, for Dorchester christenings. Hardy dreams of biting into her pale, icing-sugar-white skin; of finding the luscious glacé cherry mouth that will be his final reward for all the care and trouble he has taken with the young actress.

After all, why should a woman give up her career for marriage and motherhood?

Hardy wanders down the hill. (He was invited to the wedding but he thought it better not to attend: Florence has been getting even more jumpy lately and Hardy wants to preserve Gertrude, like the fruit so sticky and covered with a fine glaze that old Mr Bugler sells at Christmas to the good people of the town Hardy has made world-famous as 'Casterbridge'.)

Gertrude's name will still be Bugler. To Hardy, she remains the untouched virgin waiting for the ultimate role.

Florence, who confides to her friends on violet-tinged writing paper that everything about her life is driving her mad these days, she feels wound up like a spring, and the housekeeping is enough to make her feel she is 'in an asylum' – is delighted to hear the sound of bells float up in the still air. That little minx Gertrude Bugler married off at last! Good riddance to her!

But Gertrude and her hearty new husband – who will farm land in the Marshwood Vale, who will bring memories of my mother's childhood back to me when I tell you, Baby Tess, of those high-hedged lanes and rich meadows filled with waving wheat and corn – just don't move far enough away for Florence's liking.

They moved to the cottage there, on that September day in 1921 (no time for a honeymoon, there's the harvest to get in), and in that cottage by the side of the graveyard of St Mary's, Beaminster, Gertrude lived until her death in August 1992.

Hardy aches for the beautiful young actress. He gives her a few months to become accustomed to her married state. Then one day – a casual visit, Wessex will come too – Hardy calls on Gertrude and she asks him in.

It's the month of February. The landscape is dead. The first primrose shows its head on the lane from Netherbury, above Beaminster, to Waytown. A hint of wild garlic is in the air. No one in the little main square of Beaminster recognizes Thomas Hardy;

though a labourer coming red-faced from the Greyhound Inn could swear he saw the man once before, snooping about and eavesdropping at the Quiet Woman pub on the stretch of lonely road between Beaminster and Yeovil (a backward sort of a place, good for gathering rough regional accents and worldly-wise old Dorset sayings, for the great man to put in his books. For Hardy has come a long way from his humble origins: he lives in a grand new house he now pretends is his due, because of his ancestry: Admiral Nelson's Hardy was his forebear, so everyone's been told lately).

Hardy goes unseen to the gates of St Mary's Church, and beyond, to the short, steep road leading up to the Bugler cottage.

Wessex's tail wags furiously – he knows when his master is excited and reflects it in the crudest possible way.

The door opens. Gertrude, the dark-eyed heroine of Hardy's dreams, comes out and stands under the low porch.

At Max Gate Florence searches for Wessex in vain. (He is all she has now: when the dog dies at Christmastime five years later she writes to a friend that she and Wessex spent 'literally thousands of evenings together alone' and she mourns him terribly; Hardy writes a poem on the passing away of Wessex.)

But the white-haired, ferociously spoilt terrier is nowhere to be seen. Florence, so woebegone in appearance these days, so far from the sylph with the poetic face and cloud of dark hair, a sad matron now, burdened by housekeeping and by keeping at bay the crowds of Hardy's admirers, sits at her desk and puts her head in her hands.

Gertrude invites Hardy into the low, gloomy cottage. He is writing a part for her, Hardy says. There will be a dramatization of *Desperate Remedies* and he is writing it especially for her. Will she . . . ?

Florence dreams mournfully at her desk, over a pile of butcher's bills and unanswered correspondence. She sees Wessex running, turning into a squat old house by the side of a church, sees Wessex, so unfaithful, heartbreakingly disloyal, leap with delight at the skirts of the lovely young Gertrude Bugler as she opens the door.

Florence sees Hardy standing by the small, latticed window that lets almost no light into the formal little square parlour that smells of the new furniture old Mr Bugler gave the couple for their wedding, polished and dusted and unused. She can feel Hardy's kiss, as once she had known it, first on her cheek and then on the nape of her neck . . .

Florence is woken from her sad reverie by the tickle of whiskers on her cheek, as Wessex, exuberantly returned from his treacherous expedition, leaps up on Florence's table and greets his mistress.

Florence can't help giving one of her rare laughs. Wessex's whiskers tickle her extremely.

But she is already scolding, moaning, blaming by the time Hardy returns, radiating health and confidence for all his eighty-one years. Wessex has sent the bills flying all over the floor . . . Florence will never be able to sort out the asylum of this household now . . .

Desperate remedies indeed! Florence witnesses the extraordinary new vitality of her ancient husband as he prepares for the November première of his dramatization. How his eyes gleam! His wastepaper basket starts to overflow with poems again – the *Winter Words* which mark his amazing creative energy so late in life and which will be published posthumously in 1928. Florence always goes through the rejected drafts of the poems before they go out to the incinerator at the back of the house – she stands there, hands deep in the pockets of the baggy cardigan which has now become the badge of her depression, her premature middle age. Eyes ringed with circles of tiredness, she sifts through the crumpled-up slips of paper. She has been through aeons of torture this way, finding the first attempts at love poems – to Emma Gifford, of course, in her incarnation as the lovely woman with whom Hardy spent such happy weeks in Cornwall all of fifty-two years ago – and to women he has longed for, loved and lost. By the time the poems are ready to go to the printer, the pain is dulled for Florence. She can smile serenely at the compliments handed out by his admirers to TH, as she calls the great man in her correspondence: she can appear as delighted as they at the skill with which the poet delineates all his loves – except her, of course. Never a poem dedicated to Florence. She'd have to be dead for that to happen; and it seems pretty certain that, short of suicide on Florence's part, Hardy will go first.

Today, a beautiful May day with cherry blossom on the trees in the garden softening some of the ugly angularity of Max Gate, Florence has a strong instinct that she will find something particularly unpleasant among the wastepaper. She takes the wicker basket and tips it upside down, next to the roaring incinerator. On a day when the countryside dances in the pink and white blossom of magnolia and camellia – when Paradise, under a blue sky with sweet little clouds chasing around like lambs, could well be described as situated in Wessex – Florence, crouching by the flames, is in Hell.

She finds the piece of paper she knew in her heart was there. It doesn't have a poem, it's true – but, just as bad, the scrawl of an obsessed lover unable to stop himself from repeating over and over the name of the beloved. TESS TESS TESS TESS – and, yes, there it is, the entwined initials of the stupid little actress who hasn't moved far enough at all: GB, who married her cousin and lives in southwest Dorset, in Beaminster.

Florence's mouth twitches and sets in its now permanent downward droop. She tips all the wastepaper into the fire – but keeps the incriminating slip, stuffs it deep into the pocket of her cardigan. She knows now that she has a rival far more deadly than any of the others, even Emma. However many times she reads and rereads the words that are evidence of love, the pain will not be dulled by familiarity. In fact, she knows already that the pain will grow rather than diminish, this time round. Her husband – the very same man who left his first wife to die of neglect, so great was his love for Florence – has found his last love. The love of his life. Tess – who made him famous – has come to claim him at last. Tess lives.

Utterly forlorn, Florence walks into the garden and under the pretty trees. By the time the blossom has turned to fruit – and the apples have fallen to the ground – another half-year will have passed and Hardy and Gertrude will have been together all that time. Acting, rehearsing, smiling . . . Gertrude's great, dark eyes will have looked up soulfully into Hardy's for twenty-four weeks, and for at least four days a week out of the twenty-four. Florence stares at the ground and in her mind's eye she sees the apples lying there, rotting (like the other staff, the gardener is disobedient and lazy: Florence can't run the place any better than Emma could). She sees the serpent as it slithers from the core of the brown apple, half-chewed already by slugs, by the decay of the dying year. It comes towards her, hissing. Florence steps back and lets out a cry of fear. Then she stifles it, claps her hand over her mouth. Her eyes widen with a more real terror. She is going mad . . . yes, she is . . . Hardy is so cool and cruel towards her, she doesn't sleep at night. Is it her time of life? She has wondered this aloud to her corresponding friends already. She's forty-five and it's a dangerous age, isn't it? Hot flushes, migraines . . . now she's even hallucinating things! Should she confide in a doctor? But she's afraid – she has a horrible feeling that her husband wouldn't mind at all if she was locked up.

Wessex's barking causes the dejected Florence to look in the direction of the front drive.

There he is! (Oh God, time has flown and lunch will be spoilt: she forgot again to tell Cook not to put the joint in at dawn, the meat will be grey and tasteless, Hardy will throw down his fork and stare angrily, silently out of the window.) One of Florence's headaches begins to come on. And a wave of panic: she's not sure she can walk as far as the claustrophobic dining room, with its plum flock wallpaper and smell of suet and boiled parsnips. She digs her hand deeper down into the pocket of the baggy cardigan and feels the twisted piece of paper as a war-wounded might probe for shrapnel. The words hiss like the forked tongue of the serpent through her fingers: TESS TESS TESS . . . Florence assumes the martyred half-smile which has become her armour against Hardy's icy hostility. She goes to the drive to meet him.

But Thomas Hardy is happy. He's beaming all over his face. At first Florence can hardly believe it – he's pleased to see her! And so is Wessex, who bounds up and muddies her skirt with his paws.

Florence's face lights up. Perhaps everything is all right, really – it's just her silly time-of-life imagination that's been running away with her. She and TH will be happy again – like in the old days, before Emma died, all of eleven years ago now.

Florence goes up to her husband and asks him, tenderly, how his morning has been. (Even at his age, Hardy can still walk long distances and Florence has a sudden ray of hope that that is just what he has been doing, innocently taking Wessex for a good country walk.)

– Very bad news about the play, Hardy says. (But then, why is he beaming so?)

– We'll have to replace Gertrude Bugler, he says.

Florence can hardly believe her ears. There *is* a remedy to her state of desperation – simple as the lancing of a boil. Remove Gertrude Bugler! A wave of guilt succeeds Florence's sense of relief. She is somehow responsible . . . the young actress is gravely ill . . . Florence, a crone, a wicked witch, summoned up the Devil out of the ground and sent him to kill her rival . . .

– Replace her? Florence says stupidly. With her dulled eyes she stares at the happy, wizened old man who stands before her.

– Gertrude is having a baby, Hardy says.

Genesis

The baby – in the mind of the all-controlling male god that Thomas Hardy in his kingdom of Wessex has now become, is conceived out of the infatuation of a poet for his Muse. To underline his immortality, Hardy went around boasting at this time that he was as sexually vigorous as ever, at eighty-three. His biographers don't believe it – and Florence certainly doesn't, as she stands rooted to the spot on the bare windswept drive at Max Gate, with its 'uninterrupted' views across the downs to the monument of the Admiral who Hardy claims so tiresomely as his forebear. Not for Florence, the claims of potency, made over port and cigars to such as Sir Sydney Cockerell, confidant of both of the unhappy couple. Silent evenings . . . she as childless as Emma had been . . . No, TH must keep his boasts for the hour when the ladies have left the table.

The baby, in fact, suffers a different fate at the hands of Hardy's biographers. Robert Gittings, in *The Older Hardy*, informs us that Gertrude gave birth to a stillborn child at about the time of the production of *Desperate Remedies*, that is, November 1922. And that Hardy sent her a 'silver vase of carnations' on hearing the news. The vase was carried by one of the Hardy Players – yes, through the streets of Beaminster, nearly up as far as the church, but cutting off to the left up that short drive.

The pink, formal flowers, more suitable for celebration than condolence, tremble on the end of silvery-green stalks. The vase is a brighter silver – Mr Frampton, the butcher, stops in the midst of hacking out loin chops and stares at the young man, cheeks aflame with embarrassment, as he carries the votive offering into the house of the suffering Muse. (The other biographer of Hardy, Michael Millgate, reports that Gertrude had a miscarriage, but there *is* a difference: any woman knows there is.)

Hardy's stillborn love . . . his heart that beats as midday and his withered, atrophied limbs that hold him back, that force him to listen to Florence's cruel, nurse-like remarks to friends and well-wishers: he can't get around as much as he did . . . all this rehearsing makes him fuss so . . . (and after his death, Florence is to say that the excitement of *Tess* in the theatre had ended TH's life prematurely. He'd have lived to ninety if it hadn't been for *her* . . .)

Hardy sends carnations to the child that was never his, the child he longed for, who died . . . the daughter of Gertrude, the grand-daughter of the first Tess.

Incarnations

So now, Baby Tess, I tell you that one day you will understand: how the spirit of Tess – like a self-pollinating shrub or bloom, a daphne or a dandelion that blows in on the wind, came to our mother, poor Mary Hewitt. Who went mad and saw visions and then left her husband and went to work for the Dowles down there on Chesil Beach. And then, though people didn't say such things in those days, became a witch.

Our mother Mary who would carry the seed of the next Tess in her – as indeed she did.

Now you know, Baby Tess, what visions your great-grandmother Mary saw when she 'became unhinged'.

She saw the incarnations of all the women who had lived and suffered and died in this strange western part of the land: the Celts, who were free and worshipped wind and water; the Roman matrons who paced in the long, oppressive afternoons in their smart villas; the penitent, praying women in all the dusty churches in Wessex; and, of course, the witches.

Mary saw the Woman Clothed with the Sun, from the Book of Revelation. Like Joanna Southcott of Exeter just thirty miles away, Mary saw herself as the Redeemer.

The Redeemer of a world 'blighted by male domination'. As she lay in the bed where they had to shackle her down at night, so loud were her cries and lashings-out, Mary dreamed herself in a manger. She was both the female Christ and the mother of the new Messiah.

When she woke it was to the plunge of the needle or the forced administering of Largactil.

Most of all, Mary dreamed that her daughter would hang. Twisting in the breeze – how Thomas Hardy loved the public execution of a female.

And in her terrible premonitory dream, our mother wept and begged the old story not to be played out again.

When she was sufficiently subdued, when the memories of the visions had been burned from her brain, they let her come home.

And as I take you home to the Mill, Baby Tess, now the bright morning brings curious stares from passers-by, I'll tell you of the last act of Tess. Before they dig up the shale in the dip of land at West Bay for construction purposes, later today.

Listen to me, as we walk back along the ridge above Powerstock, along the top of the grassy forts that stare out at the lagoon at Abbotsbury. We stop once and look across at the land that was my mother's and her mother's – rightfully their land, that is – but, on the distaff side, there was never anything of it for them. Marshwood Vale: Canute could conquer land, it would obey him, it couldn't slip away from him and then come up and try to drown him like the sea, force him into an ignominious retreat. Lambert's Castle: he built it high and strong. And now look back at Mapperton: Ralph's land, with stone eagles to guard it and there was nothing the likes of our Tess – or Alec – could do ever to take it away from him. (Oh yes, we've risen up in our time against them: our foremothers were the angry – and long-suffering – wives of the Tolpuddle Martyrs. Look over there to the blue line of sky to the east of Mapperton, and if your misty, half-focused eyes can see across land as well as they can dream history and hear the language of the sea, then you'll see the Puddle and Piddle valleys, with their cluster of poor hamlets where the starving labourers prayed for their Napoleon, Captain Swing. Piddlehinton, Puddletown, Briantspuddle. Our foremothers fought and died for land enough to live on – all were deported across the sea to Australia, for their pathetic and brave attempt at revolt.)

There, in our mothers' heartland, Thomas Hardy built his stage for the next enactment of the tragedy he loved. As we walk on this lovely September morning, with swans already restless down at the lagoon, shuddering by the water's edge in preparation for the winter, I'll tell you how *Tess* was written again, etched in chalk on these cliffs and vales and hills.

Or maybe – for here's a lorry laden with gravel, panting its way along the narrow road that has a hedge of wild roses on the sea side and a sheer drop down the side of the hill on the other – maybe we'll hitch a ride back to the Mill and ask the driver on the way if he knows anything about the digging and excavating in progress at West Bay.

Maybe – as I climb into the high cab with you, and you look sleepily round at the stained, torn, diesel-smelling interior of the lorry, I'll ask him, too casually you might say, just how much shale has been lifted out of that pit behind West Bay, the deep saucer of land that last filled up in a neap tide in 1968.

The lorry stops and we get in. The driver isn't at all as I'd imagined him. He's a young graduate, can't find employment, working for the construction company until the job is done and the summer is over. He wears an old brown jacket and jeans. Clearly he's interested in the sights of the area – for a Pevsner guidebook to Dorset lies open on the seat beside him. He doesn't smile as I climb in (but then men don't smile at women of grandmotherly age) and I search for something to chat to the lad about, after he's said he's going all the way to Portland with the shale and he'll drop us off at the turning in Abbotsbury where we cut across the side of the hill under the chapel of St Catherine to the Mill.

My eye lights on the bulging ledge – AA book, brochures of Mapperton Gardens, and Forde Abbey, in the extreme western corner of Dorset. Then I see it. I have to smile. A little handbill: Toller Porcorum Amateur Players: *Tess of the D'Urbervilles*. The Old Church Hall, Saturday, 21st September, one performance only. A photograph of the young actress – nothing like Tess, of course, nowhere near the dark, haunting looks of Gertrude Bugler. But acting out the part of the 'Pure Woman, Faithfully Presented' in a remote village hall. And, as I grimly note, on the twenty-first of the month, on the day of the equinoctial gales – when the sea will come right up and flood the shallow pit the construction workers have emptied of the protective pebbles. When it swirls out again, what will they find?

'Tess lives' – I think this, remembering the little stone on Batcombe Down, the nailed hand, the outline of the lichened fingers. And, posing as a tourist myself, I ask the serious young driver how much he has seen of the county . . . whether he intends to go to the performance of *Tess*.

– Might, he says, smiling across at me and the sleeping baby. But I got pretty put off Hardy, having to do him at school!

I smile back at him – and I hold you close, Baby Tess, and against the roar of the engine I whisper to you, quietly and softly –

The Scandal of Tess

There were further trials in store for Florence. Oh, far far worse. She would be drawn in the end by the strength of her jealousy, to Beaminster, and to the house of the young actress whom she was sure was responsible for her illness, her fatal weakness: like a wicked stepmother in a fairy tale, she would come with her poisoned apple and make Gertrude bite deep, with those luscious lips Hardy loved so much, right into the red side of the apple. But first, the night of the woman who has risen from her sickbed and gone out to meet the poet, who promises her the part of her dreams. (No, not to act Tess yet. That's for the grand finale.)

Late November and the first snow has settled thinly on the town, making it look, in the rays of the moon that have come early tonight, throwing long blue shadows on the square and the little houses, as pretty as a postcard. Never mind that the pharmacist's wife has just died and a crowd of bewildered and miserable children stand in the small back room of Smiley's Chemist's in the main square, with a father they have never seen cry like this before. And it doesn't matter that old Tim Warren's gone bankrupt, no one wants his carriage equipment now everyone's riding around in motor cars – only half an hour ago he went past with his wife who has such terrible arthritis, with their lifelong possessions all piled high in a cart, drawn by their tired old horse. Where will they go? They'll die of cold if they have to camp out on a night like this, under the stars. Never mind. The love, the infatuation, the passion of a great man spreads its wings over the humble little town of Beaminster. The most ordinary people are caught up in it, like pilgrims when the Holy Man finally visits the shrine. A light seems to emanate from the old cottage by the side of St Mary's Church. Something wonderful and terrible will happen tonight. The light streams out from the doorstep and . . .

Everyone knows that Passion is more important than anything else.

The ordinary, the daily, the humdrum, must bow down before Passion, like the oxen knelt before the infant majesty of Our Lord.

Passion comes before family or food – or simple comforts like a bed for the night.

And Passion makes the unfortunate victim, the hapless one chosen to be sacrificed next on its altar, blind and forgetful. Deaf to the cries from those who only a moment before received the most tender love and support from the victim.

Love is All. And tonight – after the vase of silver carnations carried aloft in bright daylight by the blushing messenger to the young actress who must be Tess – comes the great man himself.

He will meet his Tess in the churchyard – well, he would choose a spot like that, because he knows that death is very close to Passion. Only a reminder, a memento, a mossy grave with the letters rubbed out long ago and the aching knowledge of the bones so eaten away just a few inches from the perfect bloom of a young cheek, will egg on the demon of infatuation. He only wants a precious minute – that's all he asks for. He can't breathe unless he sees his Tess, his darling bud, his creation, his daughter and his darling.

A minute! What's wrong with that? After all, what harm can come to anyone in a minute?

Gertrude flies out of the house – stopping for one minute by the tarnished old glass in the hall, looking and seeing the wild rose of her cheeks, the big dark eyes alive with excitement. Her hair swirls out, in the dark of the narrow little hall – then, does she shudder? – is there a goose walking on her grave? – or does she see a faint face form in the mirror behind her left shoulder, like they say comes to maids on St John's Eve if they light a candle and pray?

But the face fades again. And Gertrude races out of the door – for she can't have seen what seemed to ebb there, the face of Death himself, sunken-cheeked as all the worst pictures of Hell would have him. What has Death to do with a young woman at the height of her health and beauty? Death is no husband for her tonight.

Thomas Hardy comes round the side of a high sarcophagus and the young actress almost lets out a shriek. It's the face she's seen just a moment before – of course it is – Hardy, carrying his eighty-two years and his contiguity to the grave, looking sunken-cheeked at his tender prey, in the moonlight.

Death comes forward and kisses the maiden.

The lorry stops suddenly in the narrow Abbotsbury road, where there's a sharp left turn marked Rodden. Pea-gravel spills from the back onto the road – and I can see in the driving mirror the angry, disapproving face of a man in a German car, a businessman by the looks of him, on his way to one of the posh hotels along the coast probably, the Plumptree, where family portraits hang on the walls and the descendants of the Earl who helped King Charles II hide out in Dorset in his flight to France, serve lobsters au gratin in their shells. But the businessman looks familiar. Suddenly I have a sickening feeling that I've seen him snooping around here before:

I've seen him by the Mill, posing as a tourist, a visitor to the tropical gardens and the swannery. He even unconvincingly bought an ice cream at the van parked by the gates to our father's old workplace and then tossed it in the bushes when he thought Ella's mum wasn't looking – but she was, of course; people like us who live by the sea are always watching and looking, picking up the flotsam of conversations and pieces of tittle-tattle and scandal that come in with the tides and then are washed out again.

– He looked like he was from the CID, Ella's mum said to me that night, as I was dropping Ella back from one of our nature walks along the stretch of pebbles that acts host to a strange variety of birds – birds that must be helped to stay alive, in the face of the contaminating, polluting oil spills and sewage that get washed up there.

– And what would a policeman want with the swans? I said, and made a joke of it.

But we both knew, I think, that time was running out. Even without anyone to give information, evidence of a crime has a strange way of manifesting itself, years after the event: even a shred of an old shirt that went into tatters as a body was dragged over the stones could blow from the swampy ground behind the George pub in West Bay and land on a clothesline where a curious house-wife, handing it to her brother Fred, new in the force at Bridport . . .

But there's no point in letting this mosaic of memories come up in my mind now, throttle action, bring paralysis. Without looking again in the side mirror I tell our student driver that I've changed my mind, I'll go almost as far as Weymouth with him. We won't get off here after all.

The lorry jerks left as a blast of car horns mocks our change of mind.

– But I thought you wanted to go down to the sea here, the young man remarks mildly as he changes gear and, with another spillage of shale, we roar slowly along the road.

147

I tell him my mother lives beyond Rodden, at Langton Herring, and I need to see her. He turns sideways to stare at me, surprised – and I see I've really slipped up this time, been rattled by the businessman in the German car, who, sure enough, has taken the Rodden turning after us.

– Used to live there, I correct myself quickly – and I tell him we still have a cottage there, rented out, and I look after it for the tenants.

The young man nods but I feel his unease. Didn't I pose as a stranger to the area only a short while back? Who am I?

And I think to myself as I smile at him ingratiatingly and the plainclothesman hoots and overtakes in his little red car, that I never could explain to him that my mother isn't dead, because witches don't die – unless they're burnt or drowned – and she never was born either, if you care to go to the Bridport Register Office and search for her. So – for our driver, or for any man for that matter who believes in hard, cold facts and in facts only – my mother never existed. And if she is what our teacher Mrs Moores used to call a 'figment of the imagination', then so am I, my dear, and so are you.

Gypsies aren't prone to register their children, you see. And officially my mother never came into the world – and suffered and changed – at all. She was a lost child, from the very start.

But how could I tell our charming young student all that? Once the red car (the driver suspected nothing, he hadn't seen us at all) is a safe distance away, I ask for us to be put down. The driver looks surprised again, but I sense he's pleased to be rid of us. (He's picked up that there's something not quite ordinary about us: quite a few are like that when they come into close proximity with people like us. Or maybe he's extra sensitive and he's heard the ballad of Tess that I sing to you when no one else is about.)

– Have a nice day, the young man says, like an American, when I've assured him several times that the walk will do me good and the cottage is ready for us there, to move into.

*

And I wish him a pleasant evening at the Amateur Players' production of *Tess*.

The lorry lurches off. You're awake, and you look round at the fields and ancient forest that go down to Chesil Beach at this point, nine miles west of Weymouth and as distant from the traffic and suburban houses as the moon. You like the fresh sea breeze after the diesel stench of the lorry and a very small smile, like a thread being drawn across your face, flickers and disappears.

I will show you my mother. And I will tell you of that other Amateur Players' production of *Tess* – at the Corn Exchange in Dorchester on 26th November 1924 – when Hardy married his Tess – on stage, of course, figuratively, you might say.

My mother was two years old by then, and playing in the rough grass up at Silkhay, watching the tinkers as they worked on metal from the old scrapyard up there that even the most powerful conservationists couldn't get moved away. She didn't know anything of her past, though old Mother Hurn from Waytown – who used to bring the little dirty, unschooled children milk from time to time – was quick to see something in her. She'd take my mother on her lap and tell her what life had in store. She knew the Tess story would be played out until another order came. She saw another Tess, unborn, in my mother's life. The gypsies said Mother Hurn was as good if not better than they, at foretelling the future. But my mother just wriggled off and ran to clamber in the wrecked cars of old Rick's scrapyard: she couldn't see the tragedy that would come – nor did she see she'd end like Mother Hurn – a witch, as the old woman was widely acknowledged to be.

My mother knew nothing of the dramatization of *Tess*, nor of the infatuation of the ancient poet for his Gertrude.

Unlike poor Florence, who wished most devoutly that she knew a great deal less of both of them.

It's 1923. The play Thomas Hardy was so keen to discuss back on that November day will surely come to fruition. Florence finds him even more energetic than usual – it's as if all the loves of his life had come together, to make *The Queen of Cornwall*, a verse play which he says with a poignant air of combined melancholy and self-satisfaction has taken him fifty-three years to write – and is only eight hundred lines long. Cornwall – down there, Baby Tess, beyond the jaw of Portland, with its dangerous convergence of waters known as the Race – down to the south, towards Land's End, where Hardy and his Emma spent their happy days all of half a century ago.

The part of the Queen of Cornwall has been written for a young actress named Gertrude Bugler – who else?

The story, a Tristan and Iseult tragic passion play, with its stark elements of love, jealousy and death, has a direction 'Requiring no Theatre or Scenery' – this to show that the Tintagel setting, the Tintagel of Hardy's youth and harmony with Emma, 'an Iseult of my own', is so powerfully set in the imagination of the poet (and so inextricably bound up by now with his passion for Gertrude) that to transport the old theme of love, betrayal and death away from the amphitheatre of Wessex would be in itself a betrayal. Since *Tess*, the old story must be played out hereabouts, with a first wife as a ghostly reminder of Hardy's own first, terrible betrayal.

Florence faces backwards – and sees the past and the evergreen passion her husband entertains for Emma. She faces forwards, and sees the fresh beauty of Gertrude Bugler. As depressed wives will, she confides in the young Gertrude that the actress seems to have so much before her in life – there'll be a new baby, an acting career if she wants it – whereas Florence has everything behind her – and childless as well, poor Florence.

Gertrude hardly hears the moans of the woman in the baggy cardigan, with haunted eyes. She does indeed strain to the future – she will be the Queen of Cornwall – after that, as Hardy promised, she will surely be Tess. What has she to fear?

But the Queen of Cornwall Gertrude cannot be. She's pregnant again.

And Thomas Hardy goes about the house humming the musical setting for *The Queen of Cornwall*, he goes to Dorchester, hears the actors read through their parts, smiles at Florence and even goes so far as to ask her advice over a poem. (Florence, fresh from another rummage through the wastepaper basket, is happy to oblige: this way she can kill Hardy's still monstrous infatuation for Mrs Bugler of Beaminster, she can seize the poems at source.) 'He asked me which was the better phrase,' Florence writes to Sydney Cockerell, ' "tender-eyed", or "meek-eyed". I pointed out that "tender-eyed" is used in the Bible (in reference to Leah) as meaning "sore-eyed" – which was why Jacob didn't want her. So a little biblical knowledge is handy at times: "tender-eyed" was promptly abandoned.'

Florence looks with hatred at the scrawled 'tender-eyed' on the slips of paper that waft down from Hardy's table. She sees the eyes – the eyes of Tess – that have shone in her husband's life ever since he gave birth to the immortal heroine. And she sees Gertrude's eyes – meek, yes – is the foolish woman actually in love with a man sixty years older than herself? Could it be – no, impossible! Hardy is too old, for all his noonday heart that beats at the sight of a pretty face. But Florence vows grimly to herself that she will make Gertrude 'sore-eyed' all right, if this humiliating nonsense goes on one minute longer. She'll destroy the woman – make sure that Jacob doesn't want his Leah ever again.

Hardy sleeps badly as Gertrude's pregnancy wears on. He could be with child himself, Florence thinks scornfully, as the old bard wakes complaining of dizziness, of a craving for this or that at any hour of the night. Tiny by now, resembling nothing so much – to one of the frequent guests who pour through Max Gate to pay their compliments – as 'un vieux petit docteur suisse', Hardy lies right on the side of the bed as if half-longing to fall out, and disappear from his conjugal life with Florence for ever.

In the early hours of Sunday 23rd October as Hardy lies foetally curled in the ugly big bed with the mahogany headboard Florence has rested wearily against on so many long, deserted afternoons and evenings – he has a strange dream. You could put it down to the vertiginous position he now adopts in sleep – or not, there have been many interpretations. But it's not a dream he confides to his wife – even though he wakes whimpering like a baby. He writes a description of it instead to the wife of Harley Granville-Barker, adviser to the text of *The Queen of Cornwall*. And he sends off the letter before Florence, early in the morning, can ransack his blotter and his writing-case for his latest outpourings. Wessex bounds along beside the great man as he goes through a late autumnal mist to the little red post-box nailed to a yew tree half a mile outside the precincts of Max Gate.

Hardy wants his dream to be read and understood. This is what Mrs Barker received:

> I dreamt that I stood on a long ladder which was leaning against the edge of a loft. I was holding on by my right hand, & in my left I clutched an infant in blue & white, bound up in a bundle. My endeavour was to lift it over the edge of the loft to a place of safety. On the loft sat George Meredith, in his shirt sleeves, smoking; though his manner was rather that of Augustus John. The child was his, but he seemed indifferent to its fate, whether I should drop it or not. I said, 'It has got heavier since I lifted it last.' He assented. By great exertion I got it above the edge, & deposited it on the floor of the loft: whereupon I awoke.

Augustus John was the father of innumerable children.

Like you, Baby Tess – and like my sister Tess before you – these babies are babies of dreams, spirit-babies, love-children – never recognized or registered under law, but there all the same, born and reborn, seen by some, invisible to others.

Maybe Augustus John represented the father of these unnamed children, none of them born in wedlock – perhaps, as Hardy was the creator of Tess, he saw the baby he carried up the loft stairs to George Meredith (author of the verse epic *Modern Love*) and the promiscuous Bohemian painter, as the baby his Tess was bearing. (It's more 'poetic' to leave a real-life husband and father out of the equation.)

We cannot know how Hardy interpreted his dream. But, as he

walks back from the post-box and looks up at a late October sky that's clearing from the west, he sees a flock of wild geese coming over – and he stops and looks up, and listens.

Hardy knows that ratchet geese, as they are called – and they make a noise like a pack of hounds in full cry, as they go high over Max Gate, where Florence presides sadly over a Sunday morning breakfast table – are in legend the souls of unbaptized children, wandering through the air until the Day of Judgment.

Hardy goes into the dining room. The hotplate groans with kidneys, haddock kedgeree, fried eggs that have already shrivelled and turned greenish at the edges. But after his dream of the night before, Hardy is as squeamish as a pregnant woman. He takes a slice of dry toast – and holds out his cup for scalding coffee poured by his wife.

He had a bad night, Hardy tells Florence when she asks him how he slept (although she knows perfectly well). And she looks bleakly at him, from behind her array of silver pots and jugs, shrouded in tea cosies. Hardy feels he has already arrived at Judgment Day, as he sips the murky stuff that Cook will insist on mixing with chicory.

As it may be Judgment Day for us today – when we have to answer the questions the so-careful man in the dark suit will ask us, when he comes to the Mill: Can you inform us, please, as to the whereabouts of a Miss Tess Hewitt? If deceased, may we see the Certificate of Death? Can you please come to identify the remains of the body found in the pit behind the George Hotel at West Bay? How long have you known about this?

For now, though, let's remember it's a lovely morning, and this remote hinterland of Chesil Beach looks particularly alluring, with the stately eighteenth-century house at Rodden looking as if it's fresh out of a film where young squires cavort with fresh-faced girls in caps and striped dresses – and the little road that winds up to Langton Herring bright either side with lords and ladies, as they call those orange berries on stalks, like sentinels looking out of the hedge as we walk up there. Remember that this is the road Tess – and I, her younger sister, necessary and unwanted both at the same time – had to walk up after Tess came back to the Mill three months since she ran off with Alec and threw up in the downstairs toilet. (Our father kept it so clean since our mother left home that no one wanted to use it any more, the antiseptic smell and the swirl of highly coloured chemical, and the stiff brush in its plastic tray by the side of the lavatory seeming to stand for everything that had gone wrong with our father's life.) But this time Tess couldn't wait to run upstairs – and she said it, she choked out the words just as (as luck would have it) John Hewitt himself was walking in at the door, tired and wet from a long shift at the swannery. 'Alec's gone off, Liza-Lu. Oh Jesus Christ, what'm I going to do? I'm pregnant!'

Those were Tess's words. I'll never forget them. I don't think women ever do, even if they've been said, as no doubt Tess's have, one hundred million times before. And I won't forget our journey – hitching a lift as we did just now, Baby Tess, to the cottage my mother shared in Langton Herring. 'It'll mean going to see Mother Hurn,' Tess said. And she wept – just as we passed this field on the right here, with its orange stubble the colour of West Bay beach at low tide, when the shingle is shown to have another layer, a secret double that's not stones at all but a coarse sand, lion-hued as that rough field exhausted by harvesting. 'We'll ask Mother,' I said – for what else was there to say? 'Maybe she'll make you all right, Tess.'

The trouble was, neither of us knew what 'all right' was meant to mean. It was a state to which girls aspired in those days, not to be 'all right' could have dire consequences, as our own mother's hospital stay and electric shock treatment had grimly shown. But – with pregnancy – what was all right and what was not? To bear a child was a wonderful, miraculous – and even highly commended – thing. Yet somehow we knew that no one would think that Tess's baby was a very all right proposition (least of all Tess herself, but we'll come to that in a minute). However she did it, our mother Mary Hewitt was depended on to magic the problem away – or to transform the problem, like a bale of hay turned overnight into gold by the little folk – into a gift. We walked up the road without the slightest idea which our newly powerful – and frequently violent – witch-mother would choose to advise.

There is the tree. It stands to the side of the twisted little cottage my mother lived in before she came home to the Mill, to die. The tree is a birch, and in spring it rustles small green leaves with a sound like the dress my mother used to wear when we were children – before the inhospitality of the world sent her to seek refuge in madness. But children, famously, cling to conventional memories; and I loved the sound my mother's dress made when she ran down the stairs to greet my father, and tell him, like Doris Day in the movies she took us to in Dorchester, that his supper was on the table. After the birch tree has passed into a heaviness of summer, and then lets leaves dance away, turning only the very palest yellow before they go (as they are going now), then the tree, our mother, is at its most beautiful, the soft bruises on the trunk circling the whites of her eyes still trapped there in the silvery, tender bark.

The tree is by a small stream, and we stand waiting for the first puff of wind to get the topmost leaves dancing – like the mobiles that came into fashion just after your mother, Tess's baby, was born, and we tied them, metal scraps of silver and red, to the top of the crib. Generations of mothers and daughters run in the tree, like mercury – and she sees us, the leaves begin to move, the breeze comes to our aid, just as it always did in the days when our fore-mothers worshipped trees and water.

We'll rest here a while, and I'll tell you of the last of Hardy's monstrous loves – the love he had for the daughter of his invented Tess – and how it wanders the landscape still, waiting for the story to be played out. (And even my mother, the tree, cannot stop the old plot, played out again and again.)

This is the very last act of the incarnation of our Hardy's new Tess.

Making it Real

※※※

October 1924 – and it's the time of Florence's illness, the illness that has built up over these years of the passion of Thomas Hardy, her husband, for a young actress. It's as if the swollen gland on Florence's neck is trying to trumpet out the horror and revulsion the poor woman feels at her long incarceration in 'drear middle age', an incarceration tortured by glimpses of the youth and beauty that once had been hers. The gland – ugly, making a monster of the once-elegant Florence – has been diagnosed as a potentially cancerous tumour, and Florence must go to London and have it cut out. Hatred and jealousy signal their threat to spread through Florence – and soon, she feels morbidly, she may be sharing a grave with poor Emma in Stinsford graveyard. (Hardy has, as usual, flinched from any help or sympathy at the time of illness; his reason for not accompanying his wife to the London nursing home is that Wessex the dog would have 'broken his heart (literally) if we had both gone away'.

Florence may find scant comfort in the fact that her death could be guaranteed to provide Hardy with some poems as fine as those he wrote after the death of his first wife. But she leaves on 30th September with the worst possible forebodings: she sees Gertrude installed at Max Gate (though how could she be, really, with a husband and young baby at home in Beaminster?); she weeps as she waves goodbye to Wessex, who jumps up at the mudguard of the car like a demented beast as she is driven away. She may never come back. And Hardy, deep in rehearsals for *Tess*, will find himself a happy bachelor, married at last to the woman he brought forth, like Zeus, from his own head. Poor Florence! For all that the oper-ation went well and Sydney Cockerell wrote twice in that day to Hardy to keep up his spirits, to reassure him that his wife would come back, Florence knows that only her absence, the possible black hole of death, will revive his love. And she is right: on 9th October, when Florence feels restored enough to return from London, Hardy commemorates his feelings in the astonishingly beautiful poem 'Nobody Comes', which does indeed show the absence, the nothingness and blackness of death, the hoped-for and dreaded return of Florence.

The (unconscious) wished-for death of Florence has brought about a poem as moving as those written after the death of Emma. Now Gertrude is in danger of becoming the next Florence figure in Hardy's imagination – after all, the poet had to be in love with a dead woman, thus forcing the woman who's next in line into the prison of the no-longer-loved, i.e. middle age.

Gertrude escapes this, of course. Firstly, she's immortal, she's Tess.

And, much to Wessex's delight and bounding, barking relief, Florence returns and lives on.

It is Hardy who is weakening, growing old. He's eighty-four and a half now and his passion is burning him out. He must consummate his passion before he dies. Then Tess, any Tess, can come after he has gone – to act out the story of love, revenge, betrayal and death.

Florence, weak though she is from the operation, sees her husband dwindle to nothing more than a spark of love, a burning ember of erotic fascination for his new incarnation of Tess. Rehearsals go on all day and far into the night. They even take place at Max Gate!

The food turns to mush, the toast dries and explodes like pistol shots in the hands, doors to the garden are left open by the Hardy Players and autumn storms usher in the leaves so that the house looks like a haunted film set.

Florence's nervous tics become more pronounced. Wessex follows her closely, and snaps at anyone who comes near.

Hardy suggests to the Dorchester Amateurs that they rehearse in Wool Manor itself – the imagined scene of Tess's and Angel's disastrous honeymoon. Florence sees him off at the door of her house – where the epicentre has turned into a melodrama in which she plays no part – and she wonders in turn whether her husband will come back alive from this journey. She waits – as Hardy waited in the black night air – and Nobody Comes. But Hardy, as she bitterly knows, if he dies, will die of joy. Her death (which shadows her remaining years, so terrified is she of recurrence of cancer – in fact she survives her husband by nine years) will be a loveless, joyless thing. She stands by the gate – but the late October night air is chilly and it's ghoulish out there too, near the day of All Hallows and the roaming ghost that Florence dreads above all other: the ghost of her guilt at her betrayal of poor Emma.

Wessex runs up, white in the blackness. Florence takes him into the house and closes the door. She has a strong premonition that something is taking place at Wool Manor which will signal the end of her marriage to Thomas Hardy – be it death or, figuratively, at least, divorce.

We have to laugh when we contrast the terrible, dark and tragic scene that Thomas Hardy painted of that honeymoon at Wool Manor – when his Tess, seduced by Alec D'Urberville, mother of his (now-dead) child, trusts and confides her secret to Angel, thus losing him for ever – with the reality of the rehearsal. Poor Gertrude! Alone there with the foolish old bard and a balding Dr E. W. Smerdon as Angel Clare.

Where is the handsome, cold-hearted, high-thinking hypocrite with the looks of a pre-Raphaelite angel? Where are the diamonds, a wedding gift from the bridegroom's family, which Angel must fasten around the neck of the young bride then found not to be 'pure'? Will they really have to make do with an old silk kerchief of Hardy's – the deep red and white spotted one Florence searched for in vain during the past weeks, sniffing out with her usual uncanny instinct an object that becomes a fetish – and a fetish that has become, by another transmutation of the imagination, a part of the loved one itself?

Yes; Hardy is happy to make do. The bandana, given to him by an admiring French hostess on one of his bicycling trips to France with Emma, now has the smell of Gertrude's soft, pink neck firmly imprinted on it. Hardy will never let Florence whisk it off to the sculleries downstairs where maids scrub with square bars of scratchy soap. He will guard it, as he guards Gertrude in his heart; and, only too happy to have helped the Dorchester Players cast the unattractive Dr Smerdon, sadly short of hair, as the romantic lead opposite his darling, he goes over and knots the hankie loosely around his Tess's neck, and he smiles fondly down at her as he pulls the noose a little tighter. Does he think of the Bridport Dagger, the hangman's noose, as it closes round the neck of his first Tess, in Salisbury gaol?

– Tell him! Oh tell him you forgave *him*, so surely he will forgive *you*! – Hardy's eyes mist with tears for the thousandth time as they go through the scene. Even Dr Smerdon is almost transformed, as he kills his love for Tess ... repudiates her ... goes from the room, saying he wants to walk alone, and Tess goes flying after. Heartbroken, ten times more terribly betrayed than by young D'Urberville's casual seduction and abandonment – yes, Hardy knows this scene will live for ever. He had seen that Angel Clare, with all his 'goodness', 'sharing', 'integrity', was more damaging than a bundle of Alec D'Urbervilles put together. Men may appear to change – he thinks as he watches the pathos of the famous scene – but the old story will be played out for all that.

A fire is lit in the grate of the manor – once a fine house but now partially demolished, as depressing as the day Hardy dreamt it up as a suitable site for a disastrous honeymoon. And – as one of the Hardy Players goes out to collect more firewood, and walks across the courtyard (the farm has become the main reason to keep the house going) –

A cock crows.

This kind of thing is always happening to Thomas Hardy. What he writes takes place – years later, sometimes, but recognizably from one of his books – and people regard him with some fear and awe, some hostility, as a man uncomfortably close to the supernatural.

– An afternoon cockcrow, Hardy says and laughs and wheezes a little, standing in the doorway to cool, with a new fire going and the flames bringing high colour to Tess's cheeks. That's bad, he goes on, quoting from the book. (Of course, everyone in the room knows the quotation. Tess's Angel Clare, driving away from their wedding a few hours before arriving at Wool, hears a cock crow, right in the middle of the afternoon, a bad omen as everyone knows.) And although *Tess* is just a novel – and this is just a rehearsal of an amateur dramatization of the novel – everyone there also feels as if they've heard an omen of misfortune. It's not real, is it? But they don't like it all the same. And rumour that Gertrude Bugler is the apple of the great writer's eye makes the simple Dorchester citizens uneasy, too. Is it really the case that Gertrude's mother was the model for Tess? Will she elope with Mr Hardy – a scandal – will they be found and apprehended as Tess and Angel were, after the murder of Alec, at Stonehenge? (Here the imagination of some of the young women takes flight.) The aura of obsession which surrounds the poet makes the atmosphere more charged than many (including Dr Smerdon) feel capable of handling. And it's only a rehearsal! What will it be like on the night?

Young Fred Beazer, responsible for stage shifting and lights, wonders if the sound of the afternoon crow is a sign his elaborate sets will come crashing down, causing injury to many, perhaps, at the first night at the Guildhall in Dorchester at the end of November. There's a sudden feeling the play's unlucky – even amateur actors are ready to jump to that conclusion – and after a few more stumbling attempts on Dr Smerdon's part to show the repressed, icy anger of Angel at finding he has married someone he hadn't bargained for – a Non-Pure Woman, a Ruined Maid – there's a request for an adjournment for refreshments.

Hardy grants it willingly. He climbs the stairs of the old manor to the bedroom, where mistletoe, first placed there to celebrate the marriage of Tess and Angel Clare, hangs mockingly above the four-poster bed. He must help his Tess with her coat and hat left there, and remove the handkerchief from round her neck (the players have ordered paste gems, a great parure from Bournemouth, to adorn his sweetheart's neck and shoulders on the night of the first performance).

It's dark in the bedroom, and a low, greenish light comes in from the meadows outside – the last of the day, before the blackness in which Florence will wait so miserably sets in. Gertrude goes over to the four-poster and picks up her coat. Thomas Hardy, who has brought this place to life in the pages of a book and will spirit it away with him when he goes, walks up to her, goes down on his knees.

A commotion downstairs. Players and stagehands run in at the open door of the hall.

Hardy and Gertrude stand in the door of the bedroom, barely visible in the falling dusk.

Steps pound on the bare oak stairs that are guarded by the tall portraits of men and women Hardy describes with such attention to detail in his novel, *Tess*.

Fred Beazer runs in. He gasps out the news – a girl's been drowned – no, off Chesil Bank, down Abbotsbury way – done it herself – no one's saying over whom, or why . . .

A player walks up the stairs and comes into the bedroom with a torch. He beams it on the strange couple, sixty years dividing them, but with one and the same look in their eyes.

And everyone says later, when they go to the inn to get over the shock – it's a funny thing, isn't it? There was that cock crowed out in the farmyard at Wool this afternoon . . . and they do say that's bad luck . . .

The same uneasy feeling settles again, but not for long. The resemblance between the news of the attempt to drown herself of Retty Priddle (in the book of *Tess*), all for love of Angel Clare, and today's tragedy, is no more than that – a resemblance. Retty had been hopelessly infatuated with Angel – and it was to Tess that he proposed marriage. Of course there was nothing to connect the two – an afternoon cockcrow at Wool Manor and then the drowning of a poor girl. But there were one or two who glanced all the same at Dr Smerdon – of all the respectable, married and balding men

– and just wondered if the maid hadn't had some business with him, so great is the power of fantasy over reality.

By now, Gertrude is safely home in Beaminster in the squat little house by the church. And Hardy has walked into the freezing hall at Max Gate, brushed past Florence and gone up to his study to work.

Florence, ungreeted, unloved, turns off the lights. As she goes up the stairs, she thinks of Wool Manor – and of her husband's description in *Tess*, of the two huge portraits that hang above the staircase there – and she knows the betrothal of Hardy and his Tess is complete. She reads in *Tess* of the arrival of Angel and his new young wife at Wool Manor: 'On the landing Tess stopped and started.

'"What's the matter?" said he.

'"Those horrid women!" she answered with a smile. "How they frightened me."

'He looked up and perceived two life-size portraits on panels built into the masonry. As all visitors to the mansion are aware, these paintings represent women of middle age, of a date some two hundred years ago, whose lineaments once seen can never be forgotten. The long pointed features, narrow eye, and smirk of the one, so suggestive of merciless treachery; the bill-hook nose, large teeth, and bold eye of the other, suggesting arrogance to the point of ferocity, haunt the beholder afterwards in his dreams.

'"Whose portraits are those?" asked Clare of the charwoman.

'"I have been told by old folk that they were ladies of the D'Urberville family, the ancient lords of this manor," she said. "Owing to their being builded into the wall they can't be moved away."

'The unpleasantness of the matter was that, in addition to their effect upon Tess, her fine features were unquestionably traceable in these exaggerated forms . . .'

Florence, half-fainting, leans back against the banisters. She sees the features of young Gertrude as Tess . . . in her growing, bilious jealousy she sees the ladies of the D'Urberville family look down and disdain her, from the walls above the staircase at ugly, unromantic Max Gate.

Florence sees the portraits in one swirl of the moon that comes out from behind a cloud and makes in her fevered imagination the wall by the tall staircase at Wool. And she knows – as she goes quietly past Hardy's study (he scribbles on, so late, a moth caught in his lamp now, dancing, dying as he scratches away) – she knows Hardy has stood under the portraits with his Tess, and she has looked up at her foremothers, and she will bring the old story once more into the world, as he wants her to.

Only the next day does Florence hear about the afternoon cock-crow and the drowning at Chesil Beach. She nods grimly at the news, brought by the maid, and purses her twitching lips.

Hardy has brought all this together, as he marshals his beautiful poems, his books, his plays. Everyone, like the moth in his night-lamp, dances and dies for Hardy. They are players all.

Florence shivers, ill still, coddled in a thick shawl – as she contemplates the eagerly awaited occasion of the First Night.

We walk along the road on our way back to the Mill, Baby Tess – and I turn once and see the faces of the women in the portraits, a fine mist off the sea forming a jaw and a formidable nose high above the leaves of our mother's tree – which the wind blows away again, leaving, bare now after the last autumn gale, a simple birch.

Our mother knew of these women 'of two hundred years ago' whom Hardy brought into Tess to show, despite his insistence on his heroine being a 'Pure Woman', that there was bad blood in her: these ancestresses with their lineaments suggesting 'merciless treachery' and 'arrogance to the point of ferocity' would, by sheer force of lineage, cause the ballad of love, betrayal, murder to be sung through their descendant. Our mother Mary knew there was no escape from this. And as we look back, at the bend in the road west from Langton Herring, at the silver birch, thin and forked, striped on the silver-grey bark with the weals of time – I feel the familiar sorrow that I never understood my mother when she lived among us – and nor did Tess, that's for sure. She was trying to tell us something – but maybe all daughters feel that about their mothers – and she just couldn't get through. She tried to warn us – but we mistook her strange stories for the babbling of madness. When she sighed – or, frequently – wept in her lonely bed at the Mill at night, we heard only the mist creeping along the ill-fitting door out in the lane, or the wind in the trees.

Hardy showed the portraits of those murderesses at Wellbridge (Wool Manor as it's taken to be) to Tess, to remind her that she would never be able to elude her destiny. Any more than our mother would – who was never recognized by the world, brought up with the gypsies after her foremothers lost their rightful place in the Marshwood Vale. So she blew hither and thither with the wind – a seed carrying a seed of the next violent act of destruction.

At the sharp bend in the road, past the cottage of old Mother Hurn (still alive when our Tess got into trouble, but we'll come to that), we lose sight of the tree and start out on the long walk west. A red post-box – VR engraved on this tiny splash of officialdom in remote countryside (a century ago, in the last years of the old Queen's reign, this box was erected on its stick, now almost wholly concealed by an ancient box hedge) – and by the side of the red box stands a bus stop, no less! We'll risk it, we'll stop here – the bus along the coastal road that Tess and I would jump onto so often, to escape to the pictures in Weymouth and the pier afterwards as it grew dark and there was some danger in the air – the bus will take us home at last, to Abbotsbury and Ella and the Mill.

As we stand – and then sit on a hard bank by the side of the hedge, to wait – a flock of wild geese flies over. You look up, your eyes blue and clear as the sky, and I see the white birds reflected there, like clouds. Do you see where they go, I wonder? Where will you be when the mild air of a Dorset spring welcomes them back to nest? Will the digging men have found the body, will you be placed in care, as stumbling and piteous as young birds when they first waddle from the pile of sticks and straw? Or will you be the first to break the pattern – and change the balance of the world?

Star

What an October this is, the October of 1924!

It's not just that Florence will grieve and weep – and attack her rival for speaking 'low intimacies' to Thomas Hardy in the tea-break between the matinée and evening performance of *Tess* in Dorchester (his excuse: that Augustus John, sitting on the other side of Mrs Bugler, was the subject of discussion and would not have been amused if he had overheard).

Nor is it that all the town is abuzz now with the scandal of Hardy and his infatuation. Even the Hardy Players, no doubt because Gertrude receives so much more attention than they from the great man, spread vile gossip, giggle in corners, collect outside Mr Bugler père's confectionery shop and grunt low jokes about sweet pastries and *bonnes bouches* (they know the poet's predilection for mouths). Everyone loves the scandal, except Florence of course; and how everyone looks forward to 26th November when the world-famous poet will show his foolish love (they hope) in full view at the First Night.

No, it's none of these things that makes October 1924 so specially memorable.

It's the rise of a new phenomenon (in Dorchester, at least). A young actress becomes a Star!

And all because of the movies!

I will explain.

Thomas Hardy has seen the results of the filming of *The Mayor of Casterbridge* – he has involved himself sufficiently to accompany film and crew to Maiden Castle. And he broods, on return, that 'perhaps the cinematograph will take the place of fiction, and novels will die out, leaving only poetry'.

Clever and perceptive of the man whose last novel, *The Well-Beloved*, took the author as far as it was possible to go, into the exposure of the deepest secrets of the erotic wellspring behind creativity. But perceptive in other ways too – for surely his darling should be immortalized on screen, surely 'Tess lives' should become eerily, fascinatingly possible with the coming of this new great invention of the twentieth century? Hardy imagines visiting the cinematograph alone every day, long after the last curtain has gone down on the few performances of *Tess* at the Corn Exchange (at which he is expected to behave with dignity and propriety, as befits England's most famous living poet).

In his dreams Hardy imagines a small cinematograph at the end of his bed. He needn't leave Max Gate at all, and again and again he can see the haunting beauty, the great dark eyes of his Tess as she delivers the lines he has adapted for her.

Hardy dreams into the future, and the legendary screen goddesses, some he has not even heard of yet, dance before his eyes: Marilyn and Marlene, Joan and Barbara and Lana and Jean.

Always, though, Hardy is faithful to his Tess. In the silent films where he fantasizes that she moves so fast and so touchingly, her fate flickering in the last reel as the hangman ties the noose, Tess is Queen of them all.

Hardy resolves to make enquiries on the subject. After all, why not? With *The Mayor* in the can, it would seem quite unsuspicious to demand that *Tess* be committed to film next. (Not that anything the old man does appears unsuspicious in the autumn of 1924; but he's unaware of it.)

Then the blow falls.

A Goldwyn film has already been made! It is shown in – October 1924 – just by an accident of timing that reminds Hardy of the tragedies he loves to write. And oh dear, it shocks everyone to the core.

Hardy hurries to rehearsal after hearing of this travesty. His Gertrude must become the real, the only star – his Tess must be the only Tess, the faithful mirror of the young woman he invented – and sent to the gallows – in just one moment of creative force all those years ago when he met her mother Augusta Way. Gertrude must go down in his history – must tour the world if necessary – showing the true lineaments of Tess to the waiting public.

Hardy fumes and pleads with his Players to squeeze the best performance, on the night, from his beloved *Tess*. Famous people have been invited to the première! They will write notices of *Tess*! No one will forget the pathos of her scene with Angel in Wool Manor, Wellbridge as it is in the book – no one will go away with a dry eye from this play of a 'Pure Woman, Faithfully Presented'. Then Hardy groans aloud and gnashes his teeth. How did he allow them to get away with balding Dr E. W. Smerdon? . . . and for one whole minute the great poet considers playing Angel himself, thrilling to the grief of the audience as he spurns the woman he loves . . .

But the public outcry over the film helps to bring fame to Gertrude Bugler – that and the rumours of scandal with the author of *Tess*, sixty years her senior. It's just like Hollywood, really.

The wags giggle over the name of the star in the Goldwyn silent movie. Blanche Sweet, no less! They mouth her name outside Mr Bugler's confectionery shop on the corner of South Street where the chocolates, nougat and marzipan, and iced cakes ready for coming birthdays and wedding feasts, are laid out temptingly: Blanche Sweet. They mutter when they pass Gertrude, serious, deeply thoughtful, a young actress on the brink of the great role of her career, as she walks to the Corn Exchange, on the night of the First Performance: Blanche Sweet! It's enough to put anyone off their stroke. And they whistle a popular ragtime refrain of the day – for isn't it in a nightclub, in the film, that Tess meets Alec? A nightclub, no less!

Hardy, over the short, non-companionable dinners at Max Gate, tells Florence of the disaster of the Goldwyn film. It will take away the dignity of the book (by which he means it may take away the success of Gertrude Bugler as Tess). He has a mind to sue the Hollywood studio . . . and so on and so on.

Florence – who through all these years has been joint author with her husband of Thomas Hardy's autobiography, and whose public face is one of decorum, and of restrained anger and indignation should the slightest slur be cast on the poet's name – fails to look up from the tough wedge of meat and overcooked batter on her plate.

– It is of the utmost importance that my play is recognized as the definitive version, Hardy says peevishly, as Wessex, coming to the rescue as so often before, leaps from chair to table and scavenges on the plate of his lacklustre mistress.

Florence says nothing. But Hardy's mind is made up. Unaware of street gossip and all the hue and cry surrounding Gertrude already, he determines she shall become the most famous and respected actress of them all.

This is where, as you might say, I come in. 'My' part – played by – who else? – Gertrude's younger sister, 'Miss A. Bugler'; the role of Liza-Lu, perennial younger sister to the doomed, beautiful Tess; Liza-Lu who goes off with her Angel in the end.

Now we're back at the Mill, and the door with its rusted hinges, battered wooden panels that let in the rain and need to be replaced before the tenants drive down from London in their glitzy car, has opened and let us in to the hall, with its junk mail on the mat. Now we're back here at last, Baby Tess, I can tell you the rest of the story. The sad story of Tess and Alec and Angel – and Liza-Lu. It's close on midday, and a strong September sun lights up the leaves on the fig tree outside on the terrace – we could be in Italy, the green of the leaves is so intense – we could look up into the blue sky and see angels, climbing on ladders of rosy cloud, angels coming for the soul of the child of Hardy's Tess, a child Hardy fathered and then left to die. We could see the saviour Hardy created for Tess – the 'good man', fair as Jesus Christ, the perfect balance for her dark beauty and haunted soul; the character he had the nerve to give a harp and call Angel

Clare. Angel came for Tess – and when Tess killed herself after his betrayal of her, he came for Liza-Lu.

As he did on the stage, in the Corn Exchange. As he did, years later when the story is played out again, for me. (But no one knows how Angel and the little sister-in-law got on, of course. The book ends there.)

Maybe I'm the only one to understand how involved in the life of another a younger sister can become – how she can live through her elder sibling's feelings and forget she ever had the right to any herself. As little Miss A. Bugler did on the great night, the First Night, the night Gertrude goes up like a shooting star into the night sky of Dorchester and rises so high she can be seen in London, in America even! I can feel now for the twelve-year-old 'amateur', Gertrude's younger sister, as she helps Tess with her gown, checks everything is in place . . . (but forgets one vital thing, as we shall see) . . .

The play's a smash. Hardy has invited the great and the good, the famous critics and the literary ladies with whom he has had dalliances over the past half-century or so. *Tess* will be the talk of the big city, Gertrude will personify the tragic heroine, a young woman so much more moving than France's Emma Bovary, and already as well known as Dante's Beatrice.

This is the night of the final incarnation. The *Times* sees Gertrude Bugler has 'a most moving sincerity and beauty – more beauty, one imagines, than could have been achieved by one or two of the most eminent professional actresses who have longed to play the part . . .'

Poor Gertrude! Florence sits in the stalls with her husband. Her neck throbs, at the spot where the tumour was removed. She senses the lascivious admiration the old men feel for the pure, sincere actress on the stage; Augustus John, Sir James Barrie – and her husband, of course, the great Thomas Hardy.

And Sir James Barrie, no less, tells the Hardys after the performance that 'the girl should go on the London stage at once'.

Hardy dreams of escape, elopement. In a flash he sees himself in
the London of his youth, the horse-drawn omnibus taking him to
the shabby street at the foot of Notting Dale where he lives in
sexy Bohemian style with his mistress, the beautiful young actress
Gertrude Bugler . . .

Gertrude shall go to London! Yes, offers pour in already, there will
be a production at the Haymarket Theatre and there's talk of going
to the United States, of showing the 'beauty, calm passivity and
vulnerable innocence' of Tess to the waiting audiences of
America . . .

Little Miss A. Bugler so identifies with her role as Liza-Lu that
she bursts into tears at the end of the performance, when Tess is
taken from Stonehenge to be hanged.

– The child should be taken home at once, sniffs Florence
(who has taken to frequenting rehearsals). She dreads this so-
obvious manifestation of the dangerous substitution of fantasy for
reality – after all, she has painfully witnessed the state her husband
has been in ever since he fell into the toils (as she sees it) of
Gertrude.

Little Miss A. Bugler has fallen in love with Angel, too – but here
she has crossed further barriers in order to satisfy her adolescent lust
for unrequited love, 'crushes', passions for the unattainable matinée
idol. For even the stage-struck younger sister of the newly famous
portrayer of Tess cannot bring herself to find Dr E. W. Smerdon
handsome or moving in any way. (She's tried, especially when
watching from the wings the scene in Wool Manor when he fastens
the gems round his bride's neck – but the bald patch shines in the
arc lights and her in-love feeling fades away.)

No. Liza-Lu has chosen Conrad Nagel, Tess's co-star in the
Goldwyn film, now showing at the picture palace in Dorchester.
She has to go secretly: Gertrude, imbued with the religious signifi-
cance of her role by Thomas Hardy, would be deeply offended to
learn that her sister had sneaked off to the flicks to see Satan's
version, commercialized and trite. But she can't help it. She's

Liza-Lu – and it's with heart-throb Conrad Nagel, alias Angel Clare, that she wants to make love.

Making love is all in the air. Florence, back at Max Gate, hears Hardy scribbling poems late into the night and is by his wastepaper basket as soon as he shuffles out with Wessex for his morning walk. But so far she finds nothing: has the old Devil found a way of hiding his outpourings, his senile (in Florence's view) poetic declarations of his love for the star he has made to be born?

Florence hunts high and low. Nothing. Meanwhile, she has the Weymouth performance of *Tess* to look forward to now.

The ninth of December – the days crawl by. Liza-Lu's passion for Angel-on-celluloid makes her give up eating. The chocolates and whipped-cream confections in her father's bakery sicken her. Her mother becomes frantic with worry.

Liza-Lu starves, in the days between the Dorchester and Weymouth shows. She becomes confused, vague.

Hardy is on the verge of madness himself. His last love is his best love – it's all coming true! They'll be in London together!

The fatal combination of Liza-Lu's famine-induced vagueness and Thomas Hardy's ever-mounting passion produce the worst scandal of all, on the night of 9th December in that elegant seaside town where mad George III loved to be lowered from his bathing machine into the water. Dorset buzzes with the news; and Sir Sydney Cockerell, who comes to stay at Max Gate some weeks later, sees the effect it is having on Florence; he takes the news post-haste back to London.

Florence begins to decide to take action.

Oh, What a Cloud!

~~~❧❦~~~

The milkman comes late to the Mill today. His little red and white float moves silently along the lane and stops at Ella's mum's – as the house is known by the local kids, though I believe the Estate call it 'Footsteps' or something whimsy like that – it helps with the summer letting, when Ella and her mum have to move out and go to the caravan site. Even looking down at the milk bottles, gleaming white and pure in the sun, makes me afraid, guilty, suspicious. Why is young John (he's from Weymouth, no one around here has got to know him properly yet) running three or four hours behind schedule? Is there a hold-up on the road, due to traffic piling up at the scene of the accident?

The accident, all those years ago, in the shallow pit behind West Bay, where the Chesil Beach gravel is small as peas and the lorries are due today to take it off for building work. The accident that was no accident at all and will soon be – or already has been? – seen as a crime.

Your grandmother Tess, my poor baby, has been away all those years. Thirty years almost to the day since the shallow grave was filled in, and the coastline has been rising in the calamitous new climate ever since; but even in the worst storms never quite coming near enough to disturb that unusual depression in the land.

A lifetime has gone by, since Tess and I sat on Chesil Beach together and ran our fingers through the stones, still searching unconsciously like children for the gold ingots washed up there from the Spanish Armada, or for the brittle bones of a merman, stranded ashore, in the days when people believed that man and Nature were all one and transmuted into each other, and that humankind was made up of humours, sanguine, choleric, melancholic.

If we were there today, we'd have no need to speak as we handled, fondled the smooth stones bigger here than at West Bay, no need to talk of the game Alec made us play, all those years ago. We'd hold up a stone – and in our mind's eye we'd see the wet stain from Tess spread on the fine veins, turning pale grey to a dark sea blue. We'd know how the story began, with the stone.

Tess will come back later today. What will she say when she sees you? Where will we all be by nightfall? The milkman looks up at our house as he places two pints on the step, and already I feel he's a messenger appointed to tell us the news I've dreaded to hear for so long.

He whistles and turns away from the step, though – and Ella runs over from her mother's sad house, which always has washing on a line and cheap curtains drawn in the best of weather.

Ella is happy to see us. She wants to know where we've been. And I tell her: we've been seeing the story of the beginnings of Tess.

And now, I say, you shall hear how Thomas Hardy lost his last, great love. But not before he had (poetically, metaphorically) legalized the union – made it official that the ballad of Tess should be sung through the female of the species – until the balance of Nature is set right and we and the planet are saved.

The cold twins of Europe – that is how a great anthropologist sees the cause of the plight the globe and humanity now find themselves in: the cold, rational deadly twins, exactly balancing one another, going out into the world, dominating, destroying, forcing the unnatural faith. Nowhere else but Europe developed the doctrine of equal measurement, which in turn leads to the concept of superiority and inferiority: one race over another, one sex 'better' than another, the 'blight of male domination'.

The cold twins of Europe went to the continents of South America and the jungles and plains of Asia, and scourged and killed until they were obeyed. Peoples who had always known (as we know, the three of us, sitting under the fig tree at Abbotsbury, waiting for the crunch of the boots, the icy interrogation) – peoples of other cultures had always known that the pull and push, the constant change and mutation of men and women, nature and beast, kept the earth rolling on its axis – that a rigid system, such as that which came out of Europe and spread over North America, would kill us all in the end.

They were right, and many millions of living beings – man, woman and beast – have died at the hands of the cold twins.

Now we must find the strength to convert – if necessary, to kill – the enemy of the natural balance of Earth, before it is too late.

The daughters of the poisonous ballad of Tess must fight to evade the cold twins, as they come, dressed in the costume of Fate, to claim their next victim.

But the twins rule still with a rod of iron – and many women obey them without knowing that this is what they do. Poor Florence is one of the women of the cold twins. It's not her fault that she set out to ruin the prospects and career of another woman. (The twins like this, for one woman to pitch against another leaves the double-headed monster the throne all to himself.) And Gertrude, too – she had no idea of the trouble she caused, because she saw only with the eyes of social convention, and social convention is laid down by the twins.

Marriage Rites

✦❯✦❮✦

9th December, Weymouth

Liza-Lu, little Miss A. Bugler – who plays the part of Liza-Lu – after the two sittings of Hollywood *Tess* at the Bridport Majestic she has allowed herself for the day (one right in the middle of dinner-time, so her mother, more frantic still with anxiety at her daughter's aetiolated form, nearly goes mad hunting for the girl, a slice of apple pie in her hand) – Liza-Lu arrives at the theatre with only twenty minutes to go before curtain up. Gertrude, who needs her both for fastening her stays and for moral support, is flustered by her little sister's faraway expression and fumbling, pudgy fingers. She pushes her aside and struggles with the hooks and eyes herself. She hardly has time for make-up. A natural beauty – fresh-faced, glowing with a poetic, haunting quality unseen before – so says Sir James Barrie, lord of Fantasy, Poetic Haunting qualities and the whole gamut – Gertrude walks on stage and feels the hush, the faint orgasmic sigh she is already finding addictive, as it rises from the audience.

My God! She's beautiful! And so touching, so sincere, so truly and unmistakably Tess!

And isn't there a big rumour going round – the poet – no, not that one, silly, that's the butcher's father from Toller Porcorum – the one over there with the sad-looking lady, that must be his wife. Isn't there a lot of gossip that the writer Thomas Hardy, a figurehead for British art and letters, is so madly in love with his Tess that they've agreed to run off together?

Yes, Mary up at Max Gate who went into service there last month found the poem he's written to her – she said it was . . . well, she didn't know where to look. Then the mistress came in and seized it off her, didden she?

The whispering stops. All eyes are on Tess. And then – to the astonishment of the audience – to the dumbstruck outrage of Florence Hardy – the author, poet and playwright rises from his seat and walks down the steps of the auditorium. He approaches the stage.

Oh God! A murmur, a multiple catching of breath . . . the supreme embarrassment is more than the haberdasher's wife can stand and she lets out a shrill little scream.

Has Thomas Hardy gone senile? Or is his passion so great that he can no longer keep his hands off his creation, but must go on stage and . . . and do what? Kiss her? Oh, my God, no, surely not . . . or more, go further still . . .

175

This time an electric silence descends, like the air before the hurricane that sweeps over land, flattening, howling, shrieking in the broken timbers. Hardy mounts the stage and walks over to Gertrude Bugler. He takes her hand.

Gertrude falters and stops. Hardy looks into her eyes, pools of grief at the tragic fate that awaits her. He smiles gently and pulls the wedding-ring from her finger, slides it into his pocket and walks off the stage into the wings.

Coughing breaks out in the audience. December colds, held down by inhalations of balsam and the sucking of strong lemon and eucalyptus gums, now find a devilish release and echo round the draughty hall. The actors try vainly to regain control – the hurricane is unleashed – and it's only after the interval that a calmer atmosphere is restored.

Florence has to endure the interval, the famous old men who are friends of her husband carefully avoiding her eye as refreshments are passed round, but not as fast as the scandal – which she hears as it shrieks and moans in the rafters of the old hall.

She wants to kill Gertrude Bugler. She smiles as Barrie says he hopes they'll all dine together after the London Haymarket opening in the spring of *Tess*, with Gertrude in the starring role. She accepts graciously, she says she fears her husband may be made so terribly tired by the effort of travelling to London . . . But of course he must come, Augustus John says, roguish, chuckling.

Where is Thomas Hardy? He's outside Gertrude's dressing-room, the dolt. Like any stage-door Johnny, too nervous to knock – and he fingers Gertrude's wedding-ring in his pocket as he stands there listening to Tess and Liza-Lu going at each other hammer and tongs.

– I'm sorry . . . I truly am . . .

– You know I'm not married to Angel Clare in that scene – not yet – you reminded me to take it off in Dorchester, Annie!

– I promise it won't happen again . . .

Hardy listens outside the door to all this, with a smile like a school-boy. The ring, the gold band Mr Bugler the farmer put on his

176

bride's finger, rests in his pocket. Gertrude will start agitating about it soon . . . yes, there she is, asking little Miss Bugler to rescue it for her . . .

– I don't dare, Gertie. You get it yourself!
– I don't know where I'll find Mr Hardy when I'm on in a minute, the poor girl wails.

Hardy smirks, then goes faster than his eighty-four and a half years would normally allow, round a bend in the corridor and safely back into the stalls.
    The bell rings. The audience, thirsty for blood, longing for a full-scale scandal to be enacted on stage, come noisily back to their seats.

Florence has to endure a husband, shrunk to gnome-size by his years, bouncing with a naughty happiness on the seat beside her. He hasn't finished – she can tell it – yet.

The wedding of Tess and Angel Clare. But no one looks at poor Dr E. W. Smerdon, as he plights his troth to the lovely Tess. They look at Thomas Hardy as he walks on stage with the ring and weds his Gertrude then and there.

The story ends badly – badly for both Florence and Gertrude, that is. Thomas Hardy gets on with his life and plans, and if he's heartbroken there's very little way of proving it. (At the death of Wessex at Christmas two years later, he certainly is; and he writes a moving poem to commemorate the most-loathed dog in literary circles.) But over the loss of Gertrude – or rather, the loss of his Tess – he seems oddly unworried at the idea of replacing her (with Gwen Ffrangçon-Davies) for the London run.
    For this is what Florence did, and it sullied her name, even with the most polite of Hardy's biographers. It should be remembered,

however, that she was half insane then, with jealousy and misery, and some say the recompense she provided for the no-longer-so-young actress after Hardy's death merely added another dash of cruelty.

Sir Sydney Cockerell's journal tells us this:

> 10th January 1925. Max Gate received me very kindly, but there is a cloud over the house as TH is absorbed in Mrs Gertrude Bugler, the leading lady of the Dorchester Players, who has recently enacted Tess. FH [Florence] greatly disturbed about it. She says TH is offhand with her, a sorry business.

> 11th January. After breakfast a walk with FH and Wessie and she told me her troubles. He is eighty-four and a half and I begged her to try and look on the situation from outside as a comedy. She said that that was what she was trying to do, but that he spoke roughly to her and showed her that she was in the way . . .

> 12th January. Walked into Dorchester with FH in the morning. She told me she had been in such a fret in the night that she thought she would go mad. It was her birthday [forty-five] but he had not alluded to it in any way. She wondered if she could be in such a state of nerves on account of her age. All the company of players were talking about it. Mrs Bugler came to lunch to discuss a proposal from Frederick Harrison that she should play Tess at some matinées in the Haymarket. On the face of it there does not seem to be much harm in her. FH was very civil to her and offered to put her up for the New Century Club if she should be rehearsing in London. TH went through new scenes of *Tess* with her. FH had begged me to stay to make things easier, or I should have left in the morning.

After reading these excerpts from Sir Sydney Cockerell's journal, Mrs Bugler wrote to Cockerell forty years later in February 1964: 'Oh what a cloud there must have been at Max Gate! And I knew nothing then of the "infatuation for the local Tess". As I read those words a line from *Tess of the D'Urbervilles* came into my head: "It is in your own mind what you are angry at, Angel: it is not me." It was only in the mind of FEH . . .'

Gertrude continues: 'I well remember my visit to Max Gate on 12 January. Thomas Hardy was in a happy mood that day, and, as Mr Cockerell writes, Mrs Hardy was very civil to me; yet all the time I felt Mr Cockerell's cold disapproval and wondered how I could have offended him. And it is only now, after all these years, that I know he was defending Florence Hardy – or the Florence Hardy he thought her to be – from the woman he mistakenly thought me to be.

'A few days later there came a wire from Mrs Hardy: she was coming to Beaminster to see me. She arrived, terribly upset and agitated, and said at once that he must not know of her visit to me. Then I listened with incredulous amazement to what she had to say.

'She concluded by asking me not to go to London. So I wrote to Frederick Harrison and to Thomas Hardy to that effect. I never saw Hardy again. His last words to me had been, "If anyone asks you if you knew Thomas Hardy, say, 'Yes, he was my friend'." '

Gertrude's 'incredulous amazement' at the speech of the poor demented Florence is perhaps a little overstated. But what are you to say, with a baby crying in the next room, in a cottage with the washing catching the rain and it would be impossible bad manners to say 'Excuse me' to the genteel wife of England's most famous writer and dash out and bring it in?

What can she be but incredulous, when Florence says the great poet has written two poems describing the running off together of Gertrude and TH?

Look surprised, a tiny bit alarmed, when Florence says a journey to London could imperil her husband's life, at his age – and he had been determined to go there for the Haymarket matinées, of course.

Agree softly, quietly, while your husband comes in and hears the baby's wail and steps in quite sharp, wondering what you're at, neglecting to pick up the nipper . . .

Gertrude Bugler never forgave Florence Hardy for denying her the chance of appearing in the West End in 1925. When, with Florence's active encouragement, she did at last play Tess in London after Hardy's death, she felt that she was already too old to embark upon a professional career as a romantic actress. Comments at the time (August 1929) included the fact that critics hardly knew how to judge her out of her native surroundings.

James Agate, deploring the mistaken generosity of the audience, went further and traced her failure to the fact that she felt the part of Tess so passionately. 'Drama', he said, quoting William Archer, 'consists of imitation and passion.' Passion Mrs Bugler certainly had. 'When she wept her body shook, and one knew she had not ordered its shaking. She was "feeling her part"; and those storms of weeping caused the spectator more distress than delight.'

It was only recently that Hardy's poem 'An Expostulation' was accepted by scholars – and then by Gertrude – as a description of his feelings about the young actress and her desire to go to London. But – as you'll see – it's more likely that the verses, wooden and unconvincing as they are, were penned by the morbidly jealous Florence:

AN EXPOSTULATION

Why want to go afar
    Where pitfalls are
When all we swains adore
Your featness more and more
As heroine of our artless masquings here,
And count few Wessex' daughters half so dear?

Why paint your appealing face,
    When its born grace
Is such no skill can match

180

With powder, puff or patch,
Whose every touch defames your bloomfulness,
And with each stain increases our distress?

    Yea, is it not enough
        That (rare or rough
    Your lines here) all uphold you,
    And as with wings enfold you,
But you must needs desert the kine-cropt vale
Wherein your foredames gaily filled the pail?

Thomas Hardy died on 11th January 1928, at Max Gate, the maid
Nellie Titterington running down the stairs at nine in the evening
to call his wife.

Nellie it was who heard Hardy's last words, for she had been
sitting in the dressing-room leading off from Hardy's bedroom.
'She is such a little person yet she has seen such big operations',
were the last recorded words of Thomas Hardy, followed by the
word 'blood'. And when death came, he cried out to Eva Dugdale,
who held his hand to support him, 'Eva, what is this?'

Hardy is dead, his wife Florence sits quietly by the deathbed, and
it's time to return to the 'big operations' soon to be uncovered in
the scoop of land behind West Bay: the story of our own family,
our own Tess.

Part Four

These are the scenes I remember. Before the sun goes down, before they come for us. This is how the story was played out.

Tess and her Baby

Dr Ryall was his name. He was kind at first – 'kind', how hard it is to stomach that word, a word used when referring to a master's treatment (when he feels like it) of his slaves.

And Tess was a slave, as all women are, to her biology. There was a baby growing in her, wasn't there? And as soon as she started to throw up in the mornings (she and Alec were in a council flat in East Coker over by Yeovil then; the flat belonged to Alec's uncle, an alcoholic who worked as a hospital porter and turned a blind eye, as far as Alec was concerned: the rest of his family had washed their hands of him; he was an inveterate liar and petty crook) – as soon as Tess began to show unmistakable symptoms of pregnancy, well, Alec upped and left.

He said he was going to Bournemouth, to look for work. And – as even you, little Ella, inveterate watcher of TV soaps, could have guessed, he never came back. You've heard the ballad. People here still talk of our own Retty – who drowned herself for love. Put the big stones from Chesil Beach in the pockets of her coat and went down, down . . . they found her body washed up at Portland, battered by the rocks after being swirled round and round like a corpse on a merry-go-round by the ferocious double currents known as the Race.

Don't drown yourself for love – and Tess didn't either. She felt like a drowning woman, though – she said she saw all her life ahead of her dragging her down and down with a child she couldn't support, no love, no life, nothing.

And I didn't even like him, she said.

Dr Ryall gave an appointment to my sister Tess – she took me along for company and help but I wasn't much good to her. I felt embarrassed and kept smiling – the smile a timid young woman gives to a powerful man, and Dr Ryall got at Tess through me, because of it.

It's a life you're taking.
Have you thought this over seriously?
Is there a father?
Do you realize you've left it very late?
Your life could be in danger.
Do your parents know about this?
I said, whose child is this?

And in the street outside that gloomy great hospital in Yeovil, Tess crying, and her voice hoarse with all the sobs she hadn't shed in all the years since she'd known she'd been chosen as the next in a long line of Ruined Maids.

The man in the new Ford with the shiny covers who gave us a lift all the way to Langton Herring with Tess in front had his hand right up her skirt, for payment, while I felt as sick as a pregnant cat myself with the smell of that bright new plastic in the car.

But then I always felt what Tess felt: I caught her flu, I ended up with her life mate, I stand in for her now and tell her story. But soon you will know where she is, you may even see her and she will be as beautiful now as she was then, that's her curse, you might say.

Mother Hurn's cottage. A new smell, to my suddenly sensitive, sympathetically pregnant nose: the smell of cats, and unwashed stone flags and damp bread left lying for the cats in saucers of rancid milk.

Oh Tess, don't go in there! Don't do it!

And our mother, our witch-mother with her face a rugged weather-beaten hue from all the long hours at West Bay, shifting fish in icy bales, her eyes as muddy dark grey and brown as the sea on a relentless day –
    Our mother says, Mother Hurn will look after you, Tess. She'll see you right.

And Tess, seeing her own weakness for the first time – seeing she can't go back to Dr Ryall and plead one more time – seeing she is woman at last, someone with so few choices and all of them wrong, or 'bad', cries out in dismay and despair when we walk into the evil-smelling cottage.
    Mother Hurn must be ninety, for God's sake! This is 1963!

It's your decision, our mother says. But she has no warmth in her voice. She has shown Tess she'll support her – but both know it wouldn't work. Does she dread another Tess coming into the world? Did her own roving childhood with the gypsies turn her against the possibility of loving another nomad child; conceived in a fit of loyalty to the past on Tess's part, the whole shameful episode coming from a spring of hatred for the Mapperton arrogance?
    Who would look after this child?

I swear to you that this is true.
    Mother Hurn comes forward and leads us both into the kitchen. Yes, she has a pointed nose that comes down and nearly meets her chin.
    Yes, she has a cat that jumps straight up on to her shoulder as she cackles at us.
    And yes, there's a big pot on the stove that's bubbling away with a slurping noise like a potion horror film.

187

Mother Hurn scoops out some of the mixture and puts it in a Woolworth's mug.

Black berries of the bay tree. (Oh, who could have foreseen that the beautiful Tess, with all that promise, all that glowing free spirit, would come to this? Our mother, perhaps: for bay leaves are used for divination, the priestesses at Delphi wore garlands of bay to foretell the future of each seeker of his destiny, and my mother had the gift of prophecy, she learnt that before she could write or read.)

A leaf of bog asphodel.

Wormwood, dogstooth, juniper berries.

Jack-in-the-pulpit (*Arisaema triphyllum*). Mix them all together. Jack-in-the-pulpit certainly must not be left out – poor Tess, how will you answer those disapproving Jacks, placed in the pulpit two thousand years ago to preach and warn of the weakness and depravity of women? Those Jacks like . . . Dr Ryall? Or our father, who doesn't know yet that his elder daughter is visiting a witch to rid herself of an unwanted child?

Drink it down, Tess. There is no answer, no account of yourself that you can give which will satisfy the Reverend Jack.

The pain. I feel it too. I sit in the little room at the side where Tess lies moaning on a sofa with broken springs.

Our mother has gone back to West Bay, to collect fish for the smart new shop she manages in Bridport. Does she mind too much to stay? Does she hope a baby will be washed up to her on the shore one day, as you were, Baby Tess?

Then we see it. There has been someone here before us. This morning, it must have been. Early, while Mother Hurn picked the herbs in that wild garden at the back – all the neighbours complain, but the council can't do a thing about it.

At dawn, some poor girl . . .

The chipped enamel basin in the corner . . . Oh God, Tess sees it at the same time as I do.

Was it shame that made Tess's predecessor, here in this Devil's kitchen, come to an old woman and not go on the National Health?

Did Dr Ryall make her feel like a murderess, so she went out into the neat forecourt of Yeovil General stuffing Kleenex into her mouth to stop her from screaming?

Or had she left it too late?

The thing in the basin heaves gently in a pool of clotted blood.

Oh my God! It's alive!

Worst of all – no, it can't have been Mother Hurn's cat, they don't make a noise like that –

We're running. It's like a terrible dream, where the colours are lurid but the scene is pretending to be peaceful, with wheat stacks golden in the sun and the lanes still filled with wild flowers –

We reach the high ridge of shingle that is Chesil Beach. Tess is in agony and I feel it too, burning right through my body and turning my legs to water.

Down – down – we fall, we roll on the steep bank. A man sees us and shouts at us not to swim there.

He thinks we don't know Chesil Beach! He thinks we're just two silly girls, two townies, doing this for a bet.

Tess reaches the sea first. The man stares and stares as she plunges her head in, as she drinks and drinks . . .

The man starts to run towards us.

There, high on the shingles, Tess vomits up all Mother Hurn's terrible concoction. She gasps and she heaves and . . .

The man is just a few yards away. He shouts that he'll go for a doctor.

And he stands rooted to the spot and staring at us even more as we laugh . . . and laugh . . . and laugh . . .

– No . . . no, thanks . . . not a doctor . . . we're able to pant at last, with the tears streaming down our cheeks and the man quite put out and walking away.

*

Two silly girls, high on marijuana, he wonders . . . but what is there to tell the police anyway?

Regretfully (he would have liked to rope in male authority: there's just something too out of control, too *prehistoric* about these crying, laughing, vomiting women on the beach), he shrugs and walks away along the beach towards Burton Bradstock.

And that, Baby Tess, is how your mother's life was saved. And how you, in turn, can be here today.

Swan Song

Our mother left work and came back here to the Mill to care for the baby. Her face was always unsmiling – but she loved the child, you could tell that by the way she hummed and sang to her and held her up close as if trying to listen to the sound of the sea out of her little pink ears.

Our mother hummed.

And Tess sang. She went out later and later – often she never came home at all – and in bars and pubs and draughty halls, in marquees in fields where cows wandered amongst the stoned crowds – on platforms and in simple back rooms, Tess sang.

The sixties had got going in earnest, you see. I was too young to take part – and I looked after your mother, helped our mother Mary to make the dresses and tiny dungarees, wash the clothes that looked like rags compared to the togs of the neat rich children who had moved into the area along with the boom in tourism and 'remote retreats'. I took your mother for walks along that endless beach.

Tess sang. She had the 'best white female voice since Helen

Shapiro' – that's what the man said, and before we knew where we were, Tess was signed up for every gig in the country.

Our local Tess. So beautiful, so sad – the ballads she sang made people cry – and made the man (his name was Walter Something-or-other) wealthy and greedy for more.

The story was beginning to play itself out. Walter wanted Tess to go to London, to the States too. She could cut records, she could sell a million copies . . .

But Tess wanted to stay near her baby.

Our mother said she'd had the baby dumped on her a long time now; she'd got used to it. She told Tess to go if she wanted.

But Tess couldn't bring herself to go.

Our father left the Mill after Tess and the baby came. One night – after Tess had come in late, and she was singing, in the bath, I think it was, our father John Hewitt came in very pale and said he was going out and he wasn't coming back. (He had better manners than Alec, you could say.)

But we all knew he couldn't bear his best, his most beautiful swan, whose plumage had turned in his mind a sooty black on the day she gave herself to a man – he couldn't stand his Tess being here with a child and no shame in the world left in her, and singing too, to make matters worse. Our father hated her new-found independence, the money she earned, her gawky body, a too-thin swan who wouldn't come to his call, never had.

He would never be able to plan her nesting now – arrogant, wicked Tess, she had taken the law into her own hands – and he walked out that night and didn't come back.

– He'll be all right, our mother said, and sighed.

Secretly, I worried for our mother. It seemed her witch-strength was draining out of her every day.

And it was true. Tess had deprived her of her fierce freedom.

She had tied her own mother down. And lines had grown on Mary's forehead, over the sterilizer that didn't work properly, and the hand-me-downs old Mrs Moores gave her that weren't fit for a tramp's child, and the push-chair she said was hurting the poor little baby's back.

And all the while, Tess sang. Protest songs. Sad rural ballads. Slave songs, longings for the freedom she had taken from her own mother so as to have the freedom to travel the circuit and send her plangent, eerie songs into the heart of every man, woman and child who heard them.

But that's how it has always been. One woman will exploit another, in order to get what she wants.

One day – the child would have been about five years old by then, it was 1969 – Tess took me along to a gig in a park at a stately home, Minterne Magna, I think it was.

And there he was. I'll always remember him, standing on a little bridge that looked like it was in the last stages of rotting away, a bridge over a great stagnant lake where the necklaces of acid green weed would drag you down and drown you before a friend could give you a helping hand to climb out.

He was playing the guitar. Well, he would be, wouldn't he? He'd come with his group.

His name was Gabriel Bell. Or so he said. Maybe it was just his name in the group; it didn't really matter which, in those days.

Gabriel, the new Angel, to make Tess's life complete.

And right then and there Tess fell in love with him – and so did poor silly Retty, who'd come along even though her mother didn't want her getting in with druggy folk at concerts.

They fell in love with his blond hair. Angel the Angle. (If little Miss A. Bugler, Gertrude's sister with my part, the part of Liza-Lu in the play, had been there, she'd have fallen for him too. He was just as beautiful as the film star Conrad Nagel (in itself an anagram of Angel, as little Miss Bugler, writing it out again and again in her pre-pubescent passion on the lined pages of her exercise book, would have been well aware).)

Gabriel on the bridge, over the bright green pre-Raphaelite weed that just invited a young damsel to run to his arms and drown like Ophelia in its garlands before he could reach out and rescue her.

As Retty did drown, from the sheer misery of not being loved by Gabriel Bell of The Elastic Heavenly Band (for so they called themselves).

Oh no, Gabriel wasn't 'into' rescuing anyone, not even Tess.

It was the first time we'd seen a member of the tribe: one of the men who look like children's Bible Lord-is-my-Shepherd types. With their long sixties yellow curls, their crooks, their robes, their mantras, their caftans and beads.

The new man, the new Heavenly Light, who will lead you by the hand – away from macho, dishonest, unreconstructed men – like Alec, for example.

The peaceful man, the man with good karma, the sheep in sheep's clothing. He will love your baby, too!

The story will never be played out again! For the first time since the days of Thomas Hardy, everything has changed.

The sixties are here! The sitar whines in the apple meadows so loud that old Mr Warren claps his hands over his ears.

The Pill means no man can take advantage of you.

We are all free!

Life with Angel

Tess sang with the band. Oh, it was lovely, you'll never know what a lovely voice she had.

They had just been waiting for each other – that's what everyone said.

Tess with her dark beauty, the Spanish blood that came from the ancient invaders of Cornwall, washed into her newly found voice too, along with the gravelly sound of the shingle rubbed by the sea on Chesil Beach.

Gabriel the invading fair-haired Saxon, with the eyes of Luftwaffe blue. The dogs – lurchers, Irish setters, wolfhounds – he had always round him; the medieval doublet and hose he wore when he sang his tormented lyrics of love and loss; the jewel colours, the red wine in the goblet; the illuminated manuscript he seemed to have walked straight out of, to climb high into Tess's tower and grab her awake.

It was all new. It was too good to be true. (And Retty, handmaiden to the band, glorified groupie by virtue of being a childhood friend of Gabriel's 'lady', was tossed a bone from time to time, like Gabriel's noble pack of hounds: she could soap him in the bath when Tess was on her way over from the Mill (he stayed at B & Bs, he stayed in hotels, he dossed down with 'mates' he'd met at the gig the night before).)

After she'd pushed the loofah up and down his long, fair, rippling back, Retty would feel so horny she'd go and have a fuck with Mick the drummer – or anyone, for that matter, whom she happened to bump into on her way down from the exquisite pain of polishing the pectorals of Gabriel Bell.

Everyone was in love with Gabriel.

Except for one person, of course – as the fairy tales always have it, there has to be an impediment: a wicked stepmother, seven steep hills, a fierce animal that will chew you up if you don't know the magic word to let you by.

Our mother Mary, she was the one who voiced her doubts about Gabriel Bell.

Why don't you bring him home?

What did you say he *really* does for a living?

Doesn't he have a girlfriend already in Bridport? Annie Bowditch saw him walking arm in arm with that girl you were at Mrs Moores' with for one term – Dolly –

Doesn't he have anywhere to live?

And in those arrogant, far-off days when a new race of happy, sexually tolerant, tall, beautiful superbeings had come into a dreamy little island still stiff with class prejudice and boring beliefs – Tess could say, with a shake of her head:

– It's not *like* that, Ma!

Poor Tess! But she wasn't the only one – I was impressed too with the new wind that blew the old mist away, along with a strong smell of cannabis and patchouli. And Retty, starry-eyed Retty, believed it, too (Gabriel would always look after her, he said. You're a good chick, Retty. Hey, the band'll take you along, anytime, anywhere in the world).

Our mother was right, of course – but how she had changed since the day she left the Mill and went her own way. She could 'see' still, but she was tied down, she was itching to go: we should have been able to realize that.

Mary sacrificed herself for Tess's baby – no wonder she suspected the fact that Tess, so happy now, so radiant, glowing with love for the leader of the pack, had never once brought Gabriel home to the Mill. She suspected that Tess hadn't told the Angel who had come to save her, the basic fact of her life –

Again, our mother Mary was right. Tess never told Gabriel she had a child.

We're sitting outside the Admiral Nelson pub just near the cottage where Thomas Hardy was born. Late summer tourists are flicking through brochures at the next table. Over Gabriel's shoulder I glimpse, just for a second, the brooding profile in a photograph of Thomas Hardy, the white line of his heavy moustache. The tourists, who are Scandinavian, are staring with awe at the face of the writer, poet and dramatist: then they look across at the hills, and they drink up, and then someone suggests a cider, they all want to have the 'Wessex experience', and a girl with a backpack and a serious look goes into the pub and comes out with mugs of scrumpy.

It's to the sound of the tourists gulping the thin, sour apple wine that I remember Tess actually trying to tell Gabriel about the baby – your mother, Baby Tess, your poor mother – and I remember too that Gabriel was very full of the coming gig that night.

At Wool Manor. Where else?

– You can come on stage this time, Liza-Lu, Gabriel says to me and he laughs out loud at the way I glow with love for him, when he says that.

And all the people in the pub garden look at Gabriel when he laughs like that – and their faces light up, as if he's taken the strain of ordinary, everyday life away from them and replaced it with magic. A couple of girls squeak in recognition – they're scrabbling for paper, or the back of an old cigarette packet, or a pub napkin, and when they find something he can sign his autograph on, they come up to him and they bend low over him, so his blond, long curly hair swishes right up against their tits.

Tess is used to this kind of thing. She's Gabriel's 'old woman', he doesn't fuck the groupies, everything is cool. So she carries on saying what she was saying, anyway, and as the girls pull back and prance off with their arses rolling like pennies spewed out from a slot machine on a numbers game at the funfair, Tess tells Gabriel what our mother has told her she *must* tell him (and if she doesn't, that's it with Mary looking after the baby. It's Tess's responsibility too, for God's sake, and if she's really going steady with this Gabriel Bell, then the two of them ought to be thinking of where to settle down and bring up the kid respectably, like other people).

– My little kid, Tess is saying to Gabriel, my little girl.

There's just a split second of silence before Gabriel says, Great, how great, and bring her along to the gig tonight, babe. I'll look after the kid while you're on. Just a split second of a silence as intense as the grave – and a look at Tess that spells it all out: he won't get caught this way. And then the laughter's going again, and Dave the manager comes bobbing across the grass and throws his arms in the air and says, Shit, man! I've been looking for you everywhere . . .

And as we all walk off to the trailer, and I climb in proudly with the star Gabriel Bell, I feel for the second time a silence, and it comes from Tess.

– The pigs stopped me, said I was speeding on the road to Dorchester. This is Dave talking, Tess unaccountably gone all still and sad.

– They asked me my name. I told 'em my name and they wrote it down. Dave is convulsed with laughter now. Tess stares straight ahead at the road that takes us east, to Wellbridge, as Hardy called the lovely old house, Wool Manor.

I could swear I heard a cock crow as we slowed to leave the main road and go into the lanes that lead to Winfrith Newburgh and East Stoke.

An afternoon cock crowed, as we drove much too fast through the dazzle of cow parsley and high box hedge. Retty, sitting in the back of the trailer, stripped to the waist and swinging her breasts so Gabriel could see them in the driving mirror and go even faster round the corners, brake dramatically at the sight of an oncoming car – squealed and shouted above the roar of the engine that it was bad luck, so her old grandma used to say, bad luck to come if a cock was heard to crow after noon.

But Dave and Gabriel are laughing, rolling joints – Dave tells us what he said to the pig who stopped him on the motorway.

– I'm Sergeant Pepper, Dave said he told the cop – and how they laughed!

Fog

❦❦❦❦

In those days I used to go and see our father although I didn't tell our mother Mary – or Tess, for that matter.

He lived in a little hut, a boathouse, I suppose you could call it, except there was no boat, just a room for sick swans right on the edge of the water and a simple dwelling next to it where he slept, and cooked on an electric ring, and read his books on birds at night, with the sound of the heavy swans settling down for the night in their high nests of twigs, all round him.

My father had almost entirely disappeared from human society. He cycled into Abbotsbury from time to time and came back with a few provisions. But he spoke to nobody, except in the most taciturn way, and if people asked him details about mute nesting swans he would shake his head as if he'd gone mute himself.

Sometimes he'd take a walk in the tropical gardens, and he'd go through all the dense foliage and the spindly high trees with their strange, exuberant blossoms and fruit that could never ripen, and fetch up in the green sward where people buried their pets long ago. I used to find him there, standing by the little headstones deep in thought; and by the stone marked TESS he'd stand like a mourning owner, as if he was listening in his mind to the poem Hardy wrote for Wessex after he was dead and gone.

The most important thing in my father's life had let him down. His daughter had disappeared, in the guise that he would have liked her to remain for ever – young, beautiful and his. He needed her to be obedient, to run and trot when he called. Now she had brought her litter to his home and he preferred to sulk down by the water's edge, where the legs of the flamingos were like moving trees in the brackish water.

And besides, our mother had nothing left to say to him. It was a sad business, really.

But we none of us knew, then, where the real truth of the matter lay.

Tess was preoccupied with her grief. If she hadn't seen it coming – well, everyone else had.

It was to do with responsibility – an unfathomable word then. Alec hadn't wanted the responsibility of looking after your poor mother, little Tess. Gabriel wouldn't like to 'settle down' either. So – although you could never be quite sure what lay behind it (Gabriel was good at protesting total innocence, Retty's mother, sobbing, called him a 'shit who's learned how to be a blameless shit') – what took place that night at the gig at Wool Manor was only too predictable.

That silence, the silence Tess heard like a cold wind down the centuries, the cold wind of betrayal, abandonment and loss of love – filled the parks and gardens, the tourist pavilions erected for the music festival, the old manor itself where ticket-paying guests were allowed to wander, to penetrate even as far as the bedroom with the four-poster where the yellow mistletoe used once to hang, memento of Tess and Angel Clare, and Hardy and the object of his last infatuation, the young Tess. The silence, with its underlying violence, blocked the sound system and made Tess's voice tiny and tinny, while Gabriel's guitar sounded like a child's mandolin.

The audience was disappointed. The stench of disappointment in love hung over Wellbridge; some said it was unlucky, with the memories of the evil, hook-nosed women in their portraits on the walls and Tess looking that night so like them, unflatteringly lit by whirling strobe lights that were jinxed that night, too, throwing her features into hideous shadows on the backcloth of the stage.

And all the while the violence of Gabriel's silence, which said:

I never promised you a rose garden.

You never told me you had a kid.

What could we do with a kid in tow when I'm gonna travel, play my guitar round the world?

She'd be better off staying here with you, love.

And of course later that night – when the fog had already started down by the sea and was creeping with its white tentacles along the branches of the liana, the creepers, the palms in the tropical gardens – up in the four-poster at Wool Manor, Gabriel betrayed Tess and made love to Retty.

They lit a fire, they fucked to the leaping flames, none of Retty's loyalty to Tess was there any more either, she wanted only Gabriel Bell.

And where were we, Tess and I? Oh, quite simple: sleeping in the forecourt of the manor in the dusty trailer, with two lurchers and two greyhounds for company. But not sleeping, really. Watching the grey dawn as it brought the first wisps of the fog with it, shivering in the clammy cold of the caravan. It's in dismal, all-too-recognizable circumstances like these that the old story is played out.

Even the Thermos was broken, I remember that. Tess wept as the inner lining snapped and cut her hand as she tried to wrench the top off.

We both knew Gabriel and Retty were up there. We knew Gabriel's love for Tess couldn't include a child.

So, when you come down to it, what's new?

To top it all, when we got back to the Mill, little Mary had come down with chickenpox and our mother was grim as one of the Fates you see on an Ancient Greek vase – dabbing the poor little creature's face with chamomile and staring at the bedraggled, furious Tess as if she was something the cat brought in.

After I'd made a cup of tea our mother Mary sat across the kitchen table from us. A swan – then a formation of swans – flew noisily overhead. We all thought of winter coming on and John Hewitt sitting like a mad hermit in the freezing swanhouse by the edge of the lagoon. Then our mother said something that turned the story on one more cog, so we sat staring at each other in that terrible silence again – until the child started her feverish crying.

– Alec Field is back, she said. Mrs Moores saw him in Bridport today. He was wearing a double-breasted suit. First thing, she thought he was an American.

Fog.
The whole of that week the white sea-mist, famous in west Dorset for wrecking ships, for setting farm labourers on the wrong path as they make their way home from turnip-hoeing over the hills – the fog known right across the county for the vile phlegm that

the spit-coloured vapour brought, killing off the old and infirm, choking the lungs of newborn babies so they turn to the pillow and suffocate in a further expanse of stifling white –

The sea fog came in that week of Gabriel's silence and Tess's despair, and there had never been a summer, so folk round about said, with anything so evil, so persistent, so murderous, as that fog.

Come closer, little Ella, and I'll sing out the rest of the ballad to you. It's a sad one – and it's for you and the infant Tess here to make sure it can never be sung here again – or anywhere else, for that matter. Up to you to see that life's tape is changed, time for a new tune.

And especially in memory of poor Retty, who ran to the beach – just out there, where the stones are big as goose eggs (and the fishermen know where they've landed, even in a pea-souper, by the size of those fat great stones).

Gabriel has gone off with the band. They'll be at Portsmouth by now. A tour of France and Germany and then the big snub-nosed plane to the United States of America! There'll be plenty of girls like you, Retty, in the United States of America!

Retty loads her pockets and stands completely muffled by the mist, which licks her face and wraps her in cotton wool as if she's something too precious to lose. Why go down there to the sea with the racing current, and lie down on the sea-bed, only to rise when the sea sucks the stones from your pockets and the corpse bloats and goes dancing out to the Race?

Don't do it, Retty! There are plenty better than Gabriel about.

But Retty is in love. Tears roll down her healthy country girl's cheeks. She wades in ... she pauses ... with a shriek she rushes on forward, and she drowns.

The afternoon cockcrow had been unlucky, after all. Tess, betrayed by Retty, sees the body the fishermen bring into the cottage – yes, to that cottage next to where you live, over there, Ella – Tess sees the body with a sense of almost total detachment, as if the fog had killed her feelings for her old friend and she was staring at a hollow-eyed, dripping-dead stranger.

Tess is unhappy. Tess is in love and she wants Gabriel back. Never mind that Gabriel is on his way to the United States of America – and crossing his path is Alec, on his way back – never mind that she has a child and she should know better – Tess wants Gabriel back.

Mother Hurn tells her what to do:

Pick three rosebuds at dawn. (The fog makes the buds clammy and cold and Tess pricks her finger and sobs.)

Place one rosebud under a yew. (Easy. Tess goes to the church in Beaminster – she has to visit an old friend of our mother there anyway, has to pay a visit with her little daughter: life has to appear to go on, even when you're broken-hearted.) Tess goes into St Mary's churchyard. She stands by the wall of the cottage where Gertrude Bugler was visited by the angel of poetry and then by his indignant ex-muse; and she places the rosebud under a yew tree there as far as possible from the church.

Place one rosebud in a new-made grave. (Alas, only too easy: poor Retty, buried at Abbotsbury. How can Tess bring herself to creep in the all-concealing fog and feel the soft, new-dug earth with her fingertips, push in the pointed bud?) She can, she's in love and she's ruthless with the need to get Gabriel back to her.

Place one rosebud under your pillow.

And the spell ends. Your lover will be racked by dreams of you.

Racked indeed! Gabriel dreams, as the plane flies overhead that brings Alec back to the place where he was born, where his daughter was born . . .

Gabriel dreams of the one he loves – himself.

All the dill and cyclamen, white bryony, belladonna, henbane, what you will, will never bring him back to Tess. He just doesn't want to get involved with a chick with a child.

But here's the catch in it. Alec does! (Oh, not the chick: Tess is no more to him than any of the girls Alec knew when he was building up a stash of cash in the petty criminal underworld in Detroit.) No, the child, his child: he's one of those.

And the night after Retty's suicide, when the fog is thick over a sea that used to twinkle in the light of the stars – in the blackest air where it's impossible to see one inch in front of your face – your mother, Baby Tess – Tess's daughter, little Mary – vanishes from her bed.

Father Love

Ella – you hear the knock at the door – and then the second and third knock, the curtain rising on the last act of the melodrama, the sound of the men at the door, fresh from their find in the shallow gravel pit behind the George Hotel at West Bay.

But let them wait a minute.

Close your eyes, Baby Tess, and you, Ella, too. If you try, you can hear the sound of the sea in the shells, down there in the summer of 1954, on Chesil Beach.

You can feel our father's hand on Tess, when she comes running back from the Game of Stones, that Alec and Victor have so naughtily made us play.

You can feel his hand, as it comes down to strike his daughter (he can smell her sex, he must punish her, he must give her a few lashes with the cane that's kept in the dining-room cupboard, along with the bottle of malt whisky he takes a nip from when nesting makes him late and soaking wet at the swannery). He knows, this father of ours, that Tess has been up to no good.

He pulls down her pants ... she screams for our mother, but Mary, like in a terrible fairy tale, has gone away ... he makes me watch as he brings the cane down on poor Tess's white flesh, still goosepimply from the pea-gravel at West Bay.

And I still must watch as our father pulls out that great swollen purple thing that looks like the worms he taught us to thread on hooks when he took us fishing at Litton Bredy, and sinks it right into Tess's bottom there as she shrieks and he clamps a hand over her mouth, and I feel the fog swirl right in behind my eyes and fall down on the floor with fog-spots dancing red and white and blue in my brain.

Year after year after year it went on. No, never me. Only Tess. She was Daddy's girl. He couldn't let her out of his sight.

And that's where the silence came from: Tess's silence, as muffling and thick and white as the sea-fog: the silence you could almost hear, when she understood Gabriel would never come back to her. The silence she shared with our mother Mary Hewitt – who must have known of the abuse to her child and colluded with it, while going deeper into madness. When his favourite swan turned sooty-black and ran off with that Alec from the no-good people by the garage, it was already too late.

Tess knew, or half-knew, anyway. On the night of the ball up at Mapperton she was already well gone in pregnancy. No wonder Dr Ryall wouldn't touch her!

Your mother, Baby Tess, has her grandfather as her father. The child was the last love for our father John Hewitt, the next incarnation of his daughter Tess.

But he wasn't going to get away with it as easily as that.

The night the child, little Mary, vanished from her bed . . . didn't I hear a boat, or something like the fog-muffled outboard engine of a small fishing-boat as I lay awake at the Mill, wondering like so many other lasses, I've no doubt, where and when I could next see the heart-throb Gabriel Bell.

And instead of going to the door and taking the powerful torch our father would carry with him on an emergency trip to an ill or dying bird (he was so tender with the swans, so cruelly tender with Tess, bathing her weals when he had beaten her, 'kissing her better' when he had thrust his great cock right into her mouth so she gagged and nearly died of it) . . . instead of going out to see what kind of boat was on the water becalmed by fog out there, I went on dreaming of Gabriel – and my hand slid between my legs and I dreamed of Tess and Alec in the attic high upstairs, and I dreamed of Gabriel coming towards me, clasping me tight as Alec had done with Tess, all those years ago –

I brought myself to a climax, while the murder – the revenge killing that came years, thousands of years since the first ballad of love, betrayal and revenge was sung through a woman – was carried out. As I twisted and tossed in my narrow bed at the Mill, I never heard our mother as she raced down the stairs and out into the wall of black mist that was the night.

The knife. The fisherman's knife Mary used at West Bay for slicing off the heads of the cod and mackerel before throwing them in the basket by the lorry marked DOWLE – the screams – the running feet in the muffled lane outside.

Tess, white-faced, at my door.

And I'm running past her, down the narrow lane and out onto the expanse of grass, dry and baked from summer, where the kiosk, night-shuttered, makes a dark shadow against the dawn lifting in the sky –

And past the gleam of the white hydrangeas by the entrance to the swannery, where the brook that clatters through our garden at the Mill runs deep and brown, to its outlet into the sea –

Tess has caught me up by now, is clutching at my sleeve.

There, on the ridge of stones that is Chesil Beach, my mother stands . . .

As I told you, Baby Tess, a mother's anger is a terrible, unforgettable thing. She's prodding the body that looks as if it's made up of water and sand, it looks water-logged and already half-human, out of the bog.

A fisherman's boat. The boat from Dowle's at West Bay: my mother loads the corpse on board – and Tess helps her: I hear the silence of their collusion again. What must be done, is done.

Are the poor and unattractive, the goose-girls, the younger sisters of the pantomime princess, doomed to be the bearers of misfortune; to feel drowsy at the all-important moment, fail to wake when the prince comes along, nudge the favoured ones towards disaster? Does something in these 'unlucky' people propel them to visit their inheritance on the beautiful? Do some women, by entering a compact with the writer of the old ballad – the song of betrayal after love, of revenge and murder and death – carry the song to the next generation by accident almost, in their recital of fairy tales, their crooning of the old tunes? Is it envy for the carefree, the admired, that makes it worthwhile to go on spelling out the tale?

If so, then I have to make my confession now: I am one of these.

Did I really fall asleep on the pebbly ridge of Chesil Beach when I had care of little Mary, she a bare three years old and with the dark eyes and gypsy-dark hair of Tess and of her foremothers – did I let the sun, yellow and heavy in the sky, close my eyes and numb my legs so that I never heard the scrunch of Mary's feet on the stones when she left me and toddled away from the sea, down the steep bank to the tropical gardens and the swannery?

Did I 'accidentally' lose the child, so she could be ensnared and abused by our father John Hewitt as her mother Tess had been?

Our father John Hewitt is in his little hut by the side of the lagoon. It's high summer and the swans are moulting, so the piles of dead feathers that blow around in the light breeze make a whirling screen between us as I run, calling out for Tess's child. The birds, lethargic in the heat, walk ponderously around no-longer-wanted nests of twigs and straw. I dodge them; not one of them even spits at me as I run faster, heroine of a plot that has been taken up and played out so many times the audience is already rustling sweetpapers, clearing throats, planning an afternoon at the sales and then tea.

An old story, and I slept through it, for my role was that of accomplice to the balladeer, monkey to the organ-grinder, provider of fresh prey for the wolf. My part was written for me long ago and I sleep through the consequences. I abrogate responsibility. It's not my fault, really. Tess was the pretty one. Poor little Mary, whose father is her grandfather, will have to go the same way as her mother and all the Tesses before her. Not my fault.

Mary is sitting on my father (and her father too: it's too appalling to contemplate); she's sitting on his lap and he's fondling her hair and pulling up her little pink frock that was a cast-off from our playmate Retty all those years ago.

Our father, the father of Tess, the lover-father in the tradition of the great poet, fashions another Ruined Maid as he pushes the child down on him and he clamps his hand over her mouth as she screams . . .

But by the time I get there, of course, it's too late. Mary is just another bewildered, crying little girl who has lost her auntie by the edge of the sea. I scold her as I pull her behind me – 'Don't go off without telling me where you're going, do you hear me? – Do it again and I'll smack you, do you hear?' And all the while I know I let this happen, I'm one of the legion of women who can't stop it, connive at it by failing to stand up against the tyranny of the lover-father in our destroyed world.

You may say, what about my mother? The strong witch-mother who gouges the staring eyes from the fish at West Bay?

You may well ask. By coming back to care for her little grand-daughter, even she became trapped again, her wings were clipped, her power drained out of her until all that was left was –
Revenge.

– But what about Tess? Ella asks. She stares up at me, pale and anxious, as the knocking comes louder at the door.
And I try to explain. I say: You see, Tess had really only just discovered, in that summer of 1969, that her father was abusing

little Mary – his daughter and granddaughter, just as he had her, all those hard, suffering years. (Tess was in love with Gabriel Bell, remember, and she didn't look too hard at first. The child was in the care of her mother – what's wrong with that? It's very usual, isn't it, for an artist, as Tess undoubtedly was, to get some childcare help from her mother? Ah yes, but the most ordinary families have secrets such as ours: perhaps we're beginning to know that now.)

Tess had only a few days before, in that crazy summer of the moaning guitar and Vietnam atrocities on TV played out while she tried to staunch her aching loss of Gabriel, the New Jesus who was going to save her life and take her away from the injustices of the past – Tess had found out the truth. Her father – mine and the poor baby's too – had lures to tempt the child to the hut where he lived so alone and still by the edge of the water.

Like one of the fairy tales little Mary had read to her by our mother Mary Hewitt in the Mill, before she was taken up to sleep in the room with a round eye that looks out on the sea (the story was *Hansel and Gretel*, very probably), little Mary had only to follow the trail of sweet promises through the tropical gardens – which is a stone's throw from the Mill, here. She's a bright girl, can walk fast –

Tess discovered the lures – it can only have been a few days before.

I heard her shriek at our mother Mary, in the kitchen of the Mill.

– Did you know? Answer me, damn you! Did you know?

And Mary couldn't answer, of course. Because by then she was trapped in the old story, you see, and she no longer knew what she knew and what she didn't know. (And old Mrs Moores said she wouldn't be surprised if poor Mrs Hewitt didn't go back in that place outside Bridport again.)

Tess. A long line of the incarnations of Tess. I saw it in her face the night the little bed in the attic room was found to be empty –

I saw it in the white face Tess showed me at the door of my bedroom –

I heard it in the terrible slamming of the door as first Tess and then my mother, holding the knife she used to gouge out the eyes of the dead fish at West Bay . . .

And I saw it in the terrified face of little Mary – after her mother and grandmother had found her hiding, whimpering in the sea-grass by the side of John Hewitt's hut and brought her safely home –

Ella comes up to me at this point and leads me over to the window. The cars with their official stripes sit like a row of badgers in the narrow lane. The door of the first one opens and a tall, distinguished-looking man gets out.

Two minutes more to tell you, Ella, and Baby Tess.

I have to picture this. I wasn't there and I didn't see the killing at the end.

I have to imagine the man coming up the shingle – but then, our father John Hewitt would often walk late at night, searching for a missing member of his herd, calling a sick swan that had gone astray with a low, clucking call.

I can see the women as they came down from the ridge, two maenads, the knife held between them, two huge sea-women racing to avenge the crime. The crime of domination.

The crime of father-fuckers. I can see them, hair swirling behind them, a part of the long black tresses of the fog –

My mother and my sister Tess killed our father that night. And I came, as always, too late on the scene.

And the boat? Why, my mother saw that boat as an act of Providence, or whatever comes to witches when they're in need.

Our mother took our father's dead body all the way up the coast from Abbotsbury here, at dead of night, in the boat. She dragged him to the shallow pit at the back of West Bay, over pea-gravel the contractors started shifting last week, for the smart new bungalows.

My mother buried my father just behind the stretch of beach where she had worked as a fishwife – and had come to be a witch. She knew the tides came into that pit only once in a blue moon – and who would suspect her or her daughter Tess, then?

*

It's the time of the blue moon now, though, for the combination of the freak tides and the building men have brought him bobbing to the surface again. That's why, my poor little Ella, they will come in and take me away from this place.

Our father has been raised from the dead.

– So what happened to little Mary? Ella says – and she's looking at Baby Tess in a different way now, as if the history of her mother and all their foremothers has made her feel protective, motherly even, at her young age, towards the infant.

Her father, Alec Field, had indeed come over from America to claim his child.

It wasn't his, of course. But once the song begins to be sung with a vengeance, you don't let on too much about that.

– And Tess? Ella asks, very grave now, as if she can see the pattern unfold before her.

Open the door, Ella. Let the gentlemen in.

Yes, I can identify the body. Yes, I do agree to look at the photographs, but they may be unsuitable for young Ella here, so please hand them directly to me.

Yes, this is my father, John Hewitt.

No, I was not alone at the Mill at the time of the death. My sister Tess and my mother Mary Hewitt were here with me.

I can swear to it.

Where is she now? Why, officer! What do you expect? A woman will look a little different after thirty years, won't she? Meet her granddaughter, Baby Tess. Can I offer you gentlemen a cup of tea?

Evening

Time now to get our things together and leave the Mill. The rich film folk are due for their late summer break. They'll find the swallows gone as well as the swans but there's still some warmth in the sun and it's a magnificent view you get, sitting under the fig tree on the terrace.

I tell Ella and Baby Tess that, of course, the new tenants will be all agog over the discovery of a body higher up the coast behind West Bay. They'll look at me strangely, they'll go in the little shop in Abbotsbury to try to work out who killed the poor man, half a lifetime ago.

It's quite simple really, Mrs Hands who runs the shop now will tell them.

– Two sisters lived at the Mill, see. Tess and Lizzie – they called her Liza-Lu. John and Mary Hewitt, that was the name of their mum and dad, warn't it? An' they split up – she went to work at Dowle's Fishery down on the beach at West Bay and he . . .

– He used to hang out in that damp little hut at the swannery, comes a voice from the back of the shop, Jimmy Hands. Then he went off to live with his sister in Canada, so Mrs Hewitt said.

– Poor man. A resident of Nasebury – Ella's mum, but the film folk wouldn't know that – shuffles forward to pay for her bread and two tins of sardines. To think of him under the stones all those years . . .

No one notices there's a small smile on Ella's mum's face. After all, who looks at the woman who sells postcards and brochures in the kiosk?

– The elder sister, Mrs Hands is saying, Tess she was, got in the family way with a bad sort from the Beaminster garages . . . what was his name? I can't remember – yes, Alec, it was – but what I do know is, he came and took the child away to America. In the Big Fog of 1969.

The film people stand shaking their heads in the little store that sells stamps as well as tins and lettuces, so there's always a queue of old ladies, same bobble-hats and coats winter and summer, at the window with the grille.

– Who was the man who was killed, then?

Mrs Hands is losing patience. She takes a pension book, riffles the pages, affixes her stamp.

– John Hewitt. They said it was funny at the time – that he disappeared just like that – but he was an odd sort, no doubt about it. His daughter Tess was ever so cut up about it. Went into that place the other side of Bridport for quite a while . . .

– And the younger sister, Liza-Lu, she went off to live with that pop singer – what's he called? Mr Hands puts in. He knows he can get good custom from these folk if he feeds them titbits.

– Adam Faith?

– No . . . Gabriel Bell, that's it. Seems he'd been the lover of Tess – but when he came back she didn't want anything more to do with him. So he settled down here with Liza-Lu . . . Didn't last long, anyway. He died a few years later.

– Died? Goodness! The eyes of the new arrivals widen in pleasurable anticipation again.

– Drugs overdose, Mrs Hands says, making a tart face as she weighs potatoes and cauliflower on the scales. But we always thought Mary Hewitt had something to do with it. There was something witchy about Mary Hewitt.

– And the baby – little Mary?

– Grew up in America with her dad . . .

Ella turns and gazes upwards, to the room with the round window that looks out to the sea. And Baby Tess's eyes follow her . . .

The waiting men move forward at the sound of a light step coming down.

Tess stands for a moment on the topmost stair of the Mill. Her hair is a cloud of grey but her beauty is untouched.

She comes into the long room and takes the child in her arms, and she smiles at me.